JASON ANSPACH

ATTACK OF SHADOWS

SEASON 1

BOOK 4

Galaxy's Edge: ATTACK OF SHADOWS
By Jason Anspach & Nick Cole

Hardcover ISBN: 978-1-949731-22-4
Paperback ISBN: 978-1-949731-23-1

Edited by David Gatewood
Published by Galaxy's Edge, LLC

Cover Art: Fabian Saravia
Cover Design: Ryan Bubion
Interior Design: Kevin G. Summers

For more information:

Website: GalacticOutlaws.com
Facebook: facebook.com/atgalaxysedge
Newsletter: InTheLegion.com

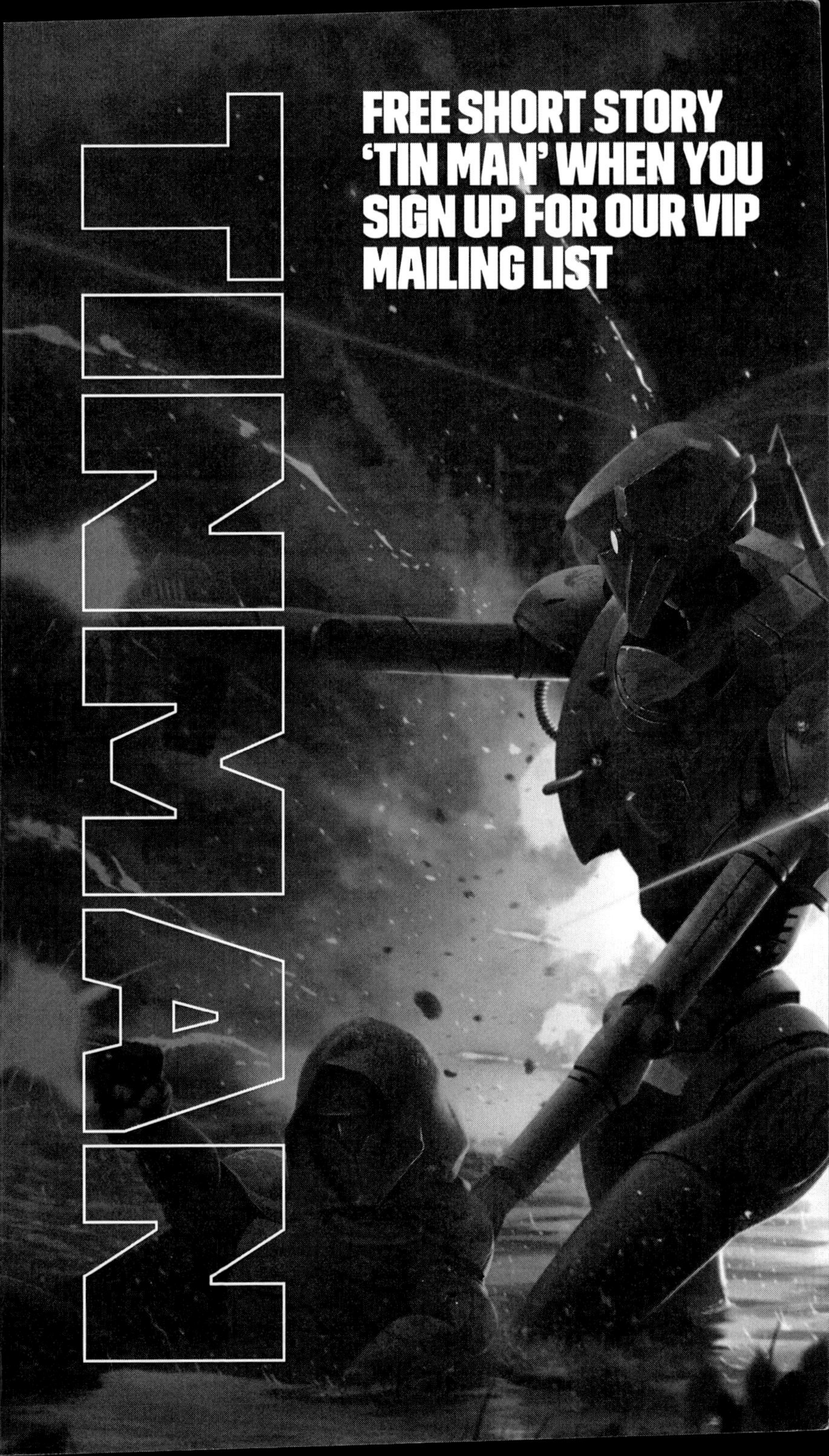
TIN MAN
FREE SHORT STORY 'TIN MAN' WHEN YOU SIGN UP FOR OUR VIP MAILING LIST

PART I

01

Black Fleet
Flagship *Imperator*
Beyond Tarrago Prime

Deep within the shadows he meditated on the coming battle. Seeing its actions. Its moments. The imminent and cataclysmic level of destruction that would signal the end of all known things. The end of the Republic. He saw it all.

And it was good to him.

Alone in a chamber on a deck to which few had authorized access—just those within his inner circle, plus the elite guard that surrounded him at all times—he watched from a simple mounted command chair, anchored to the deck of the mighty new ship beneath him, surrounded in darkness. Before him sat a matte-gray impervisteel-latticed port, staring out into the vast nepenthe of dark space beyond Tarrago Prime. A view to the coming battle.

The view to a kill.

Finally, he thought to himself, as he sat within the comfort of this darkness deeper than just the absence of mere light. Finally, the last days of a feeble and decaying Republic were at hand. Finally all would be as it ever should've been.

Finally.

The Black Fleet had made the jump to hyperspace two days ago from Tusca, just along the edge of the galaxy. *His* fleet. A fleet he had brought together out of everything the galaxy had broken, or deemed unimportant, or not realized the value of. Three massive battleships. They were utilitarian in their magnificent and terrible splendor—a stark contrast with the trim, neat, almost spindly nature of the Republic's ships. It was as though all the Republic's ships had a screaming need to convey a message of non-violence at all times.

That, he thought, summed up the very nature of this decrepit and dying Republic he was about to destroy. Warships that weren't supposed to threaten. Leaders that never led. And citizens who were really slaves.

He would destroy all that.

His fleet, the Black Fleet for now, had suddenly appeared out beyond the moon at Tarrago Prime. The moon was known simply as Tarrago Moon, and it served as guardian to the mid-core worlds and the waiting heart of a dying Republic. Of course, the fleet had dropped in well out of the awesome engagement range of the sprawling Republic fortress that guarded the approach to the massive Kesselverks Shipyards on the planet below.

The three ships, ships of a size the Republic had not seen in a long, long time, heeled to starboard and took up a course that would not attract the notice of the deadly orbital defense gun. Fortress Omicron's powerful defense system required respect.

Terror. Revenge. Imperator. Three massive, split-hulled, triangular battleships beyond the imagination of the Republic's best ship architects. Built not just for war, but for *conquest*. Unlike anything the galaxy had seen in a hundred years or more. Of course the Republic hadn't thought to build anything this massive, this deadly, or this dangerous. Or even this functional. These ships were ready for quick battle and decisive engagements.

For total warfare, in fact.

Anything that dared stand in their way was assured annihilation. These were state-of-the-art weapons systems, not discount-in-bulk cheap production corvettes meant to project the mere appearance of military business. Galactic Republic busybody business. The Black Fleet wasn't made just to start wars, but to end them. Not to maintain some faux peace that had never been challenged.

The three battleships, in defensive formation in support of one another, slowed to flank and prepared to commence operations within the system. Sleek new state-of-the-art fighters leapt away from the massive hangars across several decks.

The first wave of the attack was underway.

Still more black flight-suited pilots scrambled from their briefing rooms into those massive hangars where ground crew swarmed and prepped their fighters for launch. Shock troopers in black-lacquered armor, splashes of arterial bleeding red denoting rank, drew weapons from their immaculately business-like armories and filed toward slate-gray bulky transports and dropships while grim-faced officers watched and made sure all was ready for what was to come next. That all was going according to plans laid long ago.

Operations had begun.

War had come to the galaxy once more.

Operation Downfall was moments from commencing. Cyclopean horns resounded across the sprawling, multi-leveled decks as more new fighters were lowered from the stores racks down into the ready five positions.

Casualties would occur, and these replacements would need to be ready to move quickly. Success was dependent on this swift surprise attack that would knock out most of Fortress Omicron's defenses.

There was nothing optimistic about the organized mayhem. Instead it might have been characterized as... coldly determined. Of one purpose. As though some die had been cast, and the results must be paid for now. Must be witnessed by all.

Goth Sullus watched all of this. Watched the sleek, soulless gray of the two sister battleships just aft of the beam of the *Imperator*. Internal lighting glittered across all decks. His shock troopers were moving toward their assault ships. Pilots were receiving their final briefings. Admirals looked on with a strain that tightened their jaw muscles and showed in their tired eyes as more readiness reports came in across the two storied bridges on each ship.

But here, in this quiet inner sanctum where one could hear the souls of the damned howl, here in this private chamber aboard the *Imperator*, surrounded by ten thousand crew, was silence and the absence of life. And yet he could hear, and feel, all of them, as the three massive ships prepared for operations against Tarrago Prime.

The downfall had begun.

A long time coming. A long time in the making.

Longer than anyone alive might ever have imagined.

Goth Sullus was returning to the Republic.

Finally.

And the galaxy was now becoming what it would one day be.

After many long years lost out in the outer dark, Goth Sullus, who'd once been many other someone elses, was returning from far out beyond the galaxy's edge where things were strange and the known laws didn't necessarily apply. Out there, beyond the perimeter, things were far different. They were immaculate, and dark.

Now he was returning to conquer.

Returning to restore order.

Returning to set things as they should have always ever been.

Goth Sullus didn't need to touch the comm that lay next to his hand, embedded into his command chair. He merely whispered. A whisper from deep within the shadows of his mind, and some lost place he'd found long ago, out beyond the galaxy's edge.

"Admiral Rommal ..." he whispered. "You may commence the attack."

House of Reason
Utopion

Delegate Orrin Kaar paced alongside the brilliant picture window in his office in the House of Reason. The view was breathtaking: a top-down view of the deep blue river Eebris and the twin waterfalls that cascaded down into a lagoon like a roaring cauldron, the vast flow of water cut in two by the massive rock called *virtue*. The shallow lagoon drained into separate rivers, each watering a lush path of vegetation that wrapped around the House of Reason and the Senate Building. It was a marvel of Republic engineering, a vista worthy of a planet called Utopion.

This view was one that other House of Reason delegates employed every trick in the book to obtain. To get to the lofty pinnacle that Kaar now occupied. To have an office—and prestige—like his.

A nearby park square was teeming with Republic citizens reveling in the holiday. A rainbow formed in the mists of the waterfall.

Kaar barely noticed.

The delegate's schedule was cleared for the day. Good will visits canceled, meetings postponed, dinner plans on hiatus. Kaar's wife knew not to expect him home tonight until late, if at all. He had announced that he must prepare for an upcoming hearing about whether or not the tryk-teps, a diminutive insectoid species, should be stripped of their status as galactic minorities. Though non-human, they were statistically the most populous species in the galaxy. Thousands of them could stand wing-to-wing inside a single cubic meter of space. The issue was hotly contested; groups demonstrated and counter-demonstrated. But the hive-mind tykteps themselves were likely altogether unaware of the debate. They simply followed the directives of their queen and continually expanded the surface of their home world, which had grown nearly a kilometer in diameter since it was first discovered by Republic scientists.

Kaar had promised to study the issue in detail. To uphold his reputation as a House of Reason delegate whose intellect—he held four doctorates—had been forged into a tool for galactic justice and prosperity.

In truth, of course, he would wait until the pollsters showed the most politically beneficial decision, and he would then maneuver himself into that camp.

In truth, Kaar knew this issue would be off of the holoscreens by tomorrow morning.

Tomorrow morning, it would dawn on the Republic that the attack on Tarrago Prime was more than another Mid-Core Rebellion terrorist strike. Combat footage junkies, and watchdog media with no following, no doubt already had eyes on amateur holovids of the nascent battle, sent over comm relays by the local population. But the big networks couldn't be bothered. Perpetual war only made the top of the playlists when there was a scandal, atrocity, or disaster. And there hadn't been a good one of those in quite some time.

Kaar stopped in front of a plaque proudly displayed on the wall. The Order of the Centurion. Awarded to Orrin Kaar's most celebrated appointee, Admiral Silas Devers. The admiral gave the award to Kaar as thanks, in a showy moment for the cameras. To Kaar, a true hero of the Republic for his decades of political service. A holo of the event played in a loop next to the plaque. Something for guests to take in while waiting for the exalted public servant to meet them.

Kaar toggled the sound, and Admiral Devers's voice crisply synced to the holo.

"I'm just a warrior who fights when I'm needed. And given the Republic's might, those fights are few and far between." The gathered press and dignitaries laughed in delight as Devers handed the award over, bowing deferentially. "Delegate Kaar fights every day for the citizens of the Republic. He is my mentor and dearest friend."

The focus of the holo shifted from Devers's handsome face to his own. He muted the audio rather than listen to his own voice.

"Then why, Admiral, do you make me wait?" Kaar spoke into the air, allowing a frustrated sigh to escape.

The battle had begun. Devers was to make contact prior to his part in this grand scheme. And he was late.

Kaar looked at the comm light on his desk. "Call, damn you. Call!"

The chiming comm had an almost apologetic tone, Delegate Orrin Kaar mused. This was Devers calling. It had to be. No one else could reach him on this comm station.

Kaar had sponsored a billion-credit program designed to provide the Republic with its own version of the Legion's proprietary L-comm. If the Legion deemed it necessary to have its own ultra-secure comm system, and was too self-important to share it, then the Republic Armed Forces should have the same, he'd argued. He'd secured the funding needed. Most of it went to build a grotto on Kaar's personal moon, with a tidy amount held in reserve to grease the cogs of the Republic political machine.

For the greater good.

But a prototype did emerge before the project was shut down due to budget overruns. And it was declared unsliceable. Kaar kept it as a means of communicating the things best left unheard. Even the Republic had limits as to what it would permit. In the open, at least.

Kaar opened the comm channel. "Silas, m'boy. How goes the battle?"

"Delegate Kaar," Devers answered, his bearing rigid—every bit the picturesque Republic admiral. "It is a pleasure to speak with you again."

"How many times do I have to tell you to call me Orrin? We're friends, Silas."

"As always, at least once more, Delegate Kaar."

Kaar smiled. Devers was a man who knew his place. It was something he'd seen when the admiral was a promising lad seeking an appointment by virtue of his family's place in the Republic. It was why he would be the perfect figurehead of the new Republic. "I'll not argue with you, Admiral. But I will repeat myself. How goes the battle?"

Devers's face fell. "It hasn't yet begun. And I'm afraid I won't be in a position to say, Delegate Kaar."

Kaar leaned forward, looking at the comm with concern. "Why not?"

"Goth Sullus is withholding my fleet. My orders are to jump into the system, send out a comm signal announcing this as a jump evasion training leg, deliver shuttles of Sullus's shock troopers, and jump out of the system."

"But... the plan! With your entire fleet arriving unchallenged, a strike team could land on Tarrago Prime and capture the planetary governor before they knew what hit them."

Devers nodded. "Yes, Delegate Kaar. I relayed the plan exactly as you devised. Sullus disagreed. He said the Legion would not surrender the orbital gun even if the entirety of the planet were under subjugation."

"So Sullus intends to conquer Omicron as a first step?"

"Yes, Delegate Kaar."

Kaar rubbed his chin. "I suppose the point is moot at this venture?"

"The plans could not be altered at this late hour."

Kaar scowled. "I would have *appreciated* your informing me of this sooner, Admiral."

"I called as soon as I was able." Devers paused, as if deliberating.

"You... have something more to say, I take it?"

"Goth Sullus's army, as best I can tell, is well-trained. They remind me of the Legion. His fleet..."

"Yes! Tell me about the fleet. I'm eager to know what has become of all the credits I siphoned in his direction. Men like Scarpia deliver, but at such great expense."

Devers nodded. "The fleet is three ships, Delegate Kaar."

"Three?"

"But they're massive. Larger than a super-destroyer. He calls it his Black Fleet."

Kaar didn't like this. Sullus had always shown a defiant, independent streak. That Sullus's shock troopers were loyal only to him, Kaar already knew. But the credits given him were to be used to procure an updated design on the modern Republic fleet, not create something new out of whole cloth. This was a fluid situation. One that would require all of Kaar's political finesse if he was going to end up on the top of the new Republic's pecking order.

"Admiral, it seems to me that Sullus is intent on doing this his own way. We need to be sure that he feels we're owed a sense of gratitude when this victory is won. I want you to commit your forces to the complete destruction of Tarrago Prime's defense fleet. And then Admiral Landoo's fleet, should she respond. Draw her out and destroy her. She's no commander. Never served on the edge. She's only a political favorite that breezed through academy."

Kaar left it unstated that Devers was cut from the same cloth.

"You want me to disobey orders?" Devers asked. He appeared nervous at the very thought.

Kaar gave Devers a patronizing look that he hoped would carry over the comm relay. "We both know this is hardly the first time you disobeyed orders. You gambled your entire career on a lie while serving on Kublar, counting on that old legionnaire major to die before he had the opportunity to set the record straight. I still wonder if you fully appreciate the strings I pulled to get you out the Legion—where questions would be asked—and into the navy."

"Delegate Kaar, I didn't mean to—"

"It's fine." Kaar, satisfied with Devers's swift apology, waived the issue away. "Goth Sullus is not your commander. He is your equal. You are fighting alongside him, not for him. Win us the victory, Silas. I have complete confidence in you."

"Thank you, Delegate Kaar." Devers looked about his quarters. "I should return to the bridge. I'll forward all Black Fleet general orders and updates through this channel."

Kaar nodded. "Yes, but before you go... is there any truth to the rumor that Tyrus Rechs is dead?"

"I've been told by a number of Black Fleet officers that Rechs challenged Sullus to single combat, and that Sullus killed him."

Kaar raised his eyebrows. "Impressive. I think I'll share that bit of information when the House of Reason needs some cheering up. They no doubt will by the time this day is ended."

02

Black Fleet
Third Wing, First Squadron, "Pit Vipers"
Hangar Deck Three Aboard *Terror*
Off Tarrago Moon
0153 Local System Time

The crew chief stepped back from the hatch of the tri-fighter, ground attack variant, and saluted Lieutenant Haladis as she finished strapping herself in.

"Good luck and good hunting, Lieutenant!"

The pilot snapped back a salute, her gloved hand brushing against her thick flight helmet. She felt that familiar rush of goose bumps and emotions as she plugged into onboard life support. As the deck crew disconnected her fighter from *Terror*'s power conduits, she switched from auxiliary to internal power.

A ground crew member ahead, out beyond the cockpit glass, pulled out light batons and signaled to her. She gave a two-click acknowledgement. As she waited for the internal turbines to cycle up, she watched the rest of the flight line. Her squadron, and other squadrons throughout the massive hangar, were approaching go mode.

She finished preflight and double-checked the master weapons. They'd installed a new munitions package on her tri-fighter, replacing the standard blasters with twin 30mm chain guns capable of independent auto-targeting.

Actual slug throwers.

She took the throttle and yoke and settled her feet on the rudders.

"Viper Two, this is Viper Lead," came the squadron leader's call over internal comm. "Taxi into position and prepare for immediate departure. Once we're clear, form up on me to target."

Just as it had been planned in the endless briefings. Trained for in the months prior. And what she'd been headed toward for what seemed like her entire life.

She acknowledged. "Roger, Viper Lead."

Repulsors engaged beneath her, and the tri-fighter lifted off from its docking cradle. She moved the throttle ever so slightly forward and taxied toward the centerline. Viper Lead taxied in front of her. Other fighters were moving off the flight line into the ready position. The hangar echoed with the ghostly howls of their engines.

The tri-fighter was a wicked-looking agile starfighter unlike anything the Republic had ever even thought about fielding. Three independent deflector panels, skinned in black and angled forward like vicious scalene triangles outlined in the standard fleet gray, covered a central pilot pod and engine system. The pilot looked out the forward-looking latticed canopy, guarded by the deflectors to the sides and one above—but this provided limited visibility and was useful only for landing. It was the augmented reality pilot interface system that took this ship to the next level. With it, Haladis could see the battle going on all around her while still orienting for standard flight control. It took a bit of getting used to, but once you did, you saw all the advantages you had over fighters that relied on the pilot's visual interpretation of the battle.

She ran through the deflector pre-launch checklist and tested the inverters to standard. The deflectors also acted as impulse directional thrusters that allowed more agile maneuvering than the typical turn-and-burn heavy fighters of the Republic. Everything looked good for flight.

"Pit Vipers... you are cleared to depart," came the call from flight control high above the hangar's upper reaches, where a monumental tower hung down from the top of the cavernous deck. "Get 'em, snakes!"

"Go for throttle," murmured Viper Lead.

Haladis could barely tell he was nervous. He seemed as calm and as quiet as ever. Great pilot. Quiet leader. He'd kill you in a dogfight through sheer patience. And he'd done it many times to her in sim, back on Tusca. She was glad he'd beaten her out for squadron leader over the course of the intense, and at times brutal, training they'd spent the last year living through. Surviving, really.

Unlike in the Republic, everyone in this fleet had been trained to kill. From light infantry skills to Legionnaire training, to escape and evasion... *everyone* was a fighter—whether they were a cook, a transport driver, or even a pilot. The sadistic TAC officers had required this of them all.

But being in charge... that was a whole other job.

A tough job.

Flying a fighter in combat was also a tough job.

Doing both at the same time was more than she'd wanted.

She just wanted...

She pushed forward on the throttle and realized she was holding her breath. Suddenly what remained of the hangar and launch deck raced past her as she shot beyond the hull of the massive ship.

Breathe, Kat.

Said her brother.

Just breathe.

"This is for you, Dasto," she whispered.

And then they were out in space, the entire squadron racing toward Tarrago Moon.

Black Fleet
Bridge of the *Imperator*
Off Tarrago Moon
0154 Local System Time

"Admiral," signaled the flight ops officer. "First strike underway. Five minutes to first-targets engagement."

Admiral Rommal watched the real-time combat operations map located on the lower deck of the two-story bridge, currently set to display the Tarrago system. All targets were highlighted in red. Friendlies were identified in a ghostly blue. Targeting data and countdown bars circled and undulated, providing real-time updates for each target within the three major areas of the operation.

Fortress Omicron on Tarrago Moon would be hit first.

Then the system defense force in orbit around Tarrago Prime would respond and draw away from the planet—if the Republic's traitor followed the plan.

And finally... the Kesselverk Shipyards would be open for assault and capture.

There lay the real prize of this operation. With a fully functioning automated shipyard, the fleet could begin construction of more battleships and the planned destroyers.

The third area of operation would be space itself. The Republic's Seventh Fleet would respond, and there would be a battle like none seen in a generation. Fire would be exchanged, and people would die. That was all that was guaranteed in the admiral's mind.

Other staff officers, each in a crisp, black, almost Spartan uniform, highly polished black boots, and a small dark cap, gathered about the lower deck of the bridge. Their datapads tracked and reported on operations underway, impending, and ready to mount. They surrounded the admiral at a distance and waited for any adjustments he might offer them.

"Second strike on deck and ready to launch," called out the combat information commander, or the CIC, as everyone had taken to referring to him, just like they'd referred to the same position in the Republican Navy. Admiral Rommal had known the man from before. Ex-Republic naval officer who'd never managed to make rank because he hadn't attained the right connections along the way. "Too right-wing," they would've murmured in the hallowed halls of the House of Reason assignments department.

That he was eminently competent mattered not to them.

Rommal gave the man a nod and turned back to the real-time updates coming in from intel assets all across the system. Out there in the dark, tri-fighter scout variants running active cloak, unmanned drones, and recon shock troopers on the ground were feeding as much intel into the fleet's system as possible in the moments leading up to the operation.

The attack.

The rebellion.

The new... *whatever it would be* at the end of this very long day... whatever it would be would be new and different. And all the wrongs would be righted.

Do you really believe that? Admiral Rommal asked himself within the quietly seething cauldron of his own mind. A mind tortured by a thousand what-ifs and the responsibility for them all. A mind trying to keep painful memories and new realities at bay.

Do you?

Third Wing was now three minutes from target, and it was still, for all intents and purposes, undetected by the Republic. Scouts across the system were jamming every Repub sensor as best they could. It looked like it was working. And now if this rogue Republic admiral could deliver them the goose...

Rommal didn't trust the man. He was the worst, in that he was typical of a House of Reason point: both incompetent and ambitious. But even he should be able to handle this assignment. Down on Tarrago Prime they would be expecting nothing of what was about to happen next. Instead they were looking forward to another celebration of nothing.

"Unity Day indeed," murmured the admiral.

Yet one more opportunity, staged by the House of Reason, to shirk work and enterprise in a near-constant effort to reward themselves for the accomplishment of nothing. To make the people think they were part of something grand, instead of just a cheap carnival show run by huckster carnies who never tired of performing for power and power alone. Liars lying in order to maintain cheap power, they would give away anything they could in order to have that power for just a little while longer. And they often preferred to give away what others had worked, bled, and died for.

And how much of your involvement, his tactical mind asked himself, is because of what they took from you? And how much is because it's the right thing to do now at this moment in the galaxy?

The Galactic Republic was a slave republic. Slaves and nothing more. And very few were even aware of their indentured servitude. They just called it "taxes." Endless taxes that everyone, except those in the corridors of power, paid. There was always some exemption, or some special treatment, for the House of Reason and their family members

Like the medical care that might have saved her? that other part of the admiral's mind asked as he watched those memories of his wife dying in med bay all over again.

They'd cared only enough to send some flowers when she finally passed. Two months late. That had been like opening an old wound to him. All over again.

He pushed the thought away and watched the digital icons streaking toward their destinies. Outposts across the system that were about to be strafed into oblivion. Incoming freighter traffic that would be destroyed in order to maintain some surprise and secrecy. Across the military forces of the Republic, there would come the realization that a day never planned for had suddenly arrived. That destiny happened regardless of who you voted for. And sometimes, because of who you did vote for again and again, despite all the evidence.

And you, too, he thought as he watched all the icons representing Third Wing streaking toward Tarrago Moon. You too were once slaves in service to the elites of a Republic that cared little whether you lived or died.

Elites. What a dirty word it sounded like now, when once it had been such a high aspiration. Even Admiral Rommal's aspiration. Yes, he knew he was bitter and angry. But he was not false. Not even with himself. Not in the midnight hours of his soul or in this last moment before the revolution had begun. Before the dice were flung. He too had once wanted what so few had. He too had once wanted to be an elite.

He heard the approach of unmistakable footsteps. One leg barely dragging the boot it wore. The result of some injury in yet one more of the Republic's endless liberation conflicts.

"We've got to knock out that orbital gun, Rommal. Today's success depends on it. And so might our lives."

Admiral Crodus. In charge of fleet intel.

"I'm aware of the need for success, Admiral Crodus. And I would remind you... much of this depends on your spies and assassins. Everything is in order, I take it? We have confirmations from our teams."

Crodus nodded and studied the real-time updates.

But he was right... if Third Wing didn't knock out the massive orbital defense gun that guarded the approach to Tarrago Prime... well, it would make short work of the three technological wonders that comprised the entirety of the Black Fleet at present. Not even battleships could stand up to that kind of firepower.

But once the shipyards on Tarrago Prime were captured... who knew what would be possible after that.

231st Gun Battery Assigned Orbital Defense Command
Fortress Omicron
0155 Local System Time

Captain Thales walked the midnight corridors of Omicron. As the watch officer on duty, it was his job, and a boring job it was, to patrol the various outposts and watches within the inner fortress surrounding the orbital gun bore in the center of the defensive works that was the entire moon. His thankless job was to make sure everyone was ever alert for an attack everyone knew would never come. Never ever. There was no other power big enough, within the galaxy, to attack the Republic. It was universally agreed that nothing would ever warrant the use of the orbital defense gun that guarded the approach to Tarrago Prime and its sprawling Kesselverks Shipyards.

Nothing.

To be assigned here was a kind of purgatory.

True, it was a powerful weapon system. And an excellent one, by all accounts. But it had only been built to employ workers the House of Reason wanted votes from. One of the most great, and grand, make-work projects of the last recession, which had really been a depression, but which the media insisted on calling something less dire. Thousands of private citizen core-worlders had been suddenly forced into government contracts just to keep their families in the latest luxuries the Republic's culture of wealth had managed to tempt them with. Anything to stave off the inevitable collapse a few had been assuring everyone was inevitably inevitable.

Lock that down, Rogg! Captain Thales ordered himself as he left Turret Four after a surprise middle-of-the-night inspection. *That kind of thinking won't get you promoted off this rock.*

And Rogg Thales wanted off this rock.

His perfect assignment would be as artillery forward observer for the Legion. Or at least a Legion liaison officer.

Deep Sensors, his next check, lay thirty yards ahead down a massive hall cut into the dead rock of the lifeless moon. He'd check on them, then maybe get some coffee from the duty station farther on. It was going to be a long night.

Right now this, the "eastern" tube, was the only gun bore covering the approach to Tarrago Prime. The other three tubes bored straight into the core of the moon—referred to conveniently if inaccurately as the northern, southern, and western tubes—were considered off rotation, though they could go to general quarters within five minutes and be ready to put rounds on any targets approaching from their directions.

Targets that would never appear, of course. As everyone knew.

What other government was there besides the Galactic Republic? What other fleet was there out in the darkness of deep space that could match even *one* of the fifteen major fleets the Republic had in operation at any given moment across the reaches of all the spiral arms?

Each fleet had one super-destroyer. One carrier group. Ten destroyers, and numerous task-specific corvettes and support ships. Each carrier could launch over a hundred fighters for a full Alpha strike. And if that weren't enough, all the fleet's destroyers, the super-destroyer, and the carrier group could put together the fabled Omega strike—two hundred and thirty fighters launched from across the fleet, able to deliver a devastating blow to any ship or fleet known to the galaxy. In the past, the strike had been used to ruin small dictatorships on edge worlds. A stark reminder of why it was best not to cause trouble for the Republic.

There wasn't a fleet out there that could stand up to that kind of attack. So who, exactly, was going to attack Tarrago Prime?

No one.

He was just on the verge of admonishing himself to once again *lock it down* when he walked into Deep

Sensors and saw the two dead sensor techs. Both were slumped over their stations. At first he thought he'd merely caught them sleeping. Then he saw the burnt scoring of blaster fire on their upper backs. Neither even had a chance to turn; neither had known death was about to happen. Which meant—

There's two of them, minimum, Captain Thales remarked in some other part of his mind. Someone didn't want sensors to pick up something—and they didn't want either tech to alert the base. So both assassins had needed to fire at the same moment. Or one imminently skilled, and quick, killer could've done the job. But that was far trickier, and people who planned operations didn't like to put all their eggs in one basket. He'd learned that at Strategic War Studies College during his less than meteoric climb toward major.

He drew his duty blaster, a thing he'd never figured he would need to use as an artillery officer, and pulled the nearest dead sensor tech out of his chair and onto the floor. His eyes furtively ran across the readouts on the various screens, and he quickly ascertained all sensors were being scrambled by some sort of HK malware algorithm, probably running locally. So whoever—*whoevers,* there are two of them remember—took out the techs then uploaded a virus to knock out local access to the Deep Sensor web. Sensors the gun and the fortress needed to acquire incoming targets presenting as threats.

Because even though the gun had been one giant make-work distraction, it was still beyond deadly to any capital ship that dared approach it. Alone, the orbital gun system could knock down an entire fleet if it chose to. If it was used for such a purpose, in such a specific and inconceivable instance... it could easily do that.

But there are *no other fleets*, thought Captain Thales as he slammed his hand against the internal security alert button and got an immediate comm from Defense Command. His mind was racing through all the possibilities, and none of them were good.

There aren't any other fleets?

Really?

"Defense Six here, sir... what's the problem? I have you in Deep Sensors—"

"Go to battle stations now!" ordered Captain Thales. "We're about to be under attack!"

And as his mouth screamed this into the comm, he thought, *I'm either right and we're dead, or I'm wrong and my career is dead.*

And then he ran back toward Tower Four battery. Captain Rogg Thales was not the poster boy the Republic advertised when it needed dashing naval officers. He was shorter than average, built like a beer keg, and balding. But he was an excellent officer, and he knew the Republic was in trouble.

He would save many lives this day.

Bridge of the Corvette *Audacity*
Kesselverks Shipyards Dry Dock
0157 Local System Time

Dry dock.

How much longer?

Captain Desaix made his way toward the bridge of the corvette. He'd drunk heavily and played cards with the junior staff officers, and he was positively sure they were crying in their bunks right about now. From losing so badly, and from the hangovers he'd imparted in order to beat them. In about six hours they'd wish they'd never sat down for a friendly drink and a game in the officers' mess. In fact, they'd probably wish they'd never joined the navy.

But he'd won.

It wasn't cheating... He'd merely made them incapable of making good decisions based on the cards they were dealt.

And as he liked to say, if you ain't cheatin'... you ain't tryin'. He'd had to learn that out in some pretty tight spots along the galaxy's space lanes. And even on his first duty aboard a scouting corvette deep out in the Maldarras Reach.

That'll teach 'em, thought Desaix. Even after drinking all night he was ready for duty, and looking every inch the dashing corvette captain. He liked to joke that "looking dashing" was ninety percent of the job.

A bot sheathed in white ceramic skin and roughly configured in female humanoid shape scuttled up to intercept the captain. KA8 was his new Personal Admin and Protocol bot, just picked up on this refit. His last such bot had been eaten by Jaberwotha Merchants during a trade negotiation that had gone badly. Very badly.

"Captain Desaix," purred KA8.

It always amazed him how the Republic had over-feminized this bot to the point that its vocal programming reminded him of a Catarian showgirl he'd once... dated. Vaguely. Back when he'd been an ensign on the carrier *Freedom*. But hey... the galaxy was a weird place. Sometimes you just had to roll with things. It was the best way to gamble.

"Kate, you can just call me Captain. We've been over this. You don't need to add Desaix. I'm the only captain on this ship. If you use the word 'Captain' I'm the only one who'll respond. Sound good?"

"Probably, Captain Desaix?" queried the wide-optical sensored bot innocently.

He sighed as she deflected his attempt to reprogram her away from the Repub Navy's boorish protocols. He didn't know why... but it just jammed his signal.

"I am very sorry, Captain... Desaix. But Republic standards and protocols for personal administration specialists like myself indicate we must always denote name and rank in order to clarify any potential miscommunications. After all... we bots don't have facial expressions. The litany of catastrophes that may occur aboard a state-of-the-art ship like the corvette *Audacity* might be fatal. That would not be optimal for our next efficiency review with regard to promotion and upgrade."

They were almost to the bridge of the hammerhead corvette.

"I wouldn't call the *Audacity* state-of-the-art..." the captain said.

"Oh, but I would, Captain Desaix. She's got the latest in technological upgrades, and even though we are forbidden by the House of Reason to use such colloquialisms as 'war,' this ship is indeed perfect for high-attrition operations in wartime activities. War Studies was one of the minor elective programming subroutines I managed to secure a waiver for download during my last upgrade. This refit brings *Audacity* in statistical competition with the new Orion-class. And should the crew be killed, this ship—"

"She's a twenty-year-old ship! She'd fall apart if we weren't here to jury-rig half her systems."

But she's my ship, Captain Desaix thought in the same instant. *And age doesn't matter. She's all mine.*

"I am well aware of that, Captain Desaix. Budget cuts by the House of Reason have left many technological innovations off the table. But with our new multi-warhead torpedo launch system, and considering our standard opponent is often a pirate freighter that's marginally space-worthy and sub-optimally crewed, we are one of the best ships in the galaxy... against that type of opponent... statistically speaking, Captain... Desaix."

Halfway down the main concourse, a wall panel fell out of place and onto the deck with a sudden clang, causing the bot to jump.

"Easy there, KA8. We're just puttin' her back together after that run out to Garrumala. Don't get your wires all crossed this early on. When are we scheduled to do a final check on the new torp system install?"

The bot recovered. "The system is ready to launch now. The only problem is, the torpedoes do not have warhead packages. Those won't arrive until next week. Time to fit should take less than the two-hour minimum due to crew efficiency ratings as of 1800 hours yesterday."

Desaix shrugged. More to himself than her. He'd wanted to get that item checked off.

"We've got a long day of finishing up the refit and getting space-ready, Kate. Get me the crew roster replacement schedule by oh-six. I'll be in the engine room for most of the day supervising the portside thrust displacers."

And that's when general quarters began to bellow urgently across the ship.

Everyone froze exactly where they were.

Battle stations? In dry dock?

Every nearby crewmember looked at the captain. As if asking permission to treat this as yet another system malfunction. You got a lot of those in dry dock during a refit.

Desaix shrugged and raced off toward the bridge to find out what new thing had gone completely wrong in order to waste all of his time.

Black Fleet
Third Wing, First Squadron, "Pit Vipers"
Weapons Hot, Inbound on Tarrago Moon
0159 Local System Time

Tri-fighters streaked across the terminator of the tide-locked airless moon and emerged into the sudden illumination provided by the distant star.

"Set altitude at five hundred off the deck," called out Viper Lead over the squadron comm. "Give it a little room, Vipers. Mountain ranges ahead. Outer defenses in thirty seconds."

Lieutenant Haladis dialed in the terrain-following altitude and pre-heated the cannons. She scanned the gray and lifeless horizon of the tiny moon and saw little more than jagged leaden mountains and shallow impact craters across an unending airless sea of dust. Ahead and above loomed Tarrago Prime. Even from here, Kat Haladis could see glittering cities sparkling across the night side of the lush tropical world.

It was a beautiful planet. And it was about to fall to a new order.

One in which everyone would have a chance.

She pushed away thoughts of Tarrago Prime. That was up to Task Force N. Knocking out the defenses at Fortress Omicron was Third Wing's mission. Her mission.

Do that, and get your next mission.

Streaking over the wasted surface of the moon at high velocity, Kat spotted the lone Republic observation tower on a ridgeline of low broken mountains ahead. It was skinned in the standard gleaming Repub white, standing out like a beacon in the unending lifeless gray regolith of the moon and the midnight drop cloth of the galaxy beyond.

"Viper Two! Contact!" alerted Nova Lead over squadron comm.

"Got it," Kat replied matter-of-factly as she tapped the tri-fighter's thrust rudders and aligned her angle of attack. With her gloved thumb, she flicked open the safety cover for the guns and began to spool up.

Repub Army, 231st Artillery
Fortress Omicron, Outer Perimeter Observation Tower 16
0159 Local System Time

Sergeant Durmmond Mactay liked things to run smoothly. And smoothly meant orderly. And orderly meant by the book. The men under his watch had learned that well, and often, under his tutelage through a series of surprise inspections and Dongalore fire drills—his personal specialty. They knew he was tough, but fair. Yeah, this post was the absolute dead end of upward mobility within the Republic, for NCO and officer alike. But it was Durmmond Mactay's post, and things would run dress right dress even if it was Unity Day in all its House of Reason silliness.

They were in the middle of a thirty-day rotation out to Observation Sixteen. By the time they got back to Omicron and down to Tarrago Prime, Unity Day would be well over.

All his little gun bunnies would be so sad knowing they'd missed yet another drunken bacchanal to end all drunken bacchanals until the next state-sponsored drunken bacchanal. There'd be others. There always were. The House of Reason would provide endlessly until one day it couldn't. Mactay had been around long enough to know the House of Reason was already queuing up some new holiday to celebrate something ridiculous and give everyone another day off from the drudgery of serving the glorious Republic. There would always be something historic to celebrate, even if they had to make something up.

Always.

His favorite attempt at unity through diversity had been Revision Day. A weeklong celebration of history, as the House of Reason wanted everyone to view it. It had been full of massive floats redefining the Savage Wars. Floats that had verged on the ridiculous with respect to historical authenticity. Mactay had traveled to as many of the old battlefields as he could from the dozens of duty stations he'd served at over the last twenty years, so he knew full well the zhee had never fought in *any* major Savage War battle. Yet to look at the prismatic digital-display floats on Revision Day, one would have thought they'd won the wars singlehandedly, all by themselves.

Like the stupid donk savages could do anything other than blow themselves up for their gods.

Ridiculous, he thought as he took another sip of his black coffee and watched the rest of the men sleep blissfully in their bunks. He'd been up for two hours to take over the watch. Done PT. Filled out all the necessary reports. Scheduled a day in full armor as a reward for the two privates he'd caught sleeping on watch a few minutes ago in the observation tower. They wouldn't be doing that again.

He'd dust-drilled them into the Stone Age.

"What the hell!" he'd screamed at them just after midnight. "This is an observation post. We *observe*. We observe in order to defend the main gun. We do not *sleep*. Sleeping is the opposite of what we do when we are on duty observing. Then it would be called a sleeping post and it would be useless to the Republic!"

He screamed, and growled, all this and much, much more, with the two men in what some called the push-up position, and what the Repub and the Legion chose to call the front-leaning rest position. He alternated this with dust drills. For upwards of twenty minutes he had their full focus in order to draw their attention to their many deficiencies as gunners and living beings. He watched their muscles shake while pools of sweat gathered beneath their trembling frames, and it warmed the cockles of his heart.

Exposed vacuum training for the whole day just after first chow was what was needed now. That would get everyone's mind right about what exactly went on at a forward observation post surrounding the most state-of-the-art gun system ever designed by the galaxy. What, exactly, did they think this was all about? And when he opened the airlocks, they'd find out that any of their gear that wasn't locked down—as it should be according to Standard Operating Procedure—would be vented all over the place, and... probably, and hopefully, be sucked out into deep space.

He delighted in the expectation of this moment of chaos and loss of their personal possessions.

That'll get their minds right.

Sure, thought Mactay, it was the worst post in the system. But it was his post, and things would run dress right dress until the time clocks reached 0600. He'd done lots of cruddy, boring gunnery and observation duty all across the Republic. He'd received his checks, he was assured of a pension someday, and he would do his damned best until it was time to clear post. That—

In the half second of life remaining to Sergeant Mactay, he watched the mug in his hand suddenly explode. He may also have heard the heavy glass in the observation tower above shattering into a thousand pieces. He may have. It was all so sudden and violent. Perhaps he might even have heard the distant hollow thrum of two heavy-duty chain guns spitting out over four thousand 30mm rounds that laced the superstructure of the observation tower along the lunar ridge, tearing through armor plating, gunners, the two observers who'd gone back to sleep, and finally the mug and coffee... and Sergeant Mactay.

Sound does travel in space and low atmosphere. That's the myth you have to constantly dispel when you work for the Repub Navy. The stars even sing if you know how to listen.

But a second later all was a howling venting of oxygen rushing into an airless void beyond walls suddenly turned to holed cheese by an automated rail gun system. Mactay was at once pulled off his feet and hit by three supersonic rounds moving at well over a thousand miles an hour. It was a sudden and horrible way to die.

But it was quick.

03

Black Fleet
Third Wing, First Squadron, "Pit Vipers"
Tarrago Moon
0200 Local System Time

Lieutenant Kat Haladis caught her breath while the tri-fighter beneath her bucked and pulled, spitting out supersonic high-velocity 30mm rounds. Slugs. Old-school Savage Wars rounds that left little whole, and did devastating work on vessels and equipment that needed to maintain atmospheric integrity in vacuum-exposed environments.

The results were brutal.

Blasters were cheaper to outfit, but they also had a slower rate of fire. They also often sealed any damage they did by fusing internal systems and armor plating. Damage control teams had a much easier time with that class of destruction. They'd trained for it almost exclusively.

But four thousand rounds on target could not be patched by even the most diligent of specialized bot-assisted damage control teams. Too many tiny holes in too many places. Not to mention explosive decompression sucking everyone—along with all that precious oxygen needed to sustain life—out into the unforgiving void of space.

In the aftermath of the apocalyptic Savage Wars, the House of Reason had classified slug throwers as weapons of mass destruction and outlawed their use, production, and ownership. Twenty-year gas mining sentence on the nearest giant if caught with any form of that type of weapon system. A mandatorily enforced living hell.

As the black and gray tri-fighter streaked past the ruined observation tower, just a few hundred feet from its exploding octagonal observation windows, with bodies, debris, and burning oxygen shooting up and outward across the dead moon's surface, Kat understood why the Black Fleet eschewed such restrictions.

One pass with these guns on full auto had done the trick easily.

The standard twin blasters the tri-fighter carried would've only managed a few hits in such a fast flyby. Instead she'd literally sprayed the tower with target-assist active. The tower was now venting into vacuum from a thousand places. There was no amount of damage control that would fix that. Especially if it was lightly armored. Everyone down there in that tower, she thought as the rest of the squadron two-clicked their congratulations over the comm, was dead.

Just fly the ship, Kat.

Just fly it.

"Good shooting, Viper Two," murmured Viper Lead across the static-washed ether.

Behind them the rest of the wing, hundreds of tri-fighters skinned like black and gray demons, leapt the ridgeline above the ruined tower and broke formation, peeling off to knock out as many outlying observation towers and auxiliary power supply facilities as they could. Up ahead across the long lunar valley in which this particular gun tube of Fortress Omicron lay, they saw the beginnings of the outer defenses that guarded the fabled orbital defense gun.

Best-case scenario, thought Kat as she switched to her secondary target waypoint, was that they got in a few passes before the turret defenses surrounding the main bore automated. Right now some tech was getting a check systems alert from the observation tower she'd just killed. They'd do a system malfunction check, cross-check, and verbal confirmation comm. But by then it would be over.

Worst case... someone was doing their job, and the defenses were online with turret guns charged and ranged to repel the strike. And if that was the case... they were flying into a shooting gallery.

Bridge of the Corvette *Audacity*
Kesselverks Shipyards
0201 Local System Time

"Captain... we're getting an emergency alert order from Admiral Bula. Stand by."

Desaix leaned over the helmsman's station and tapped the comm. Both the pilot's and co-pilot's seats were empty—a clear violation of shipyard SOP, which stated that at least one pilot needed to be on duty at all times. The comm officer was one deck up and the only one doing her job at present.

Still, Desaix was not totally unconvinced that something was wrong. Yes, everybody was slacking for Unity Day. Everyone knew it would be a half shift, followed by a wild drunken party in the afternoon and evening. But the alert wasn't internal. It wasn't coming from the *Audacity*.

It had been ordered by the shipyard commander in charge of refits and construction.

"Patch me through to the OIC on duty," Desaix asked the comm officer.

He began to boot up the flight controls. According to orders, the ship had to be ready to depart within three minutes of receiving a general alert. His fingers swam across the engine panels, flicking master switches to get the cold start sequence going. He muttered when he came to the portside thrusters. They were still disabled and needed a balance test before they could be cleared for operation.

"Can't get through, Captain!" came the comm officer's emphatic reply. Engine sequence to main startup climbed into the green. Desaix twisted back to find his command chair, and then remembered it hadn't been installed yet. So he leaned forward over the flight controls and tapped the pilot's comm for ship-wide broadcast.

"This is the captain. Prep for departure. Clear all mooring lines. All crewmembers, report to battle stations. We're not sure if this is a drill yet."

I *hope* this is a drill, he swore under his breath as he felt the tremor of the ship's massive engines coming slowly to life.

Desaix knew that the comm officer would be listening in on shipyard and orbital approach control traffic. She'd have a good idea what was really going on out there. If, anything *was* actually going on.

"What's this all about, Lieutenant?" he barked irritably. Maybe he should have gotten a few hours rest.

There was a long pause.

"Captain, low-orbit sensors are detecting three unidentified ships just beneath the atmosphere. Approach is saying one minute there wasn't anything near the defense squadron, and in the next second they were there. Wait... now they're reporting thousands of contacts falling toward the shipyards. Could be some kind of bombing run by a rogue MCR fleet that just jumped in. No one's sure of anything."

And we can't get deflectors up until we're airborne, thought Desaix grimly.

**Black Fleet Shock Troopers, Third Group
Tarrago Prime Atmosphere,
Altitude 110,547 Feet and Falling Fast
0202 Local System Time**

Sergeant Bombassa did not like falling through atmosphere. No, he didn't like it at all. He preferred ground combat. He preferred blasters on full auto, and even knives up close and personal.

And jumping off the back of a Republic destroyer seconds after it had jumped in, skimming atmosphere, in this new armor he'd been issued, was even worse than an ordinary jump. It was like being sucked out into the void only to fall all topsy-turvy longer than you ever thought possible. And much longer than you've ever wanted to. It was exactly like when a hull decompressed in deep space and vented in the middle of battle.

A thing that had happened to him only once.

An experience he'd never wanted to repeat.

But you've done a lot of things you haven't liked just to get off Kimshana, he reminded himself in an attempt to distract his mind from the seemingly endless fall toward the planet below. And you kept doing them because you never wanted to go back to that hot, stinking jungle world one of your ancestors colonized on nothing more than hopes, dreams, and old grievances. So you joined the Legion. And you sent all your paychecks back to your family, and your extended family, so they could continue their little back-to-nature experiment. An experiment that resulted in little more than an unbelievable death toll from the Gray Plague—what the rare viral biologist who visited called "hyper-malaria"—or due to bites from any of the four hundred different indigenous and highly poisonous two-headed snakes that called that world home long before your tribe showed up. Never mind all the endless and petty strongman warlord politics and superstitious voodoo your ancestors dragged out there, or the mean daily temperature of well over one hundred degrees in "winter."

Anything was better than Kimshana.

So, occasionally, as a part of the Legion, you'd allowed yourself to be thrown off the back of a drop shuttle. For as bad as this seemingly endless freefalling moment is... it ain't Kimshana.

But this ain't the Legion either, Bombassa had to remind himself as he gritted his teeth and dropped below ninety thousand feet, screaming like a burning comet through hard atmo. Thousands dropped alongside him at this very moment, and statistics indicated, as Bombassa well knew, that some weren't going to make it to the ground safely. They'd just burn all the way in and crater. The numbers required that *X* amount did exactly just that.

He could never push that thought out of his head every time he jumped.

"Bombassa!" growled the platoon leader over S-comm. Another ex-legionnaire. "Tighten up. You're drifting out of the LZ window. Stay within the target squares inside your HUD. It's almost over, big man. Hang in there."

Bombassa shifted his weight inside the special armor they'd been issued in the last days of training out there in the wastes of Tusca. Just like modern leej armor, but better. The gear he was wearing now was modified for high-orbit low-opening drops, and it was black, like his skin. A skin that was literally gushing cold sweat as the massive planet raced up at him through his HUD. He was so far up he could see the curvature of the planet in all directions. And to be honest, that freaked him out on levels he couldn't address without going stark raving mad.

He reminded himself that this was not his best work environment. That would be at the end of this fall.

"KTF, sir," whispered Bombassa once he was back within the digital glideslope of their approach to target, the massive Kesselverks Shipyards on Tarrago Prime.

He got a two-click acknowledgment.

In addition to the thousand shock troopers in this group, more were dropping on the capital itself, the Legion barracks, and other high-value objectives across the populated peninsula. But Third Group had the primary mission: to secure the shipyards and defend them against counterattack. And they were bringing some pretty heavy-duty equipment to do just that. Bombassa watched as a light mech, currently folded into its boxed-shaped transport mode, fell past a stick of shock troopers. Its modularized thrusters adjusted its flight path toward the pre-selected LZ.

General Nero had ordered them to take the massive shipyards... or die trying. Because if they didn't, then what was being accomplished would die before it even began to start. And every one of them had shouted back the phrase they'd been re-trained to use, the phrase that affirmed every command within this new Legion. This new... *Dark* Legion, as it were.

"Death to the Republic!" the general shouted on the desert floor of Tusca where the winds howled like lost ghosts.

And the eighty thousand of the Black Fleet had roared back, "DEATH TO THE REPUBLIC!"

The Republic hadn't been so bad, thought Bombassa as he continued his fall. If they hadn't thrown him out of the Legion, he would've stuck until he made sergeant major. Then retired to some nice little planet with lots of water and tiny islands.

Seventy thousand feet now and falling like a rock.

"Death to the Republic!"

Fifty thousand feet, and Bombassa remembered some old joke the jump masters in the Legion liked to crow in the minutes before a drop. In the minutes when Bombassa was rigid with fear and wanted nothing more than to throw up—or better yet, be somewhere else altogether.

"If my chute don't open wide, look out, world, I'm a-comin' through!"

They liked to sing that as they checked everyone's rig.

Fun times.

Not so much.

"No suh," whispered Bombassa in his deep bass voice, into the ether of his fancy new armor that smelled all new and high-tech. All industrial in its rubber and padding. "Chute goin' to open like it's supposed ta!"

Positive thinking. Just like Legion NCO Development School had taught him. You don't mind, they won't either.

Bombassa liked tricks. Especially tricks he could play on himself to get him to do things he didn't want to do.

"What's that, Sergeant?" asked the LT over the comm.

Bombassa still hadn't gotten used to the new software the suit ran. They called it S-comm instead of the Legion's L-comm. It was exactly like the software the Legion ran inside their armor, but not quite as reliable.

"I say—"

Sudden turbulence began to buffet the falling armor at forty thousand. Bombassa checked his stick. The rest of the men who'd dropped behind him—really gotten sucked out into nothing behind him—were being thrown all across the sky, fighting to maintain their orientation to the ground and the target. The turbulence wouldn't last, Bombassa reminded himself. The briefing had made that clear. Just weather and temperature layers playing their games.

"I say," began Bombassa again, his voice shaking from being thrown about. He hoped his compact assault blaster was still secured to his armor. The shaking was getting more violent now. "KTF, sir."

"We don't do that anymore, Sergeant," came the reply over S-comm. "But I copy all the same. And... roger that. KTF, Sergeant."

At a thousand feet, Bombassa was screaming in so hard he thought if he waited one more second he'd splatter all over some high-rise sky crane or mammoth construction gantry—even *if* his chute deployed. A thousand feet above the massive shipyard, in Bombassa's mind, was way too low for things not to end badly. And for a second it did seem as though he'd just continue straight on into the ground, where he'd bounce off one of the big corvettes under construction down there. Or even go straight through a hull.

But then the graphene micro-fiber SmartChute auto-deployed.

And blaster fire from the anti-air turrets opened up.

As the thousands of floating shock troopers drifted down into the oh-dark-middle-of-the-night shipyards, men all around Bombassa were burned straight through by high-intensity blaster fire that suddenly seemed everywhere all at once. Seared chutes collapsed and dropped armored shock troopers into the heavy cranes and ships under construction. Klieg lights searched and air raid sirens wound up into their urgent doomsday howls, warning everyone against the attack.

Fine, thought Bombassa. And then he forgot all about bad points who made themselves heroes and got good men thrown out of the Legion, or outright killed, just so they could advance their pathetic careers. Or wretched Kimshana. Or dying in the atmosphere. Or dying in space.

Once he reached the ground, everyone was going to pay the price required for him to live the life he wanted.

He executed a perfect parachute-landing fall on a wide spot along the hull of a half-painted corvette. His armor made a loud metallic gong, and he rolled his body with the impact. The gel-shock layers within his armor did their best to cushion the fierce blow and negate the brutality of physics. Bombassa slammed his glove against the auto-disengage and rolled away from the chute harness, coming up with his compact blaster rifle ready to engage targets. Ready to kill his way to the other side of another day.

He forgot about all the terrors that plagued him before this moment, and set his mind to not dying in the next.

And to do that he would have to kill everyone who stood in his way.

"K... T... F," he said slowly, scanning for targets across the midnight shipyards.

House of Reason
Utopion

Orrin Kaar looked gravely into the holobot, his hands folded on his desk. "Of course I agree that a meeting of the House Security Council may be warranted, but not at this juncture."

Aletha A'lill'n, the Security Council's vice chair, restated her case. "Delegate Kaar, every indication received so far suggests that the attack at Tarrago is something beyond what the Mid-Core Rebellion is capable of."

Kaar gave a wan smile. "Now where have I heard that before? Was it Kublar?"

A'lill'n pulled back slightly. "I don't mean in terms of military threat. There's a risk in every attack, I understand that. But these comm reports..." The delegate picked up her datapad and read from it. "Legionnaire-like ground forces in black armor. Starfighters of unknown types..."

"Delegate A'lill'n—"

"If there is a threat to those factories, we should ready a battle fleet with full Legion support, and we can't do that if the Security Council doesn't first convene."

"Delegate A'lill'n..." Kaar tried again.

"Military comms aren't reporting, suggesting localized jamming. Perhaps by a fleet of unknown affiliation focusing on the moon and planetary factories. Or sabotage of the comm relays, or—"

Kaar spoke softly, his voice warm. "Aletha. We both know there isn't a force large enough in the galaxy to withstand the might of the Republic."

"And what about the reports of Republic destroyers firing on one another?"

"In the confusion of a terrorist attack, it is often difficult for those observing to deliver accurate information. And, should friendly fire have occurred, tragic as those times are, they hardly necessitate an emergency meeting of the Security Council."

The Security Council's vice chair surrendered with a sigh. "Of course you're right, Orrin."

Kaar smiled. "That the MCR is capable of the occasional coordinated attack is a persistent and sad reality. After Kublar, they nearly pulled off a terrorist bombing of the House of Reason itself. Let's wait for the Legion to repulse the assault. If the MCR acquired more capital ships, let them come and see firsthand what our orbital gun emplacements can do."

Delegate A'lill'n nodded slowly, her conviction seeming to grow with each second. "Thank you, Delegate Kaar."

"It's my pleasure, dear Aletha. If Tarrago doesn't report the situation under control within"—Kaar glanced at the chrono-display—"two hours, I'll arrange a meeting and we'll make sure the Legion and armed forces are doing their jobs to protect the Republic."

The transmission ended, and Kaar leaned back in his chair, the leather releasing a *blurp* as his hips shifted. He tapped his chin twice, then leaned forward to activate a secure comm transmission.

Kaar arched an eyebrow as the face of a young woman with platinum-blond hair appeared. She seemed to be recovering from a pair of black eyes.

"Sentrella," Kaar said, passing over any discussion about *how* she came to look like that. "Get me your employer. Immediately, if you please."

Black Fleet
Third Wing, First Squadron, "Pit Vipers"
Tarrago Moon, Over Fortress Omicron
0205 Local System Time

The battery towers that encircled the massive gun tube opened up on the swarming tri-fighters in the dark space above the base.

"Watch that north tower, Viper Six," called out the squadron leader over the comm.

His warning was too late.

Targeted turret fire found its mark. The massive quad barrels of the turret opened up in their *tom tom* motion on Katazzo, a guy Kat had only barely known. That tri-fighter exploded, leaving a smoking debris trail that ended somewhere out in the gray dust of the long lunar valley.

Someone called out a targeting spot report.

Kat was doing everything she could to evade heavy concentrations of green-hued streaking turret fire in order to set up a strafing run on any tower she could get an angle on. But it was verging on the impossible. The firepower coming from the base had gone from nothing to completely overwhelming in seconds.

She picked up Viper Lead's six and fell in as his wingman as he streaked across the base once more, trying to draw turret fire so the others could attack.

"Break off, break off, break off!" he was calling out to her when a turret burst caught his dorsal deflector and sent him spinning off course. He screamed just before his ship smashed into a monolithic gray wall that surrounded the fortress below.

There was no surviving that.

For a moment, Kat did nothing. Felt nothing. She was stunned and empty. She let her tri-fighter streak out across the barren surface of the moon. Away from the battle.

Someone in the squad was calling for her.

Asking for orders.

Needing help.

"What're the orders, Viper Two?"

And then it hit her.

She was in charge.

She came to and pulled the tri-fighter back around in a hard-banking turn, coming straight back at the fortress on the horizon. She dialed in a broad-focus setting on the target-assist for the 30mm cannons that hung below her ship.

Spray and pray, she thought as she increased to attack speed. She streaked just over the outer wall of the sprawling fortress, jerking the fighter hard first this way, then that to avoid fire. Doing everything she could to dodge the heavier clusters of interlocking turret fire all around her.

The 30mm barrels spun up and began to spit out short bass-note thrumming bursts of depleted uranium ball ammunition in mass quantities. She barely saw her wild strafing line rip a turret to shreds, but she heard the distant detonation through the hull of her fighter and saw the sudden light flare lit up the inside of her dark cockpit.

"Got one!" she grunted into the ether. Radar lock warnings screamed across her controls, and she banked hard and pushed the throttle full forward to evade. Turret fire tracked ahead of her, anticipating her position, and behind her in case she tried something tricky.

Over the comm, came the sounds of screaming and dying. She watched other tri-fighters get knocked down, or plow into the fortress complex. A few climbed to avoid green chasing blaster fire. It was setting up to be a slaughter.

Some part of her wanted to scrub and run. Get everyone out of here, or at least as many as she could. They'd lost the edge provided by surprise, and now they were being swatted from the skies like darting and annoying insects in some light show shooting gallery.

She was out over the lifeless gray wastes of the moon once more. She diverted power to the deflectors and ran for cover behind a series of low jagged hills beyond the complex.

"Viper Two!" shouted someone over the comm. "Bad guys inbound. Break off?"

She checked the comm traffic identifier and her available ammo in one quick look. Then she cranked her helmeted head to scan outside the starboard cockpit glass to visually identify the targets. She clocked several Lancers inbound on the tri-fighters that still swarmed the gun towers. Less than there had been, but some of the squadron was still in action. Still on mission.

A mission that had begun less than a minute ago.

"Negative, Viper Five. Re-form and stagger attacks on the towers. We've got to take them out before the bombers arrive. Otherwise this whole op is a no-go. Fleet's depending on us, boys. Make your shots count."

She yanked the ship into a climb and watched the battle below.

"Viper Two... Warlord Actual." Comm from the strike commander's traffic coordination officer—the air boss. "Bombers inbound. Two minutes out. Status on towers?"

"Active, Warlord. But we'll have them down."

There was no reply. She knew the air boss would be apprising the strike commander. There was still enough time to call off the bombers.

Which would be a failure.

And failure was not an option today.

"Talk to me, Dasto," she whispered.

Black Fleet
Second Bombardment Wing,
Ninth Squadron, "Black Jacks"
Tarrago Moon, Inbound on Fortress Omicron
0208 Local System Time

"Throttle back to targeting speed," said the flight lead over comm.

Easy for you to say, thought Lieutenant Fasio. Easy for you to say... as though this were anything but real live actual combat and you're riding lead bomber. Me, I'm stuck down here in the bomber's cupola just a few feet beneath your butt. I'm gonna see it happen. I'm gonna *see* the bolt of blaster fire as it comes up at us. The one that's going to get us.

"Easy for you to say."

Those were the things bombardier Fasio was thinking, muttering really, as he looked down at the pockmarked surface of the moon far below. And at the battle over the fortress in the distance.

"I can hear you over internal comm, Fasio."

"I'm just saying... if those towers aren't down, we won't be able to dodge even a little bit and still line up for a perfect drop on the bore. Just saying, sir."

Bravo One ignored his testy bombardier and concentrated on lining up his ship for the attack. If they didn't hit that orbital gun guarding the approach to Tarrago Prime, the fleet was doomed. And everyone knew there were fates worse than failing. If the rumors about who was behind all this were true, that was enough to make you want to do your job just to avoid meeting *him*.

The man in black.

Everyone had their recruitment stories. Everyone had ended up on Tusca, training for the war that was coming with the Republic. They'd signed the datapad, sworn the oath, and settled in. But in their year of training, there really hadn't been that much about who was actually in charge beyond the people immediately above you and the grand inspections by the senior admirals.

There had been rumors, however.

Everyone called him "the man in black." If hushed whispers over your shoulder counted as calling someone something. People had seen things. Some people had even disappeared—and not always because they failed at some task or couldn't handle the intense training.

"Fasio, set drop altitude at current flight level. Let's lock in the targeting solution before we're over the target, roger?"

The bombardier grumbled a bare acknowledgment and set to his instruments. In just a moment he'd arm the munitions. Drop 'em. And then they could get the hell straight out of here.

And if those towers weren't down... well then what did it all matter anyway?

Safe House
Somewhere at Galaxy's Edge

Aldo Kimer was sweating by the time his conversation with Orrin Kaar was over. He'd relocated everything to avoid the retribution of Goth Sullus, only to find out that his single best client was in league with the man. Had that saved his life the first time Sullus came to him, seeking the location of Kael Maydoon? Would it save his life now? Or had Wraith left Kimer's name out of things?

The questions only added to his pounding headache. Too much stress along with a roaring hangover. He needed to be more moderate with his end-of-night libations, he knew, but the constancy of looking over his shoulder since that last encounter with the bounty hunter wore on him. A few drinks were all that seemed to settle his poor nerves.

Perhaps this job would stabilize things once more. After all, the price for both tasks was enough to get him into a core-world business park, and there was no telling how much his business could grow from there.

"Sentrella," Kimer called out.

His receptionist-bodyguard entered the makeshift office immediately, as though she's been standing just outside the door. She probably had.

"We're brokering a job from Delegate Kaar. He wants the comm relay network around Tarrago shut down. No comm traffic in or out of the planet. I think Sanatole Krenz is the one we need for this... given the circumstances."

Sentrella nodded. "Spare no expense, Mr. Kimer?"

"Spare no expense," Kimer echoed.

Levenir Orbit
The Galactic Core

The comm burst came from Utopion. Cade Thrane was sure of that. The slicer had triangulated the ultra-encrypted messages through the comm relay. Whether coming or going, an end user was always in Utopion.

But who?

Thrane moved around the lounge of his orbital space yacht. No one would mistake the old luxury boat for one of the mega yachts owned by the core's wealthiest beings, but it *was* a luxury craft, no matter how old, and at one time, it had been coveted. Who knew what sort of debauched parties had taken place here? For Thrane, it was a symbol. A code-slicer for hire, he vowed to live in luxury, even if it meant doing so by degrees.

Now he orbited the core planet of Levenir, because core rent was too high, but a satellite bearing was within reach. He lived in a ship that only hinted at its former decadence. But one day... one day he would live *on* the planet. And his ship would be gleaming, straight from the showroom.

Thrane drummed on an imaginary kit to the sound of screeching nova-metal. Good thinking music. "Okay, so the comm burst initiates as a basic Repub holo-strand," he said, scribbling notes on the lightboard in the middle of his lounge. He kicked a pile of clothes off the side and examined his notes. "That's as far as most people would look. But then it switches to UE..."

Ultra-encryption. L-comm level stuff. The truly unbreakable coding, though Thrane liked to fancy he'd gotten close to cracking the ever-changing L-comm once or twice.

But this *wasn't* an L-comm transmission. This was something he hadn't seen before. Until today. And it was driving Thrane up the wall. So much so that he had been neglecting his paid work—and now he was going to have to pull an all-nighter to finish doing a UE decrypt for a client, a paranoid military type sure his junior officers were plotting against him. Not the most difficult job in the world—crack into a few datapads, see what's there—and enough credits to make it worth the time. If he actually got around to doing it.

Thrane looked back at his computing station. He really should get going on that job...

A shipboard chime sounded. Another comm burst from the mystery encryption. They had been buzzing back and forth all day. Something was definitely going on.

Thrane went back to his lightboard to jot down his thoughts on the puzzle. The paid job could wait a little longer.

Black Fleet
Third Wing, First Squadron, "Pit Vipers"
Tarrago Moon, Over Fortress Omicron
0209 Local System Time

"Negative... negative hits on Tower Four, Viper Two. We'll have to go around again."

Viper Three had followed Kat over the target and recorded hits. Of the four massive squat turrets that had once watched over the Republic's sprawling orbital defense gun complex, three were ruined and venting atmosphere. But one was still active and knocking down any tri-fighters that dared attempt to take it out, including

Kat's. She had taken hits on two of her three deflectors and had barely gotten away with a damaged ion engine.

But she still had enough ammunition for one last pass.

And the bombers were due in seconds.

"Coming around again," she said as the tri-fighter howled all around her. She adjusted the throttles and dialed in more reserve power to the forward deflectors. The massive engine of the tri-fighter screamed like an obedient banshee from the nether regions of some nightmare.

"Viper Two... are you sure about that?"

"Got to, Viper Three. Those bombers will be sitting hoopas if we don't."

"I'm on your six, Viper Two... here they come!"

Six Repub Lancers swept off the moonscape floor and scattered to engage, fighter-to-fighter. Their powerful twin nacelle engines made them faster, but harder to maneuver.

"Slowing to maneuver speed and lining up my guns!" shouted Kat over comm as blaster fire from the Lancers raced over her ship. "Keep him off my back, please."

"Roger that, Two," replied Viper Three.

Kat danced her tri-fighter nimbly across the surface of the moon. The hiss and screech of close fire against her hull shook her tiny ship as she dived toward the one tower still hurling bolts at anything in its firing arcs.. She rolled her shoulders and leaned forward toward the dim red glow of the targeting halo. She pulled the trigger and unloaded on the ground turret, staying on target, throttling back as the high-speed rounds lanced out ahead and smacked the turret's base like a swarm of angry mummybees, chewing the superstructure to shreds.

She added some reverse thruster, causing the nose of the tri-fighter to pop up, then she added another burst from the guns that smashed into the turret proper.

Incredibly, the turret continued to fire back at her.

Viper Three went up in a debris cloud alongside Kat, throwing her ship hard to port from the force of its exploding ion engines. And still she held target and emptied her guns into the defiant turret, landing hundreds of hits in a bare second, watching plating and machinery come apart as internal cooling systems from the turbo blasters vented and suddenly exploded.

And *still* the damn gunner kept firing back at her.

"Die already!" she screamed at whoever was in that turret.

Her ship took a solid hit. The forward deflector screamed high-pitched bloody murder and collapsed. Kat's fighter rolled hard, suddenly uncontrollable.

Kat heard herself shriek, then fought it down as she struggled to get the wounded ship back under control. Internal systems shorted out and fire control kicked in. Her panel blinked and went down. For a brief moment she was flying blind with nothing but the metal-laced front view for guidance. She watched as the moon abruptly turned on its side and then began to hit the ceiling of her ship.

Is this what it was like, Dasto?

She grunted through gritted teeth, seeing her dead brother as she yanked on the lifeless yoke, willing it to obey her. Now she was stalled and ready to dead spin back into the moon's gravitation well.

A Lancer shot past her, its engines humming wildly. For a moment she had a perfect sight picture on the larger fighter. A perfect kill for her guns. For a moment...

before the moon would reach out to embrace her forever, pulling her down to her death. For eternity.

The fighter's AI reconnected with the controls and rerouted operation to her HUD.

Kat fell back on her training. She backed off the engine as she took the controls in her gloves once more, fighting the instinct to right the ship and save her life. That way was death, with no speed and precious altitude above a celestial body. As the moon's surface raced up at her, she leveled and brought the engines back online. Then she punched it and shot toward the horizon, climbing for space as soon as she had speed. Climbing for the distant fleet in a wounded bird with no fangs.

Black Fleet
Second Bombardment Wing,
Ninth Squadron, "Black Jacks"
Inbound on Fortress Omicron
0208 Local System Time

The flight lead had time to drop his weapons package—two STG deep cluster bombs—from his tri-fighter bomber variant before that lone remaining tower began to take out the bombers. A few others managed to get their bombs off. Most got knocked down.

Fasio watched both his cluster bombs fall away and fire their internal jets to adjust final targeting. They'd race for the massive maw of the main gun tube in the dead center of the fortress and streak down into its deep darkness, where the rail gun assist mechanisms made its cataclysmic shots possible. Somewhere along its length the bombs would explode—hopefully taking out the critical maglev components that made the weapon so fierce against any approaching capital ship. It would also be a good hit if the bombs took out those systems that allowed last-minute guidance. If the weapon couldn't be aimed, then it was almost useless.

A moment later, Fasio quickly scrambled backward as much as his harness restraints would allow inside the tight bombing cupola beneath the tri-fighter variant. He willed himself into the seat behind him. Anything to get away from the blaster bolts the tower turret was flinging up at them.

But there was only so far one could go in a tri-fighter bomber variant.

The first bolt missed, but the second smashed straight into the bomber—killing both Fasio and the flight lead.

Of the Black Jacks, only three ships would return to the fleet.

The orbital defense gun was still operational.

04

Bridge of the Corvette *Audacity*
Kesselverks Shipyards
0214 Local System Time

Audacity climbed away from her docking cradle among roving bone-white searchlights and throbbing emergency alert strobes. Desaix leaned over the helmsman's shoulder and stared out at the sprawling shadowy shipyard below. Dark figures were running across the gantries and long platforms between the various ships. The unmistakable bright flash of blaster fire was everywhere.

"Clearing three hundred, Captain," reported the helmsman. The ship's co-pilot was busy getting local nav info and seeming to make little sense of what was going on across the comm net.

"Captain," said the comm officer, her voice static-filled and distorted over the bridge comm. "Admiral Bula on visual. High priority message."

In the absence of his command chair, Desaix had to make his way to a screen panel off to one side behind the helmsman. As he held onto crash handles mounted into the low ceiling, the entire ship was shuddering, and Desaix couldn't help but wonder not if, but *which* crucial repairs hadn't been effected before takeoff. They'd still had another thirty days of refit to undergo.

Now they were making for atmosphere and under some kind of attack.

The Tennarian admiral, Bula, appeared within the tiny screen. Vocal synch was bad, so his words followed three seconds after the squid man's lipless mouth moved.

"Captain Desaix!" shouted the humanoid squid, apparently unsure if his transmission was being received. One of the admiral's tentacles brushed sweat, or blood, from his uniform.

"Desaix here. Admiral?"

It was clear Admiral Bula was aboard the flagship of the sector defense group. Behind him emergency lighting undulated in reds and shifting shadows, and Desaix could hear the ship's damage control klaxons resounding ominously, as well as some kind of automated damage control alert indicating a hull breach in progress.

The transmission broke up for a second, then cleared suddenly, synching the admiral's words in real time.

"... we're holding a jump corridor for your ship, Captain. Get clear of Tarrago and rendezvous with Admiral Landoo and her fleet. Coordinates incoming. Inform her ... situation ... dire. All system transmissions are being jammed."

Suddenly the *Audacity*'s navigator was swearing.

"Captain! Collision alert! We've got a massive piece of debris falling out of orbit and inbound on an intercept course. Looks like a ship of some sort. One of ours. Plotting evasive—"

"I see it!" yelled the co-pilot.

"It's coming straight at us!" shrieked the helmsman as he fought to adjust the departure heading *Audacity* was currently tracking to reach orbit.

Desaix turned to see what looked like the burning engineering section of a Republican destroyer falling straight toward them out of the sky. Thick white smoke trailed behind it high into the distant reaches of the silvery clouds and the night above. Escape pods jettisoned, and crewmembers and debris fell away from the burning hulk.

"Emergency power to forward deflectors!" shouted Desaix, knowing they would do little against a direct hit from another ship. He had a sudden dark vision of the wreckage smashing directly into his ship and carrying them down into the cities below.

"Hang on!" yelled the helmsman.

"Don't use the starboard thrust deflectors. They're—"

"I know!" cried the pilot in tense exasperation.

The *Audacity* shifted over to starboard in one brief instant, barely missing the streaking bulk of burning space debris. The entire flight deck watched as more debris, and crew, trailed past in its wake.

Desaix turned back to the admiral on screen.

"We're under attack, Captain," the admiral was saying. "Alert the fleet and get them back here as soon as possible. We'll hold them off for as long as we can."

"Who's attacking us, Admiral?"

"Unclear at this time, Captain. The attack seems to be coming from three unidentified and very large battleship-class vessels out beyond Tarrago Moon. They're keeping their distance, most likely due to the orbital defense gun. But ships impersonating ... Repub ... jumped in ... attacked us in low orbit. We're transmitting a targeting data package with everything we've acquired."

Small bits of debris began to slam into the hull of the *Audacity* as it climbed into the upper atmosphere.

"We're launching fighters to give you a jump window now, Captain," continued Admiral Bula. "Good luck and good hunting."

Then the admiral was gone.

Deep Space Orbital Platform
Tarrago System

Sanatole Krenz couldn't believe his luck. He'd thought Aldo Kimer would never send him another job after the way things went down at Bocccy. But now, he was about to make more money from one job than he'd made in the past ten years combined. At least, theoretically. Time was of the essence. He'd only receive the full payoff if the job was done within fifteen minutes of tender. The reward would drop exponentially every minute thereafter.

Krenz figured he could change into his Republic maintenance coveralls and find the right ID pass in ten minutes. Another twenty minutes of travel time, maybe eight minutes through the comm relay station. Eight more minutes back... still a pretty payday if he brought the relay down in that amount of time.

More money than he needed.

Krenz smiled at that.

There was no such thing as more money than you needed.

House of Reason
Utopion

The light on Orrin Kaar's comm station pulsed, indicating an incoming comm. Admiral Devers. Kaar shifted in his chair and returned his eyes to Delegate A'lill'n. The vice chair of the Security Council had been after him yet again to call a meeting. Word had reached Utopion that Tarrago's orbital defense fleet and the moon itself were now under attack. The time to stall was finished. If he put this meeting off any longer, he himself might come under suspicion from some hotshot young delegate looking to weasel his way into this office.

"Delegate Kaar?" A'lill'n asked, still waiting on a response to a question. Though Kaar could not recall what she had asked.

"I'm sorry," Kaar said, doing his best to look bewildered, as though the events and his age were conspiring against him. "The magnitude of what may be before us is... has me lost in thought. We've worked so hard to avoid another Kublar for our Republic, and now..."

Kaar let the sentence linger, leaving it open to the hearer's interpretation.

"So you agree that a meeting of the Council is required?" prodded A'lill'n.

"Yes," Kaar said, a sudden resolve ringing clear in his voice, a reminder of the tremendous oratory ability that granted him perpetual election. "Please inform the other members that we will meet in thirty minutes. I have much to do. I'll see if I can obtain Legion Commander Keller's assessment, assuming he is aware of the situation. Admiral Devers's fleet is near the system. I'll call upon his expertise."

"Admiral Landoo's Seventh Fleet should be stationed near Tarrago as well."

"Yes," Kaar said somewhat absently. "We'll make sure the pieces are in their proper places."

A'lill'n signed off, and Kaar immediately took Devers's comm message. "You have news?"

"I've engaged Tarrago's defense fleet, causing crippling damage. They won't last long."

Kaar nodded grimly. "I wonder what will come of reports that it is *Republic* destroyers assaulting the planet..."

Devers was confident. "At this point, my super-destroyer is more than capable of scrambling comm relays. I intend to broadcast over all Republic channels, announcing that the defense fleet was mutinous, and that I have been sent to restore order."

"Good. That message needs to be broadcast galaxy-wide. I'll announce it at the meeting of the Security Council."

Devers smiled weakly. "It will do until further reports of the attack reach Utopion."

"I've arranged for Tarrago's comm relays to shut down momentarily. The truth will never reach Utopion. You are the hero of the Republic, Silas. Send your message, then remember a lesson from your time in the Legion: kill them all, and kill them first. Leave no one alive to challenge your narrative."

"Understood, Delegate."

Comm System Relay Command and Control Station
Tarrago System

Sanatole Krenz whistled as he made his way through the comm relay command station in the Tarrago system. Each system had at least one manned comm relay station, or more depending on size. Tarrago had just the one, along with several satellite relays. Of course, these were all redundant, and the network was designed to continue working with the loss of up to sixty percent of satellites and the manned relay station itself.

The Republic comm system—private, public, and military—was an engineering wonder. But it wasn't flawless.

Krenz stood outside the secure control room. Inside, there would be one Republic employee monitoring the comm relays for overall health. He would be unarmed.

The control room's exterior security protocol sprang to life as Krenz approached. It gave a low, singsong chime. *Dee-dah.* This meant that Krenz had ten seconds to sing the six-note tonal response. The genius of this security check was that it was so unique. Sure, some species in the galaxy had tonal or singing dialects, but most did not. Intruders without the necessary layers of training, voice lessons, and know-how that came with being an employee of the Republic Comm Section simply would not know what to do when greeted with the security chime.

And then they would be vaporized with particle atomizers recessed in the walls.

The Republic might be a lot of things, but clueless about the need to protect its comm relays from disruption was not one of them. That's why the job paid so well—though gambling *did* have a way of cutting into that salary—and why Krenz had been forced to go through multiple psychiatric and character evaluations, background checks, bio-temperament scans, and an eighteen-standard-month wait period just to get the job.

It was also why an independent investigator was to monitor all comm section employees no less than twice per year.

When Krenz first succumbed to Aldo Kimer's offers of big money for easy work—his first job involved forwarding comm relays between a low-level senator's aide and the senator's mistress—he was sure that the control room door would blast open and a kill team would take him away, never to be heard from again. He didn't realize then that he was far too small a fish to attract a kill team. But when no one noticed, he did believe Aldo Kimer. The integrity inspectors near Tarrago were lazy, and no one paid him any mind beyond a cursory interview.

"Have you been a good boy, Sanatole?"

"Oh, yes, sir."

"Excellent."

End of interview.

And so things went swimmingly for a while. Krenz helped to report comm messages of all types, even black-channel contracts, and always got a cut of the action. If it weren't for those crossed wires at Bocccy... No. That was in the past. Kimer called on him for this, and that meant the good times—and the credits—would keep coming.

Krenz sang the tune to disarm the security, then keyed in his authorization code. The door swooshed open and the shift's controller, a family man named Lariot, swiveled around lazily in his chair.

"Oh, hey, San, I thought you were off duty for Unity Day?"

Krenz gave a sour frown he'd been practicing the entire trip. "I was supposed to be, but Victor said there'd probably be additional comm traffic, and since I wasn't doing anything, I should come in and help. So how is it?"

"The traffic?" Lariot swung around in his chair. "Actually pretty jumpy. There's something going on by the shipyards, but I can't get an idea of what. MCR hit and fade is my guess."

"Interesting," Krenz said, as he pulled a stinger pistol from his belt. He aimed the tiny weapon at his co-worker and shot a dart into the back of his neck.

Lariot slapped at the wound as if he'd been stung by a hiver, then slumped unconscious onto the control board. He wouldn't remember the last fifteen minutes when he woke up. And once Krenz falsified the security logs and holocams...

Krenz pushed Lariot to the side and frowned. Lariot was a good guy. He had a family. He would probably get fired for this.

Krenz shrugged and began working the comm station. He would pay off the man's mortgage once his payment came in.

Sanatole Krenz sped through the comm station, his work finished. Before the Tarrago comm relays had all gone dead to the rest of the galaxy, he received a message from Aldo Kimer. A Nimbus Rover performance ship was waiting for him at the port docking station. Kimer made a point of saying he'd spared no expense. And with a ship like that... he wasn't lying.

Practically bounding up the narrow docking tube that snaked out from the comm station to the waiting ship, Krenz saw the brilliant yellow sunburst paint of the ship. It was breathtaking. And hopefully it had a decent AI. Krenz wasn't much of a pilot.

His fears were allayed when a congenial bot with pilot's wings stenciled on its chest plate greeted him at the cabin door. "Hello, sir. Where shall we go?"

"Someplace with white sand beaches and beautiful humanoids," Krenz said, shouldering his way past the bot.

"I will enter those parameters into the ship's navicomputer," the bot said as it sealed the cabin door. "If you'll excuse me, we must make haste."

Krenz dismissed the bot with a wave of his hand. The robotic pilot entered the cockpit, and seconds later the ship began to hum.

Flopping into an amply stuffed leather lounger, Krenz fished around a chiller for a bottle of chamblisies. He found one, popped the cork, and poured himself a frothy glass of the magenta liquid.

The ship gently detached from its docking station and drifted into space before activating repulsors. Krenz lurched slightly, just enough to spill a little chamblisies on his uniform. "Should I buckle in?" he asked the pilot. "Or are you going to get the inertial dampers adjusted to a level adequate for humans?"

"That won't be necessary," the bot said over the shipboard comms. "I will attempt to adjust the dampers. They have been troublesome."

"Fine by me. Those belts are never comfortable." Krenz took a drink, and immediately went into a coughing fit. This was a bit stronger than he was used to.

"Mr. Kimer asked me to relay a message to you, sir," the bot said.

"Oh yeah? What's that?"

There was a loud thunking from somewhere in the rear of the ship—then a rumble that shook Krenz in his seat. He dug his hands into the folds of his seat looking for a safety belt, but found none.

A roaring alarm sounded, and Krenz felt a drastic change in cabin pressure. A rush of wind swept past him, and he found himself ripped from his seat, along with every other item not strapped down. When he flew out of the open cabin door and into the vacuum of space, there was chamblisies in his eyes.

Aldo Kimer had spared no expense.

And, per Orrin Kaar's instructions, he had left no witnesses.

Nebula Cloud Apartments
Tarrago Prime

As Vigdis watched the local holonews, she felt a heaviness over what might have been. Image after image flashed past. Republic assault shuttles landing around key supply depots and the shipyard itself. A pitched blaster fight between legionnaires in odd black armor and the local security forces. Dead revelers on the streets. It seemed as though the entire planet was under subjugation. And the journobots were reporting still more casualties—citizens who had found themselves caught in the crossfire or crushed beneath Republic tanks.

Vigdis's and her husband's shifts at the shipyard were supposed to have started nearly thirty minutes ago. The couple had been irritated over the fact that, in spite of requesting this time off nearly a month ago, they were nonetheless scheduled to work on Unity Day. But that job in the shipyard, inspecting impervisteel for impurities, had saved her life. Her husband's, too. Had they not been at home preparing for their shifts when the fighting started...

Vigdis shuddered.

"Any luck getting a comm transmission off-system?" Vigdis's husband Edward called from the window. He carried a single-action blaster rifle in one hand as he peered through an opening in the electromagnetic shutters, watching for danger. "Your mother is going to be worried sick."

"No. I can't get anything beyond Tarrago, and most of what we receive are prerecorded messages advising comm use for emergency purposes only."

"Not sure what else you'd call this..."

Vigdis smiled. Edward could find humor in anything. It was why she'd fallen in love with him.

Every holoscreen in the couple's modest apartment lit up with the crest of the Republic. Vigdis gasped at the sight of the handsome man that appeared: Admiral Devers, the Republic's greatest living hero.

The admiral spoke with confidence and authority. "This is Admiral Silas Devers of Republic Navy, Third Fleet." He paused as if to let the weight of his position sink in. "I have been sent by the Senate Council and House of Reason to put down a terrorist rebellion seeking to capture or destroy the Kesselverks Shipyards. The Mid-Core Rebels have infiltrated the local security forces and the planetary defense fleet and are actively fighting against Republic forces. Do not be alarmed by the legionnaires in black armor. They are a new evolution of soldiers serving in the Third Fleet. They will not harm you. Citizens of the Republic, I urge you to stay in your homes until Republic order is restored. And to the insurgents I say: You will not have the victory this day."

The message ended, and the screen reverted to the crest. The message would repeat every five minutes.

"Well," Edward said. "I guess we stay put."

Vigdis nodded, fingering the necklace resting against her chest. "Yes. I feel so much better knowing the admiral is here fighting for us."

Black Fleet
Bridge of the *Imperator*
Off Tarrago Moon
0216 Local System Time

A sick feeling was beginning to grow deep inside Admiral Rommal's stomach. And truth be told... it had been there for as long as he could remember. Some kind of unspoken fear and anxiety that had always been his constant companion.

Of course, in any operation there were bound to be mistakes. But that buffoon Devers had just ruined everything.

"We'll have to inform... *him*," Admiral Crodus had murmured as they sat reviewing the status updates.

Yes, thought Admiral Rommal as he stepped away from the bridge's real-time holographic tables and over to his personal comm station, the fault will be yours. You, after all... are the one in charge.

He touched the comm and tried to wash away the image of Devers jumping in three destroyers to shoot up the sector defense fleet. They'd scored direct hits and knocked out critical systems. But that hadn't been the plan. The plan had been to jump in *one* destroyer full of shock troops and drop them over the shipyards for a surprise attack. Then that destroyer would've jumped out to re-form with the rest of Devers's fleet—just another Repub ship transiting through—instead of attempting to shoot everything up, thereby alerting the rest of the in-system forces.

Devers had shown all their hands far too early. The idiot. Was he attempting to frame himself as some kind of victorious cavalry officer who wins the battle in one swift stroke? Instead, his actions had resulted in the activation of system-wide defenses, including the gun batteries around Fortress Omicron—which in turn had stopped the fleet's bombers cold.

There are no contingencies for a fool in your own ranks, he thought.

Goth Sullus appeared on screen—as much as he *could* appear. All that really showed were blue shadows and darkness, and just the barest outline of the lower half of his shadowed face. The rest remained hidden by the hooded cloak he wore.

Shrouded.

The man in black. That was what everyone called him when no one was supposed to be listening.

Rommal knew what went on among the troopers.

"I have an update for you... my Lord." Admiral Rommal never was quite sure what to call Goth Sullus. Nothing seemed appropriate. Nothing seemed natural. Nothing had been required. What was respectful had seemingly eluded the high command staff who interacted with this wraith.

"Go on," whispered the sepulchral voice of Goth Sullus.

Rommal could feel the entire bridge of the *Imperator* watching him now. Even though they shouldn't be. And yet, secretive and furtive glances were cast quickly, and ears strained to hear things they probably should not. Things they would *wish* they had not heard in the years that followed.

Admiral Rommal straightened and cleared his throat. "Our strike against the gun has failed. The local fleet in orbit is engaged with three of Admiral Devers's destroyers. As of this moment, we have not achieved the total surprise we had planned for. Nor, I fear, shall we."

Long pause.

"This does not alter my plan, Admiral," Goth Sullus replied. "Proceed with the landing beyond the main gun's defenses."

The screen went dark.

And Rommal began to breathe again.

Black Fleet
Flagship *Imperator*
Beyond Tarrago
0230 Local System Time

With a wave of his hand, the massive locks disengaged, and the doors parted. Beyond, within the octagonal chamber, it waited. The air here was reverential. Sacred even. Throbbing with power.

Sullus stepped within the chamber and approached the design table where the armor had been re-forged, improved, and made whole again.

The armor of Tyrus Rechs.

Where it had been beaten and burnt, gouged and gashed, and still noble, now it was made new, or almost new, and really... far more dangerous than it had ever been. It gleamed in the darkness like the sleeping body of some mythic monster carved in dark steel, polished like a mirror reflecting the soulless void of the darker regions of the galaxy.

Goth Sullus lay one hand against it.

He had not expected to need it this day... but things were changing. And if need be, he would don it and go forth into battle just as Tyrus had so tirelessly done so many times. Except this time, the outcome would be far different. Far more terrible.

Beneath his hand he felt power... and it was good to him. The power that waited inside his own skin craved all this and so, so much more.

The mythic armor was a thing of dangerous beauty to Goth Sullus. And a tool for the means to an end a long time coming.

Where Tyrus had failed, he would not.

Bridge of the *Carramo*, Republic Sector Defense Flagship
Off Tarrago Moon
0217 Local System Time

Admiral Bula spun about as the bridge began to collapse all around him. Concentrated fire from the three "enemy" destroyers was tearing his ship apart. He had no hope against a pair of Republic destroyers and one super-destroyer. Klaxons sounded as a catastrophic collision alert horn bellowed across all decks, alerting crewmembers to secure themselves and brace for collision.

A moment before the ceiling collapsed in on the command deck, Admiral Bula's yeoman dragged him into the corridor beyond the blast door that sealed the dying and the dead on the bridge. Fire control teams raced past them to rescue and repair what they could.

"Are the fighters away?" gasped the admiral, his mind reeling.

The yeoman nodded as he urged the admiral down the passage to the next blast door.

"Tell Commander Luq to clear a path for *Audacity* to jump. At all costs," coughed the admiral. "He must clear a path for that corvette to get through!"

How could this have happened? Those three destroyers were Republic ships. Ships he *knew.* All assigned to Admiral Devers's Third Fleet battle group.

Carramo reeled to port as the sound of two hulls colliding tore through his ship. Bula and his yeoman went sprawling.

The prow of the destroyer *Triumph* had ripped away the forward command structure of the flagship, exposing all decks forward of the third bulkhead to deep space—though these were details Bula would never know in this life.

He watched in horror as far down the central passage leading away from the bridge, blast doors began to iris shut. The howl and scream of venting oxygen shrieked in his ears.

And still, his last thoughts were... how had this happened?

First Squadron, "Gray Wolves"
Assigned to Republic Cruiser *Carramo*
Above Tarrago
0217 Local System Time

Squadron Commander Luq pulled up hard on the flight stick to thread the narrow gap created by the two destroyers smashing into one another. A moment later the forward command structure on the *Carramo* tore away, and internal explosions blossomed across all decks.

There were no enemy fighters to deal with. Just massive ships engaged in close-range volley-fire as waist gunners targeted enemy batteries in vicious broadsides. How one ship had managed to collide with the other would remain a mystery. But such things happened when ships fought at broadsides.

Three of the sector defense auxiliary corvettes had already gone down in the atmo. Another one was on fire and burning in. Escape pods were ejecting in all directions.

Bad day, thought Luq as a ship flared and exploded, illuminating his cockpit in a bright flash. He checked local radar and searched for *Audacity*'s transponder image. Of his squadron, only three Wolves had made it off the *Carramo*.

Three Raptors against the one remaining rebel destroyer.

Bad day, he thought again and cranked his head around to make sure both his wingmen were on station.

"Wolf Squadron Leader to Wolf Squadron... Form up on the *Audacity*... she's coming through now. Her jump window is marked in your HUDs. Let's try to give her enough room to get out of here, kids."

The hammerhead corvette surfaced from the atmosphere surrounding Tarrago Prime and went to full thrust. Luq crossed her beam and rolled off to port. She looked fine—no apparent damage.

"Captain of *Audacity*... this is Wolf Squadron Leader. We'll get you to the jump. Maintain course and heading. Keep your speed up."

"Roger that, Squadron Leader. Starting our jump solution now. Sensors indicate interceptors inbound."

"We'll take care of that," replied Wolf Squadron Leader. He increased to full throttle to get out in front of the slower-moving big ship.

Up ahead, a group of three-deflector-shielded fighters swarmed toward him like a nightmare of banshees suddenly howling out of the nether of space.

Bad day, thought Luq again.

Bridge of the Corvette *Audacity*
Above Tarrago Prime, Heading to Jump
0219 Local System Time

"Got a jump solution... feeding it to helm now," announced the navigator. His voice was calm, but Desaix could hear the fear. "Gonna be tricky. That destroyer's moving in to intercept us. She gets in the way..."

Holding on to the crash bars on the ceiling with one hand, Desaix reached down with the other and patted the kid on the shoulder. "Hang in there, Mr. Taun. We've been in worse before."

Ahead, three of the slick Raptor interceptors, the latest acquisition in the Repub Navy's fighter arsenal, streaked forward, engines glowing like the fires of hell. Their hulls were Repub white and streaked with unit gray.

"Contact!" yelled someone back in sensors.

"Talk to me," ordered Desaix as he watched the pilot set a course to the jump. From the corner of his eye he kept an eye on the damage control panel. It was lit up like Christmas tree. Much of it because of the unfinished refit.

"Multiples... fast movers inbound for intercept. They came out of deep space. They're trying to cut us off."

Desaix leaned down and scanned near-space out the bridge window. In the distance he could see a swarm of fighter-like craft inbound and moving fast. Faster than he'd seen any fighter move before.

"Time to jump?" he asked.

"Two minutes, thirty-seven seconds," came the reply.

First Squadron, "Gray Wolves"
Republic Cruiser *Carramo*
Above Tarrago
0219 Local System Time

"Jasings, Merca, lock foils into attack position and prepare to engage. Break up and take on as many as you can. We'll try to distract them from focusing on the corvette!"

A second later he got replies from both.

"Can do, Wolf Leader."

"Good hunting, Wolf Leader."

Luq's HUD was highlighting at least twelve interceptors. Not great odds by the longest of shots. Whoever these guys were, they had some kind of military training. They weren't just pirates or MCR rebels.

He set the foils on the Raptor to attack position, visually confirming that both his wingmen had done the same. Now the forward-swept wings of the arrow shaped fighter had retracted to the rear, allowing the wing-mounted blasters more range and target coverage.

"OU7," said Luq over internal comm.

His onboard bot beeped and clicked in the affirmative.

"Jam their comm and try to detect any loose signal we can hack our way into. If you do... run an HK on their deflector shields. That might make things a little more even."

The bot crooned a high eight-bit melody whose inherent melancholy assured the squadron leader this would not be as easy as requested.

"Gotta try, little guy."

The bot did not like being called "little guy."

Two seconds later, the wave of odd-shaped fighters came at them like the rushing tentacles of a tyranasquid. One second all was the deep dark velvet of space, and the next, enemy fighters were everywhere. Luq yanked the

Raptor around hard and tried to pick up one of the enemy fighters. As soon as he had a brief sight picture as he squeezed off a series of blaster shots. Two went wide, and one struck one of the deflectors. The craft shook from the impact and sped off. Luq dove after it, never mind he had two on his tail, according to the bot.

"Pop chaff pods now!" he ordered the bot.

He caught a glimpse of Merca smoking one of the enemy fighters. The kid landed solid hits until the thing came apart. Two more swooped in on his tail, and he dove away.

Luq let go of the fighter he was chasing and maneuvered in to save Merca. Both enemy fighters were unloading with full blasters on the kid, dancing all across Merca's rear deflectors.

"Hold your course for two seconds, Wolf Three... I'm on 'em."

He passed across their pursuit axis, blasters blazing. He landed hits on the first and caused it to break formation. Then he backed off his throttle and fell in behind the remaining pursuer. A moment later he was shooting into the central pod's engines. It exploded, sending deflectors and explosive gas-propelled debris in every direction.

OU7 whooped with eight-bit joy.

"Never mind that! Get me into their systems."

"Three of them have broken off... they're going for the corvette!" announced Wolf Two.

House of Reason, Security Council Chambers
Utopion

"I'd like to thank you all for being here." Orrin Kaar nodded at each of the five other members of the powerful Republic Security Council. He stopped at Delegate A'lill'n and proffered a smile. "And special thanks goes to Delegate A'lill'n for arranging this meeting on such short notice."

"Thank you, Delegate Kaar," A'lill'n said. "We have Senator Jasu Hendrexyln observing over holocomm, as well as Legion Commander Keller from the *Mercutio*."

"Good," Kaar said. "Our purpose for this meeting is to determine the necessary response to the unfolding developments around Tarrago Prime."

Kaar turned to Delegate Tye, a senior member who oversaw Republic intelligence. "What does Nether Ops have to say on the matter?"

Tye shook her head slowly. "Nothing officially. It's possible some agents were following this development, but none reported an imminent threat. They have no assessment, and agents in or around the Tarrago system are currently unreachable."

"I'm afraid that's true of all comm traffic to Tarrago," Kaar said, adding a touch of sadness to his face. "The comm relay seems to have been disrupted."

A junior delegate stood up in surprise. "But how—"

Kaar gently cut the man off. "We don't know. The comm relay is supposed to have such redundancy as to make this impossible. We have a clever enemy."

"So you believe this is the work of the Mid-Core Rebellion?" Senator Hendrexyln said through his holocomm.

Kaar gave a half smile. "I believe it is an enemy of the Republic. But I would caution against blaming this on the MCR. I received a comm transmission from one of our finest appointees, Admiral Devers."

The other council members leaned forward. "What did it say?"

"It is meant for this council only, though I think with your approval, the Senate and Legion Commander Keller should be privy to the message as well."

Consensus made it so, and Kaar played the message the admiral had recorded for the benefit of those in power on Utopion.

"Delegate Kaar, honored council," Devers began. The klaxons and frantic scurrying around the bridge where the admiral recorded his message made it clear that Devers's ship was engaging in battle. "I don't have much time. I was performing training exercises when I received a distress call from Fortress Omicron. I jumped into the system and discovered that Tarrago's defense fleet was firing upon the orbital moon, and Tarrago Prime security forces had seized the shipyard."

"On Unity Day!" bellowed a delegate. She slammed her fist on the table, the audacity of an attack on such a day was apparently too much for the House of Reason member to cope with.

"I maneuvered three of my ships between the defense fleet and the moon in an attempt to protect the legionnaires stationed at Omicron. It looks like a ground assault has also been initiated on Tarrago Moon, and I am scrambling my shipboard soldiers and marines to reinforce the company stationed at Omicron. By all appearances, the attacks are coming from Republic-made ships and are being carried out by Republic soldiers. I'm unable to raise the Seventh Fleet, but if you reach Admiral Landoo, advise her to find my flagship and form up on my command. The enemy has a considerable advantage given the—"

The holo shorted out, ending the message.

"Given what?" Delegate A'lill'n demanded of the empty comm channel.

"My aides believe the message ended with the disruption of the comm relay," Kaar said. "At this point we have no way of knowing the tactical situation beyond what the admiral has said." He looked mournfully downward. "Nor do we know if the admiral has survived the surprise assault he's stumbled upon, though he no doubt is fighting valiantly."

Legion Commander Keller spoke up from the comm. "This does match the intelligence the Legion received from its legionnaires stationed at Fortress Omicron. Before the relays went down, we received deep space transmissions warning of a friendly fire incident. Those reports evolved to say that the attacks were intentional."

The disgust on the faces of the delegates could not be hidden.

"One wonders," Kaar said, speaking on behalf of the whole, "when the Legion intended to share this information."

Unfazed, Keller replied, "Given the severity of the attack and the circumstances, the Legion had no such intentions. This looks to be the beginning of a civil war, delegates."

The Security Council sat in stunned silence at this proclamation.

It was A'lill'n who spoke next. "And what steps is the Legion taking to put a stop to it?"

Keller was matter-of-fact in his reply. "I've authorized a kill team to infiltrate Tarrago Prime and destroy the shipyards."

A furor arose among the delegates. Even Senator Hendrexyln's voice could be heard in protest over the comm. "This is unspeakable!"

"Tarrago Prime is a world entirely dedicated to the construction of Republic capital ships!"

"Destroying that shipyard would disastrous to our ability to—"

"Why not take the damn thing back, Keller? Aren't you legionnaires supposed to be fighters?"

Keller waited calmly for the voices to die down. "I trust the reports of my legionnaires. They are hopelessly outnumbered, and Tarrago Prime's security forces are farcical. Whoever is after this shipyard wants it whole; the opportunity to destroy it through orbital bombardment was available and went unused. The other side wants ships."

Kaar slammed both palms against the table. "Unacceptable. Your solution is unacceptable, Legion Commander Keller. I believe I speak for all of us when I say that you need to call off this kill team immediately."

Keller set his jaw. "If that's the will of the House of Reason—though I'll say on record it is strategic folly. The battle for Tarrago is already lost, no matter what Admiral Devers or Admiral Landoo might think. But if that's the House of Reason's decision... I'll see what I can do. The comm relays in that system have been... uncooperative."

The holo of Keller went offline, but Kaar imagined he saw a grin on the legion commander's face as his projection scrambled and disappeared. Kaar would need to reach Admiral Devers to warn him of the incoming kill team. He thanked Oba that his prototype comm would remain operative even with the relays down. The Republic really *should* have kept funding that project.

Bridge of the Corvette *Audacity*
Above Tarrago, Heading to Jump
0220 Local System Time

"Time?" asked Desaix.

"Here they come!" shouted the co-pilot.

"Activate point defense turrets. Gunners fire at will," ordered Desaix over the chaos coming from along the narrow bridge. And then he repeated his unanswered question. "Time to jump?"

"One minute fifteen seconds, sir."

Off beyond the moon he could barely see the three massive capital ships that were what was being called... the enemy. He'd never seen anything like them. They were massive. This was the full-scale war no one had ever expected. And Desaix knew right there, at that moment, that the *Audacity* had to reach the main fleet if Tarrago was to have a chance.

"Taking damage! Auxiliary batteries offline!" announced someone back in damage control.

"Never mind!" shouted Desaix. "They weren't reconfigured to interface with the new energy displacement absorbers. The deflectors will hold."

In moments, the enemy fighters were all over his ship.

"Destroyer moving in to cut us off. Thirty seconds and she'll block our jump window!"

"Maintain course and heading," announced Desaix calmly. "Stand by to jump!"

"We're not gonna make it," muttered the helmsman.

05

231st Gun Battery Assigned Orbital Defense Command
Fortress Omicron
0155 Local System Time

Twenty minutes prior to the *Audacity*'s attempt to jump...

After he'd found the two dead techs and sounded the general alarm, protocol dictated that Captain Thales was to report to the nearest gun battery to organize the defenses. So he ran. Emergency lights gyrated from every corner and all along the massive cut-into-the-dead-rock-of-the-moon gray walls.

When he reached an armory, he skidded to a stop and entered. He suited up for vacuum operations in the standard Repub Navy battle armor. It was nothing like what the legionnaires were issued, but it was enough to stand up to hard vacuum, and maybe a child wielding a plastic knife.

A link to base commander General Daalro appeared on his datapad. He clicked it and winced in anticipation of the storm that was coming. Which didn't look great in combination with him trying to shrug into his armor.

"There had better be a damn good reason why you just woke the entire base, Captain!" shouted the irate general.

Thales could see that his commanding officer was still in bed. Sitting up. His iron-gray hair and mustache, normally every inch the typical Repub general, looked wild and disheveled.

"I'm almost certain... *sir*," grunted Thales as he struggled to pull on his boots. In another part of his mind he told himself that he really needed to stop binge-reading at night and start hitting the gym. "That we are about to come under some sort of attack. Both the techs on duty in Deep Sensors are dead. They look to have been assassinated. Someone then scrambled our systems with what most likely is some type of hunter-killer malware designed to make sure we don't see what's coming."

"Balderdash!" barked the general. "Listen here, Captain... uh?"

"Thales," prompted Thales.

"That's right. Thales. The thinker. Well, bonehead, if this isn't a full-scale attack, then your career is over. And truth be told, son, we haven't had high hopes for you. You don't even look like an officer."

It was at that moment that some gunner in one of the batteries began to fire back at the wave of incoming tri-fighters now swarming over the base. The look on the general's face changed from venomous outrage to shock and horror in an instant.

Thales cut the link, pulled on the ridiculous, wide-flaring gunnery helmet—its odd shape supposedly provided better hearing protection for those who operated the high-intensity quad turrets—and grabbed a blaster rifle off a rack. By the time he left the armory, gunners and officers were flooding into the halls, racing for their stations. Thales noted that very few had decided to suit up as per artillery defense SOP.

They're relying on the blast doors, he thought. He'd railed against this false trust in something that couldn't stop hard vacuum from killing those on the wrong side of the door. Many had argued back at him that the Repub now had force field technology systems that could be hard-wired throughout ships to immediately seal as soon as breach occurred. Thales's reply had been, "Yes, that's true." Except that, one, none of that tech had actually been implemented, other than a coming-soon campaign waged by the House of Reason; and two, if power systems failed on the ship, or even within that section, then the force fields couldn't activate. And usually, during battle, power was a tricky thing at best once you started taking internals. Alas, very few listened, and his constant preaching had actually— and he knew this because he was honest with himself about his career—negatively affected his chances of further promotion.Now he ran for all he was worth to get back to Battery Four, which he'd just inspected before discovering the horror show in Deep Sensors.

He arrived beneath the ladder that led up into the tower, atop which the squat hexagonal turret rotated and fired. He could hear the coolant rattle and hiss, indicating the battery was operating as it should. And above all this he could hear the muffled shriek and whine of the quad blasters, their *tom tom* cadence chasing down whoever was attacking.

It was a long climb up into the turret, sweating inside his armor, and hearing the strange ominous *BRAAAAAAAAAAAAP* coming from the airless skies over the moon didn't make things easier. And because he was an amateur historian of the Savage Wars—he'd written his university thesis on Historical Gunnery Tactics of the Savage Wars and was a firm believer in the lessons he'd learned studying that apocalyptic conflict—he recognized this sound as the report of a weapon consistent with that time.

Slug throwers.

If it was pirates, they'd hang for sure.

With one more rung to go before he reached the security landing that would allow him access to the turret, some of the clues he'd been working out in his ever-spinning brain began to make more sense. Could this be another Savages outbreak?

Had to be.

He'd always suspected it could happen again. Even though the House of Reason had gone to great lengths to make sure everyone knew it couldn't. That it never would, ever again. No one knew how many of those old light-hugger colony ships from fabled Earth had been lost out there in the darkness of sub-light speeds before the advent of the hyperdrive. Way out there in the dark, with years upon years to perfect their perfectly mad societies...

Of course, this had to be another outbreak of Savages.

Too bad for them, thought Thales, because they just walked into one of the most heavily armed Republic ports this side of Fleet Headquarters at Baltrado Maroon.

He found the security door to the turret wide open. In combat it was supposed to have been dogged shut and locked from the inside. Code pass sign and counter-sign to enter, with the sergeant on duty carrying an assault blaster. He found none of that as he keyed the pneumatic hatch and climbed up the last narrow rubber-lined conduit into the turret proper.

He did find three gunnery crewmen at their stations, manning the massive air-defense gun system. The gunner sitting in the targeting chair, the spotter at the sensor station, and the sergeant watching everything—with nothing in his hands. No blaster rifle as per SOP. In fact, his hands were in his pockets.

And then Thales heard the ominous howl of an enemy fighter coming close, and that sudden lethal *BRAAAAAAAAAP BRAAAAAAAAAPPPPPP* that sounded more intimate and personal than all the rest Thales had heard up until this point.

Hundreds of rounds punctured the turret. One smashed through the sergeant, who was instantly sucked toward the roof. The gunner avoided being hit, but he died anyway, as he wasn't in armor and he too was pulled from his chair—a chair he should've been strapped into, according to protocol.

And that was the last thing Thales saw before he dropped back down into the access conduit to avoid being holed. His suit gave him a vacuum exposure warning, and he knew that everybody in the turret was dead. None of them had been in armor.

Some thinking part of himself was telling him to crawl back down the conduit and get to safety. And then there was that other part that reminded him he was a gunnery officer in the Republic Navy. And that even if the crew had been killed, it was his job to see if the gun system was still in operation—and then to operate said gun system to the best of his ability until relieved of his position.

Reluctantly, and still covered in cold sweat, yet determined, he climbed back up and out onto the deck of the turret. He struggled to his feet and staggered toward the gunner's chair, once again reminding himself he needed to get in better shape.

As he slid into the gunner's chair, he performed a systems check. Other than a coolant leak that was currently not a danger to further operation, the gun was still functional. He connected his targeting software to the turret's limited AI and charged up the gun for action.

He hadn't acted as a gunner since his officer basic course in artillery, but he knew what to do. And he remembered some acid-voiced NCO telling all the newly minted junior officers that the gun could be operated by a child.

Targeting engaged.

Gun to power.

He acquired several targets and spent a moment studying the strange alien fighters in the spinning holographic display. All the normal intelligence that accompanied such targets was missing, and instead small electronic question marks blinked back at him. Thales was still convinced that this was some kind of Savage Fleet come in from the deep dark. Some colony ship that had developed an alternative form of technology and design in their almost thousand-year flight.

Then he took aim at one and began firing. He pushed away all the ramifications presented within the history of his mind, and instead chose to simply kill them as best he could.

He knocked down three ships in fairly short order. It was just like the games he'd loved to play as a kid. Games about math and trajectory combined with intuition. He'd always questioned why he'd been assigned to Artillery after taking the Republic's mandatory testing assessment. He'd secretly wanted to be a legionnaire officer, though even he knew that he didn't exactly scream Legion material. But now he was seeing, once more, why their assignment had been right.

Three minutes later he got a comm from main gun fire control.

"Captain Thales. This is Lieutenant Charu in main gun operations. We have negative contact with the general. You're the only OIC I can reach, and I need to inform you that we're detecting at least three battleship-class vessels in near space."

One of the enemy fighters came streaking in at the turret, guns blazing. Thales targeted and tried to lead, but the ship was all over the place. Around him he could hear armor-plating coming to pieces from a thousand rounds suddenly penetrating its bulk.

Some distant thought reminded him he might die right now. But he knew the RF-D77 battery system shielded the gunner from blaster fire, even Savage Wars slug-throwing tech. If the gunner had been in armor and strapped in, he wouldn't be dead.

One of the gun's charging batteries shorted out and exploded with a terrific electrical *CRAAAAAAAAAK*!

Must've taken a hit, thought Thales. He swapped out targeting to reroute battery power from the auxiliaries down below.

Meanwhile the lieutenant down in fire control was still asking him for orders. "Sir! Tell me what to do. We've got fighters everywhere. The general's missing, and I'm *not* kidding. This is for real!"

Power rerouted, Thales brought targeting back up and prayed the guns wouldn't explode on him. Lancer interceptors had joined the fray now. That was good. He tagged them and set the guns not to engage if they came in too close to his targeting reticule.

"Sir! Did you hear me?" screamed the LT over the hiss and wine of the battery cannons.

"Say again," grunted Thales as he tried to target a fast-moving enemy fighter going for a kill on a Lancer. He winged it, and it spun off into the dirt of the moon. Thales rotated the gun, looking for more targets.

"We've got three Repub destroyers tearing through our sector defense group," the lieutenant said. "Tagging them now. Could be rogue ships the MCR hijacked. Admiral Bula's ship is burning up in the atmosphere. Sir, what are my orders?"

Thales didn't have enough time or brains to wield the battery guns *and* figure out what to do tactically. Literally he was doing a gunner's job. And the general's job. The only job he wasn't doing was his own.

"Listen, Lieutenant... Are you saying I'm the current ranking OIC?"

"Roger that, Captain," replied the kid nervously.

Thales waited. Tracking and firing on more of the strange alien fighters. This was a decision he did not want to make.

But as he'd learned back in officer school, a bad decision was better than no decision at all.

He'd always doubted himself.

But he called on that bit of training from way back when, and it helped to free him from that constant struggle of doubt. It gave him the permission to do anything, as long as he did *something*. To do nothing was to submit to death.

"Warning alert!" came an automated voice over general comm. "Unidentified bomber craft inbound."

"Lieutenant, are you tagging those inbound starfighters as bomber-types?"

"Yes, sir. Defense AI says they're consistent with type configuration."

Good move. You're making a decision. Sorta.

"All right... get me firing solutions on every unidentified capital ship. Tell me who we can hit in the next two minutes."

There was a long pause.

"Sir... are you talking about firing the main gun?"

"I am."

An even longer pause. Thales rotated the turret skyward and began to range the incoming bombers well before they could drop their payloads. His was now the last turret active across the sprawling base. *Don't think about that*, he screamed at his own mind as he led the first bombers, tossing high-intensity baster fire up at their slender frames.

"Launch detected," announced the battery AI. A moment later his HUD tagged two bombs falling directly at the base. At him. And some part of him wanted to fling himself out of the gunnery chair and take cover. But his body refused to obey, and instead he returned as much fire as he could.

KTF, he thought. Just like the legionnaires. And if he hadn't been wearing a helmet, any casual observer would've seen the iron-set sneer of a real killer as he tried to knock down as many fighter-bombers as he could in the time that remained him. Even as two bombs fell right toward his position.

KTF.

"*Kill them FIRST!*" he screamed into the comm ether.

The first bomb hit the fortress about half a kilometer away from the battery turret. Lunar dust and sand went flying in all directions, and even the hardened turret, set on gyroscopic hydraulic-assisted platforms, shuddered with a sudden end-of-everything violence. Across the base, military vehicles went flying and lesser buildings were flattened by the impact wave.

The other bomb disappeared down into the gaping maw of the main gun bore tunneled into the side of the moon. A second later there was a titanic detonation deep below everything, and the ground began to shift.

And still Thales continued to knock down the bombers above. In the end they broke off and scattered, some dropping their bombs wildly beyond the perimeter of the base. One smashed into the outer wall and destroyed a vast section of the defenses.

And then silence.

There were no targets in the sky.

Everything was quiet.

Thales brought up comm and contacted fire control.

"Talk to me, Lieutenant."

Nothing.

"What's going on down there?"

Nothing.

"How bad is it?"

If the orbital gun was down, then this was over. For the base, and for Tarrago.

"I'm here, sir. We're fine." The kid sounded shaken. And giddy at the same time. "We've got some damage, but we have firing solutions on all ships. We can't hit the battleships. But we can hit those rogue destroyers."

Thales climbed out of the turret. His whole body felt like it was made of rigid iron turning to sudden warm gel. And then his body began to dump sweat as it shook uncontrollably.

That's just the fear, he told himself as he sat down on the floor of the turret to catch his breath. It'll pass.

"Sir," began the lieutenant in fire control. "We will need some kind of authorization to actually engage, won't we? I mean, we never fire this gun but once a year, and the entire House of Reason comes out just to watch it."

That wasn't totally true, thought Thales. But the kid was right. Firing the main gun *was* a pretty big deal.

And then some other part of himself reminded him that the base had just been bombed and that there were enemy ships in the system the size of which no one had seen in a generation. *And*—and this was probably the most bizarre aspect of the whole situation—the Republic's own ships were attacking the system defense group.

He tapped his comm. "Contact Admiral Bula and confirm that he's under attack by unknown enemy forces. Specifically, clarify we mean the destroyers currently engaging his group."

"Can do, sir."

Good kid, thought Thales.

He was having trouble breathing. He leaned back against the gun. He felt better. He took deep breaths now.

A moment later the lieutenant was back.

"Admiral Bula's first officer confirms they are under attack, and he has confirmed our targets. He's also requesting fire support. Admiral Bula is dead. The first officer is in an escape pod. The *Carramo* went down."

Thales felt his eyes close. He was sleepy. It was just after two o'clock in the morning, local time.

"Target lead enemy destroyer and fire for effect."

Bridge of the Corvette *Audacity*
Above Tarrago, Heading to Jump
0221 Local System Time

"We've lost the deflectors, Captain. Guns six and seven are offline. Taking casualties in engineering."

Desaix ignored the report and concentrated on the jump. That was their only hope now.

"Can we get any kind of window with that destroyer in the way?"

"Negative," replied the navigator.

"More enemy fighters inbound!" someone in sensors yelled over the din.

"If we alter course in the slightest we're looking at a total recalc for jump solution," finished the navigator. "Sir?"

A collision alert horn began to bellow. The destroyer was now directly in the way of where they needed to go.

"Brace yourselves!" screamed the pilot. "She's firing on us!"

Ahead, the big waist guns of the destroyer began to open up on the corvette. A Raptor chased one of the enemy fighters across the cockpit windows, blasters blazing away for a kill.

"Time to jump?" asked Desaix, hearing the quiet desperation in his own voice.

The round from the orbital defense gun that hit the destroyer just ahead of the *Audacity* had been accelerated by a rail gun system that urged the guided round—a piece of forged impervisteel the size of a large tree trunk—up through a cascade loop that pushed its velocity to the edge of light speed. The city block–sized magnets also provided some initial guidance until onboard independent targeting and tracking took over.

The round hit the destroyer well below the forward command structure, but just off the port beam. The lieutenant in fire control had planned it that way, with the help of the targeting computers—a series of banked systems three stories high, deep inside the moon's dead core. And with little gravity to slow the round's departure from the launch system, its effortless flight continued right through the destroyer's aft engine compartments.

It literally gutted the ship from stem to stern.

The crew of the *Audacity*, in the moments before the larger ship's explosion in every direction, watched the hyper-ballistic round tear straight down the beam of the destroyer in a diagonal course. First it struck the forward torpedoes. Then it gutted decks twenty-two through twenty-four entirely, destroyed the starboard hangar, killing everyone there instantly, and traveled another three hundred meters, hitting munitions magazines and targeting systems, resulting in huge explosions all along the spine of the ship. It slammed through—not into—engineering, where it hit the reactor, which didn't explode until the batteries went up a picosecond later. Finally the round punched out the back of the massive ship, carrying a debris trail off into the nether reaches of space.

All this took about a second and half, but to the bridge crew of the closing *Audacity*, it seemed slowed down for their viewing horror.

The ship exploded violently directly in front of them. Debris scattered in all directions, including directly into the path of the oncoming hammerhead corvette. In the moment before Captain Desaix ordered the jump by shouting, "Jump *now*!" they saw several fighters from both sides go up in a wave of destruction.

A half second later the *Audacity* executed an uncontrolled jump with only a partial solution. This was generally considered a fatal proposition, never to be undertaken unless the circumstances were incredibly dire.

But what other choice was there?

House of Reason
Utopion

Orrin Kaar waited for Admiral Devers's return call. The admiral's aide had assured Kaar that he would retrieve Devers from the bridge within ten minutes.

Under normal circumstances, Kaar would have refused to even speak with any but his principal players in this intrigue. But the entirety of the Third Fleet was loyal to Devers, every officer appointed, every enlisted man's loyalty unwaveringly certain. They would provide the backbone of the New Republic.

And Kaar would be its head.

The comm chimed, and Devers came online. "Delegate Kaar—"

"I was somewhat alarmed to hear that the initial attacks went so poorly," Kaar said. In truth, the delegate was irate. Devers and Sullus had both the initiative and the element of surprise, yet the forwarded communications had shown an ineffective opening assault.

"My ship's attack on the defense fleet is going well," Devers replied. "Hyperdrives were targeted first, and battle projections indicate destruction within moments.

Sullus's fighter and bomber squadrons were torn apart by the base defense systems."

"Surely at least one bombing run was successful?" Kaar asked. "Has the main gun been disabled?"

Devers looked around his room, as if looking for answers. "No one is sure. All ships are staying out of range until Omicron is captured. A total ground assault is planned."

Kaar contemplated this. A ground assault against a company of entrenched legionnaires was no easy feat. The cost of men and materiel could be staggering. And if the kill team was not called off—if they destroyed the shipyard...

"Silas, I spoke with Legion Commander Keller. A kill team is en route to destroy the shipyards on Tarrago Prime. This... must not happen."

Devers smiled. "It won't. I'll tell Goth Sullus of the plans personally. Between my destruction of the defense fleet and news of the kill team... things will unfold as you've planned, Delegate Kaar."

Kaar felt nowhere near as sure of this as he had before the day began.

Levenir Orbit
The Galactic Core

Admiral.

The ultra-encrypted transmission Cade Thrane had just decompressed and partially decoded definitely said "admiral." Either that or "I'll borrow." The quality was... not ideal. It was like listening to someone speak while clearing phlegm from their throat three rooms away.

But the slicer could hear *something*. And "admiral" made the most sense. Who else but the Republic military have such sophisticated comm encryption? And why else would all transmissions involve Utopion?

Thrane looked to a crudely drawn map of the galaxy he'd scribbled on his lightboard. The transmissions were all either to or from the Republic capital. On at least two occasions, they went to a backwater planet at galaxy's edge, but most of the time they traveled between Utopion and the Tarrago system. And that was intriguing. Because Tarrago was—somehow—down. Comm relays weren't working in that sector. The Republic claimed that such a thing wasn't possible—but that was probably just Republic propaganda. Thrane could think of at least five theoretical ways to shut down a comm relay system at the sector level.

Another UE burst, this time inbound to Utopion, crackled through.

"All right, back at it," Thrane muttered, entering new decryptor keys into his datapad. "I can hear your voice, now let's see if I can get you to speak more clearly..."

PART II

06

Eastern Gun Bore
Fortress Omicron
0302 Local System Time

Still several kilometers off, the HK-PP mechs lumbered toward the eastern defense wall of Fortress Omicron. Behind them moved heavy main battle tanks, with swift-moving combat sleds in the rear.

"Oba." The legionnaire captain lowered his field macros and prepared to call in his findings to the heart of the fortress, deep inside the moon. That was something a lot of people didn't understand. They saw the four defense walls, one erected just behind each of the massive gun bores, and assumed that Fortress Omicron was actually *Fortresses* Omicron. But the walls were merely firing positions, observation posts, and a last line of defense to prevent any would-be ground attackers from reaching the true heart of Fortress Omicron—its underground complex.

"This is Outlaw One for Omicron Command."

"Go ahead, Outlaw One."

The captain licked his lips and transmitted the macro recordings his bucket captured. "I'm sending in visuals on several HK-PP mechs, MBTs, and combat sleds. Estimated time to arrival is twenty standard minutes."

There was a pause, probably just long enough for eyes in the command room to verify what the captain was saying.

"Confirmed, Outlaw One. Prepare your men to defend the eastern wall."

"Copy. Outlaw One, out."

This was it. Whoever was attacking Tarrago Moon was looking to finish the job. The air attacks had failed, with virtually no bombers getting their payloads off before getting dusted. A ground force assault launched away from the anti-air emplacements was the only move left. Well, other than orbital bombardment. But no one would be dumb enough to get close enough to the big gun to try something like that.

Mechs, tanks, and combat sleds. The same armored elements that Outlaw One had served alongside during his tours at galaxy's edge. And now they were coming for him and his men.

Civil war. That's what this was. What else could it be? And why not? The entire galaxy had been at war with the Republic ever since the Savage Wars. It was about time for the Republic to finally go to war with itself. And Outlaw One knew where he stood.

With the Legion.

Black Fleet Assault Force Scythe
Tarrago Moon
0305 Local System Time

The sergeant found it humorous that his first major piece of action as a shock trooper would be sitting inside a combat sled. He'd spent countless hours inside the vehicles while serving in the Legion. Could still handle a sled assault with his eyes closed. And he knew the men in his squad were very much the same.

Some of them, like him, had walked away from the Legion. Lifers who realized that the way things were going, there wasn't a life to be had in what the Legion had become. At least, not a long one. Others had been forced out. Dishonorable discharges. A lot of them, probably, unjustified. Just another legionnaire sacrificed for the sake of a clueless point. The sergeant had seen it himself. Had *lived* it himself.

Each new point forced upon the Legion was like a single drip of water landing on a slab of sandstone. Eventually it made an impression. Split stone, carved canyons where cliffs once stood. That was the Legion now. Hopelessly eroded by the Republic and its system of appointing unqualified men for the sake of politics.

The sergeant smiled to himself. Everybody ever run out of the Legion blamed it on a point. It was like prison—no one was ever guilty. But the sergeant knew better. Some of the men serving as Goth Sullus's shock troopers possessed training unsuited to their temperaments. Killers looking for a killing field. These types would actually flock to the points. They'd serve as the remorseless muscle for the points' clueless decisions. And in exchange, the points would look the other way when the bad times started. Maybe even join in.

But not in this army. The sergeant loved the Legion, and he'd be damned before he'd let the shock troopers become anything less than the *true* Legion. He was fighting his brothers to *save* his brothers. Because sometimes, in a family, you gotta fight just to show how much you care.

The sergeant cared deeply.

The Black Fleet combat sled chimed, and the image of General Nero came online.

"Shock troopers!" Nero bellowed. "Now is the moment of your victory. You are trained and equipped to do what must be done. Take Fortress Omicron, and pave the way for the Black Fleet to conquer the Tarrago system—and then the very Republic itself." Nero held out his arms. "Death to the Republic!"

No one in the sled echoed the call. They never did. None except the true believers, and this sled didn't have any of them. The sergeant had made sure of that.

The comm burst ended, and the sergeant stood from his jump seat. "You guys think the general's real name is Nero? Who does that? Who names themselves after an insane Ancient One?"

Nervous laughter sounded among the shock troopers. Good. The pucker factor would come soon enough. May as well enjoy life while you have it.

"Listen. Nero—he's right about you all. You're professionals. Former Legion. You know what we're going up against, and you know what we have at our disposal. We go in hard, and we KTF."

A shock trooper raised his head. His bucket was still on. All shock trooper buckets were required to remain on whenever the soldiers weren't in their barracks. "Sarge, we have general orders not to use the Legion expressions."

"Screw that," the sergeant answered. "Look, I don't know about you, but I'm here *because* of the Legion. I realized a while ago that the gangrene of the Republic needs to be removed. You can't amputate without a sword, and we're the sword that will save the Legion's life."

This was an impromptu speech. A speech, the sergeant knew, that could get him court-martialed if word of it left the combat sled. The officer corps of the Black Fleet wanted loyalty to Command. But although they were light years more capable than the points stinking up the Legion, the sergeant believed that the *true* legionnaire officers still had the advantage when it came right down to it. Black Fleet officers were tactically smart, but fearful. Afraid of the man in black.

"So I'll say it again," the sergeant continued, raising his arms as if he were pumping up a crowd. "KTF?"

"KTF!" shouted the shock troopers.

"Ooah!" The sergeant paced down the middle of the combat sled. "Now listen, we know what we're facing. Leejes don't go down without a fight. But this moon is protected by a single company. They'll be dug in like a nix, but that's two hundred leejes against two *thousand* shock troopers. That's textbook. HK-PP's gonna blow us a hole in the wall, we're gonna speed inside and dismount, MBTs are going to take out the defense systems, and then we good."

A shock trooper raised his hand. "What's the word on taking prisoners?"

The sergeant had thought long and hard about this. Thankfully, his lieutenant was of the same mind as him, and Command hadn't said anything to the contrary. "If it's a leej, treat 'em with respect and take 'em alive. We take Tarrago Prime, give Goth Sullus—"

There was a murmur at the use of the supreme commander's name.

"Yeah, I said it," the sergeant boasted. "Goth. Sullus. Ain't no thing. Anyway, when he starts cranking out the ships—because why else take over a shipyard?—and we start spreading the news that the Legion is alive with *us*, I'm telling you... they're all flipping sides. We took an oath to protect the Republic from enemies foreign and domestic. We've dusted plenty of foreign threats. Now we end the domestic, criminal reign of the House of Reason and Senate."

To this, there were no objections inside the sergeant's combat sled.

Command Center
Fortress Omicron
0314 Local System Time

"Could it be a feint?" asked the company commander's staff major. He pointed to the line of HK-PP mechs marching their way to contact on the eastern wall. Mechs that were still coming.

Commander Yoon, in charge of the entirety of Hotel Company, 80th Legion, studied the holo before shaking his head. "No, I don't think so, Major. And I'll tell you why. That fleet out there, minus the Republic destroyers fighting it out between us and Tarrago Prime, has one approach vector. They have purposefully avoided getting close enough for us to use the main gun. Their bomber raids resulted in superficial damage to us and heavy losses for them."

Yoon waved his hand at the holodisplay, causing it to zoom out and show a real-time three-dimensional plotting of the moon and the three battleships, just out of gun range. A series of red arrows pushed outward from the ships and toward the planet.

"This is the most direct route for drop shuttles to deliver mechanized infantry and support vehicles."

The holodisplay's AI followed Commander Yoon's words, its processors showing what it imagined would best complement the briefing being given. The arrows impacted on the moon's surface, and the POV rotated to show a possible landing zone.

"From here they have two options: move toward the east wall and gun bore—approximately a sixty-minute drive—or attempt to traverse to the western wall. This moon is small, but that trip would still take nearly four hours, giving us ample time to prepare defenses."

"So the fight is at the east wall?" the major asked.

"I'm sure of it," Yoon answered. "If they had the resources to send in more than what's already down here, they'd drop right on our heads. This is the best punch they've got, and they can't afford to lose it by getting in close to our anti-air defenses."

"Shall I reinforce the eastern wall?"

Yoon nodded. "I want each wall to send me one hundred legionnaires. That will give the eastern wall five hundred men. That should be enough to keep what's coming at bay. We only need to hold out long enough for reinforcements to arrive from the Seventh Fleet. Or for them to do something stupid and get a taste of our big gun."

"We should be so lucky." The major paused. "Permission to speak freely, sir?"

Commander Yoon nodded.

"Are we at war with the Republic? I mean, is this a civil war? I know that what we're seeing coming our way are Republic mechs, tanks, and sleds. But why?"

Yoon had been wondering the same thing. It was an open secret that the House and Senate despised the Legion. For its part, the Legion didn't much like them back. But Legion Commander Keller had always sought the greater good of the Republic. Civil war was genocidal folly. If acquiescing to a few points could stave off conflict... so be it.

Yoon thought all this, but he wasn't afforded the chance to put these reflections into words, because the all-channel comm sounded, and a holo of Admiral Devers of the Third Fleet appeared.

Yoon didn't think much of the admiral as a military commander. He had served a few rotations in the mid-core with the Third and had found the admiral's strategy and judgment to be... lacking. But if his fleet was here to lend him a hand, Yoon would take it.

The holo of the admiral began to speak. "This is Admiral Silas Devers of Republic Navy, Third Fleet."

The pomposity Yoon had come to know while serving with the admiral was clear. Devers was delivering this wartime emergency transmission as though he were giving a speech while working the stump.

"I have been sent by the Senate Council and House of Reason to put down a terrorist rebellion seeking to capture or destroy the Kesselverks Shipyards."

Terrorists. But how could anyone—even the zhee—get ahold of so much Republic weaponry without the Legion issuing an all-points briefing?

Devers continued. "The Mid-Core Rebels have infiltrated the local security forces and the planetary defense fleet and are actively fighting against Republic forces. Do not be alarmed by the legionnaires in black armor. They are a new evolution of soldiers serving in the Third Fleet. They will not harm you. Citizens of the Republic, I urge you to stay in your homes until Republic order is restored. And to the insurgents I say: You will not have the victory this day."

"Shut that off," Yoon said, though the message had already ended.

"What do you make of it, sir?"

"Are you in league with the MCR, Major?" Yoon asked.

"No, sir!"

"Neither am I. And if Admiral Devers thinks otherwise, if those are his point-led troops advancing on our eastern wall..." Yoon cracked the vertebrae in his neck. "We'll make 'em pay."

Eastern Gun Bore
Fortress Omicron
0319 Local System Time

"Yes, sir," the legionnaire captain answered into his L-comm. "We'll draw them in."

Reinforcements from the other walls were already pouring in to bolster the eastern wall. And while legionnaire majors and lieutenant colonels drew up battle plans, the captain thought over his own part in the battle. He'd been ordered to disrupt the enemy attack formations. The question was how he could do that without taking heavy casualties.

The repulsor pool had twelve of the wall's fifteen combat sleds, and only half of those were equipped with anti-vehicle missile launchers. The rest sported the ubiquitous twin blaster cannons. Not much good against mechs. The sleds were fast and nimble, but wouldn't survive a well-aimed shot from the mechs or main battle tanks.

"They'd love that," the captain mumbled to himself.

A light went off in the recesses of his mind. They *would* like that.

The captain looked around for his communications officer. The second lieutenant was right where he should be. "Can you work it so that I can speak with Commander Yoon?"

A leej captain on the front had no chance of being patched through direct to the company commander, and the captain had no intention of broadcasting what he was thinking over L-comm. But the second lieutenant would have friends in the Command Center comm section. Maybe he could make arrangements.

"I think so..." the second lieutenant said, somewhat hesitant. "I may have to offer a few favors..."

"I'll make sure you get whatever you need," the captain answered. "Just get me a conversation with Commander Yoon."

Black Fleet Assault Force Scythe
Tarrago Moon
0322 Local System Time

The HK-PP mech driver checked his chronometer. Five minutes. Five minutes until they'd reach close weapon range.

The massive bipedal machine took another lumbering step forward, causing the driver to lurch from side to side in his seat. These beasts were slow and ponderous—but the firepower! Nothing in the galaxy could match it. Destroyer captains could call down orbital assaults, and featherheads could flick off seeker missiles and snap away with blaster cannons. But the sheer feeling of power that came from annihilating whatever stood before you with the hull-chewing blaster cannons mounted on each arm of the mech... the noise and surge that came with every payload rocketing from the shoulder-mounted launcher—so powerful that an unskilled driver would have to take a few steps backward from the blast… these were true expressions of power. And they were exhilarating.

The mech driver moved forward, maintaining a textbook battle formation. Mechs spread out to avoid collateral damage from artillery—not that there seemed to be any on this moon. The bombers had done that much. Tanks filled firing lines, with combat sleds in the rear, ready to exploit any opening the HK-PPs made.

The S-comm jumped to live. "Giant Three, this is Giant Four, you seeing what's coming your way?"

The question was accompanied by a manual grid-pulse sent by Giant Four.

Squinting through the forested terrain and attempting to peer above the hills between his mech and the eastern wall, the driver of Giant Three followed grid-pulse until his eyes saw motion. "I see something, Giant Four," he said, switching to thermal image. "Any idea what?"

"Try combat sleds, Giant Three."

Combat sleds? The Legion was sending combat sleds against a phalanx of mechs with MBT support? The driver couldn't decide if they were crazy or just stupid. "Are you kidding?"

"Negative," answered Giant Four. "I just couldn't quite believe my eyes and wanted you to verify before I called it in."

"Well, I see it, too. Going hot with weapons in case they expose any more of themselves…"

Giant Four called in the sighting to the other drivers. "Giant Four to Giant Team, I have confirmed sighting of multiple Republic combat sleds. Say again, multiple Republic combat sleds coming inbound."

"Copy, Giant Four," replied the team leader. "All mechs: you are clear to fire on the sleds, just don't let them distract you from taking down that wall."

This was a welcome development, the driver thought to himself. A chance to unleash some hell before reaching the eastern wall. It was shaping up to be a good day.

"I'm seeing some more sleds on the right flank," came the warning from another driver.

Alarms sounded, and the driver of Giant Three could see missile trails billowing toward the line of mechs. "Incoming anti-vic fire!"

The sleds that had made themselves so visibly alluring had been a distraction.

Giant Three swiveled in his seat to watch a salvo of missiles—they must have been slave-fired to come at one target so fast from so many directions—streak toward Giant One's mech. The lead HK-PP popped heat chaff and sensor scanners, but Legion ordnance was not easily fooled. Only a few missiles arched upward or veered harmlessly into the ground or trees. Most found their marks.

Giant One erupted in a ball of flames. The mech's driver pod didn't eject. They'd lost their leader.

The driver of Giant Three refocused on the battlefield in front of him. His HUD showed that the tanks had stopped, as had their own combat sleds. But the Republic combat sleds were darting about like a swarm of gnats. He tracked one sled mounted with twin anti-personnel blasters and raised the gargantuan arm of his mech. Spiraling blaster-fire rained instant death, as the rounds ripped through the sled, cutting the vehicle in half. Nearby, a second sled erupted in flames; a fellow mech had homed in with a shoulder-mounted gauss gun.

Two sleds down, at least a dozen more in the field.

The sleds managed another volley of missiles. These struck the leg of Giant Two, blowing it nearly off. This time the driver-pod did eject into the air—but it was quickly shot to ribbons by a legionnaire manning the twins on another combat sled.

The concentrated firepower of all these sleds was proving to be a match for the mechs. And their tactics were clear: they intended to take down the lead mech and each subsequent replacement.

Who was in command of the mechs now?

Giant Three realized it was him.

He shook his head. He wasn't about to get taken out by bunch of leejes flying around in combat sleds like teenagers racing their parents' speeders. The driver throttled his controls forward, causing his lumbering mech to enter a full run. This depleted fuel at a daunting rate, but they were close enough to the wall that he could spare it. So long as a retreat wasn't called, the driver wouldn't have to get out and walk.

"Take back the initiative," Giant Three called into the S-comm. He began firing his arm cannons, destroying sled after sled. The other mechs followed suit, and soon the main battle tanks joined the pursuit, their repulsors bouncing up and over the rocky terrain.

The Republic sleds knew they were beaten, and attempted to return to the safety of the eastern wall. They were putting ground between themselves and the advancing line of mechs and tanks, but not without paying a toll. More combat sleds exploded in towering balls of fire as the mechs continued their sprinting pursuit and the tanks' repulsors roared at their limits. These bastards weren't going to get away.

Giant Three watched as the sleds took the speed track around the massive gun bore cavern. This gave them the fastest route around and back to the still-open impervisteel gates at the eastern wall.

The mech driver pushed the sticks forward so hard he thought he might break them. "You're not getting away," he told the retreating sleds. "I've got you. I've got you."

Eastern Gun Bore
Fortress Omicron
0334 Local System Time

The legionnaire captain watched as his sleds sped homeward, the mechs and tanks in hot pursuit. There wouldn't be time to let the sleds back inside and close the doors before the enemy attack vehicles arrived to send a devastating volley of missiles inside the eastern wall.

There didn't need to be.

"Now!" the captain shouted into his L-comm.

It dawned on him that he'd never yelled at a company commander before. And he probably wouldn't get the opportunity again.

Command Center
Fortress Omicron
0351 Local System Time

Commander Yoon heard the voice of one of his captains give the word. This was a matter of trust, and Yoon trusted his front line legionnaires completely.

"Fire cannon east," Yoon ordered.

"Firing cannon east," confirmed the gunner.

The ground shook as the gun bore hurtled a projectile designed to destroy a capital ship in a single shot.

Black Fleet Assault Force Scythe
Tarrago Moon
0352 Local System Time

The shock trooper sergeant monitored the battle from the holoscreen mounted inside his combat sled. The mech and tank drivers seemed to have bloodlust, and if there was a commander on hand capable of giving an order to keep back, it wasn't being heeded.

"They're being drawn in," the sergeant said to no one in particular. "Need to slow up and let those sleds get away. Today ain't gonna be won or lost because of a few extra combat sleds getting dusted."

"Unless it's ours," chimed in another shock trooper.

"Ooah," answered the sergeant. But distantly. His mind was trying to comprehend what was before him. The Repub sleds were moving full speed toward the eastern wall's vehicle entryway. The sergeant didn't need his bucket to tell him that the mechs pursuing would get multiple missiles fired into that opening before the leejes on the other side had the chance to seal it up. It looked like an enormous tactical error by the Legion. Exactly the sort of thing a point would do.

And therein lay the problem for the sergeant. A point would send out sleds against mechs, spouting some kind of nonsense like "Speed defeats strength." A point would also leave the back door open and get leejes killed. What a point *wouldn't* do is launch a coordinated missile attack through slave-fire controls. That was some impressive shooting, taking down two HK-PP mechs with a concentration of aero-precision tank-buster missiles.

So did the point get lucky… or was this a trap?

The sergeant heard the *dat-dat-dat-dat* of his combat sled's twin blaster cannons. They were joining the fight. Unlike the Republic models, these Black Fleet sleds had automated turrets controlled from the cockpit. The sergeant didn't like that. No driver could shoot like a leej—like a shock trooper.

The sergeant hailed his sled driver through the S-comm. "What's going on, buddy?"

"We're moving to engage the enemy," the driver answered. "Giant Three has identified an opening in the eastern wall. All sleds are requested to shoot the gap."

Shoot the gap? Before the mechs and tanks can really pound the leej defenses? Gonna be a tall order.

"Listen," the sergeant said, hoping that he'd finally learned how to pick his words carefully. "I've served all throughout the galaxy, and I can see a potential sketshow when I see one. This is one. That opening isn't gonna close up with the way the mechs and tanks are positioned. But that doesn't mean the Legion won't blast our sleds to hell if we rush in too quickly. Slow it down a bit and wait for the heavies to lay down some damage. At least give my guys a chance when the doors drop. You under orders to go in now?"

The sled's deceleration provided an answer before the driver even spoke. "No orders, just a request from Giant Three. I think you're right, though. I think—"

If the driver finished his sentence, the sergeant didn't hear it. He was thrown down hard onto the deck, then tossed into the shock troopers still strapped into their jump seats as the sled rocked and spun out of control.

The S-comm was little more than white noise from some sort of catastrophic distortion.

As the S-comm system rebooted, the whine over the comm gradually gave way to frantic communication between shock troopers. The sergeant tuned it out and pinged his driver. "What happened? Did we get hit?"

"No! But almost all of our armor did!"

"What?"

"They fired the main gun! The mechs and tanks were right by the edge of the bore. They just—incinerated."

The sergeant pulled himself to his feet and stared at the blank holoscreen. "Can you feed me combat visuals?"

"I think so..."

The screen came to life with a chaotic picture of the battleground. The sergeant controlled the holocam. There didn't seem to be a mech left on the field. And not more than a few tanks. At least the Black Fleet combat sleds were mostly intact, not having had the chance to get in the blast zone before the Legion opened the gates of hell.

A trap, then.

The sergeant saw legionnaires manning the battle stations along the top of the wall. Incoming fire began to rain down on the surviving vehicles. Leejes fired the familiar aero-precision missiles from shoulder launchers. For now, the tanks took priority, but that wouldn't last.

"Get us up against that wall!" the sergeant yelled to his driver. "We're sitting targets out here, and you know we can't go back the other way. Just don't get too close to the gun bore!"

The sled sped forward, and the other sleds did the same. Retreat was not an option. That had been made perfectly clear in the Black Fleet training leading up to this assault. Fight until you win. Period. The sergeant thought it was the foolish blustering of idealists... but the Legion needed saving. The prize was worth the fight.

For their part, the tank crews were dedicated to the last. They focused their main guns on high-value targets, blasting away at fortified emplacements and making life end too soon for the legionnaires manning them. But the aero-precision missiles kept coming. Eventually the tanks ran out of bafflers, chaff, and interceptor bots. They began taking evasive maneuvers, concentrating their fire on anti-personnel weapons like N-50 nests. And when they could, they sent high-explosive blasts into the wall's vehicle entryway. These made little more than a fist-sized dent.

The sergeant watched all of this from his holoscreen.

"Thirty seconds," the driver called out as the sled swerved and juked to avoid the maelstrom of incoming fire.

"Get ready, STs," the sergeant called to his men. "There won't be time to sound off and move. When I drop that door, you know your numbers. Get your asses outside and set up a squad perimeter. KTF! Because you can bet for damn sure that's what the brothers on the other side are aiming to do to us!"

The sled fishtailed to an abrupt stop. "Here!" cried the driver.

The sergeant hit the ramp release. "Go! Go! Go!"

Eastern Gun Bore
Fortress Omicron
0411 Local System Time

This was all going well. Better than the Legion captain could have hoped. The swarming combat sleds led the mechs and tanks perilously close to the gun bore, and the Legion made 'em pay. But the battle was far from over. Enemy combat sleds were now using their own speed and maneuverability to reach the wall, and several of the enemy's combat-effective main battle tanks remained.

"You'll make major for this, sir," the communications lieutenant said as the captain surveyed the battlefield.

"Gotta survive first," the captain replied. But he sheltered hope that it would be so. Fate had left him—a captain—in charge of the one section of Omicron's walls that the enemy had chosen to attack. And he'd risen to meet the challenge.

But now the tanks were the priority. Each well-aimed shot from their heavy main guns denied the captain the further use of a defensive emplacement. Several of his anti-vehicle batteries had been destroyed, which would pose a significant problem if another bombing run came in this direction.

The captain brought up his supply hot list and smiled. They were still flush with aero-precision missiles. As long as he had legionnaires to fire them, they could at least make sure any incoming featherheads only had a one-way flight.

"Get me a status update on the remaining enemy battle tanks," the captain ordered over L-comm. The north and west walls had their own tanks, and the captain wished he could send them out to deal with the mechanized rivals.

"We're tracking five enemy tanks left," came the answer. "We think they've expended their internal anti-missile defenses, but they've managed to find natural cover to avoid direct missile fire. We keep trying to pop 'em when they sneak out to take a shot. Rat-and-croaker game, sir."

"All right, keep on 'em."

The captain turned his attention to the combat sleds beneath the wall. The soldiers inside the sleds wore black armor. Almost like Dark Ops, but with different buckets and a high gloss. That, and the blood red paint that really made them stand out. Dark Ops would never go for that sort of thing. These dark soldiers were exchanging small-arms fire with the leejes of the eastern wall. The captain's bucket assessed the troop strength at fifteen hundred—still three times what he had, even with the reinforcements being sent his way from the other walls. The enemy had the numbers, but the Legion held the wall. And the result at the moment was a standstill.

Not for long, the captain thought to himself.

The legionnaires on the wall had to be careful about exposing themselves. The fire coming up from below was accurate and deadly. Whoever these guys were, they had Legion training. The real stuff, not the "Legion" hit squads full of point lackeys that the Republic sent to collect taxes. These soldiers had to be former Legion. Dark legionnaires. And they'd come to fight him.

The protected blaster cannons at the top of the wall and observation towers had either been destroyed by the tanks or simply weren't firing and thus were unable to target the dark legionnaires. And those weapon emplacements dug into the walls themselves that *could* shoot down on the gathered horde were priority targets for the enemy. Every time a leej went to man them, they were cut down within seconds.

A sense of sadness came over the captain, for two reasons. First, that he might never know the reason for this schismatic fight. This civil war, it would seem. And second, because he was going to win. And in a fight like this—perhaps like every other fight in the galaxy—a victory comes with the cost of Legion lives.

And now that number would be doubled.

"Gather up your fraggers and any satchel charges you can find," he ordered over L-comm. "Time to make it rain. KTF."

07

Black Fleet Assault Force Scythe.
Tarrago Moon
0415 Local System Time

"Sergeant Gutierrez! Command Sergeant Major Caleb Gutierrez!" A shock trooper who'd somehow lost his bucket came running over to the sergeant.

"That's me," said Gutierrez.

"Sir," the helmetless runner said breathlessly, "I've been sent to discuss command by First Sergeant Bule."

The S-comm, Sergeant Gutierrez noted, was nowhere near as reliable as the Legion L-comm. This close to the wall, they were being jammed hard by the Legion and could only communicate via S-comm within a five-meter radius.

Sergeant Gutierrez spied a leej attempting to man an N-50 positioned toward his line. He squeezed off three bursts from his rifle and watched the leej fall from the emplacement. Points for persistence, at least. "What's the message on command, then?"

"You're it, sir!" the shock trooper answered.

"What about Lieutenant Mercer?"

"Dead," the shock trooper replied. "All dead or missing. You're it by rank, and you're it by the choice of the STs. If you hadn't convinced your driver to hold the sleds back, none of us would have lived to this point."

Sergeant Gutierrez had done almost all there was to do in the Legion. He'd served in countless combat tours.

Even spent some time with a kill team. But he'd never had command of anything beyond a squad.

Still, he was ready.

"I need to know what we've got for demolitions and engineering," he said without missing a beat. "We're protected well enough against blaster fire, but we need to get inside and take this fortress out of the hands of the Legion."

As his mind shifted from squad command to theater command, a series of small explosions began to ripple out among the shock troopers taking cover at the base of the wall. What was this?

"Fraggers!" someone called out. "They're dropping them on top of us!"

Sket. This would be a serious disruption. And there was nothing they could do about it.

First things first. Gutierrez needed a way to communicate with his shock troopers and then maybe beg for some air support from the fleet. He scanned through his bucket, toggling his search metrics in an attempt to see where the jamming was coming from. If he could find it and pull back out of its broadcast...

Wait. That was unexpected. He could clearly see a Sigmar-A3 black box positioned at the top of the wall. Perhaps two hundred meters away.

"Someone bring me an A-P launcher!" Gutierrez called out, amplifying his external speakers in the hopes that someone might hear through audio what they couldn't through S-comm.

A shock trooper brought forward the weapon. "Only two missiles left, Sergeant Major."

"I'll only need one." Gutierrez shouldered the weapon and switched off the automated targeting system. It would get spoofed by the jamming.

"Wait," a shock trooper protested, probably following Gutierrez's aim through his HUD and seeing the impossibly small and distant target. "You're trying to take that black box out on manual fire? There's no way."

"You're right," Gutierrez answered. "Ain't nobody good enough to make this shot... *'cept me.*"

The launcher fired, and the missile propelled away, leaving a laser-straight trail of white smoke. There was never any doubt. Never any need for the second missile. The black box erupted in an explosion of sparks that reminded shock troopers and legionnaires alike of a Founders' Day celebration.

The S-comms immediately came back online. It felt like hearing again after being in a sensory deprivation hood. Everyone began to talk at once.

Sergeant Gutierrez used his command codes to mute every shock trooper but himself. "This is Command Sergeant Major Gutierrez. I want all shock troopers to pull away from the vehicle entry door. Let's see if the featherheads have any more bombers to help us out. KTF, shock troopers. For the Legion."

Black Fleet
Flagship *Imperator*
0427 Local System Time

"My Lord..." Admiral Rommal hesitated. How many more times would he be forced to bring dark tidings to Goth Sullus? "The assault on Tarrago Moon has stalled. We are scraping together the resources for air support, but it will require the assistance of Admiral Devers, who insists he needs all of his fighters for operations against the defense fleet."

Goth Sullus looked to his aide. "Prepare my shuttle."

Black Fleet
Third Wing, Fourth Squadron, "Pit Vipers"
Hangar Deck Three Aboard *Terror*
Off Tarrago Moon
0429 Local System Time

Already on standby, Viper Twelve hurriedly jumped into his tri-fighter. Part of a reserve squad, he was being brought into the battle.

Already.

"What's the mission, Ten?" he asked as he strapped himself in. "No time for briefing, huh?"

"Escort duty for a bombing run on Tarrago Moon."

"Scuttlebutt was that we didn't have any bombers left." Viper Twelve looked around the hangar as his tri-fighter's engines roared to life. "I don't see any..."

Vipers 10 and 11 lifted off on repulsors and formed up to leave the hangar. Vipers 12 and 13 were right behind them.

"We're flying to the Republic Third Fleet that defected," Viper Ten said, continuing the briefing even as the tri-fighters exited the *Terror*'s hangar bay. "Stay alert and listen up. A squadron of Republic tri-bombers are launching from Third Fleet. We're meeting up and providing escort down and back."

"Doesn't Third Fleet have its own Raptors or tri-fighters to pull escort duty?" asked Viper Thirteen. "Why do we have to do it?"

"Gee, I dunno, Thirteen," Viper Ten answered, his voice dripping with sarcasm. "Why don't I just call up the admirals and ask? Now shut up and do your job."

"Sorry, Ten."

The squadron flew in silence to the rendezvous coordinates.

The thing is, Viper Ten thought, escort duty *should* have started at launch from Third Fleet. Had they lost all their fighter support in the battle with the defense fleet? Were things really going this poorly?

"I'm picking up incoming tri-bombers on the scope," called out Viper Eleven. "Only two? Should be ten, right?"

The bombers roared toward Pit Viper Squadron, hailing them on the open comm. "Get these guys off our tails!"

"I'm seeing three vampires in pursuit," Viper Twelve announced.

"Engage and reform when you've dusted them," Viper Ten ordered.

Viper Twelve acquired missile lock on the incoming Republic raptor. The fighter had been so intent on chasing down the last of the fleeing tri-bombers that it was taken completely by surprise. Viper Twelve hoped the same would be true of the other craft. He wanted to run this mission and get back to barracks. No one in Fourth Squadron ever claimed to be war heroes.

"Missile away!" Viper Twelve pulled up hard to get away from the concussive blast of the warhead. His HUD showed it detonating a meter away from the raptor's left wing, just as the enemy craft attempted to spin up in avoidance. The ship was shaken apart by the explosion. "Vampire down."

"Vampire Two down," called out Viper Thirteen.

That meant one left. Viper Twelve peered around his open cockpit to spot the enemy Raptor.

"Vampire Three is on my tail," Viper Eleven announced calmly. "Need someone to swing behind and pick him off."

"I'm dropping in, Eleven," Viper Ten said before dropping his tri-fighter behind the raptor. "Juke hard starboard, I'm opening up blaster cannons."

Unlike First Squadron, the Fourth still had standard-issue blasters. Maybe Goth Sullus had run out of money...

"He's got missile lock!" Viper Eleven shouted, a bit of panic now in his voice.

Viper Eleven rolled hard starboard as commanded. Viper Ten unleashed a salvo of blaster fire that tore the final Raptor to pieces. But through the extinguishing gases and debris, Viper Ten could see a seeker missile turning hard after Viper Eleven. "It's after you, Eleven, deploy countermeasures!"

A cloud of signal chaff dropped from behind Viper Eleven. The missile continued through it undeterred. "No good!" Viper Eleven cried out. "Deploying intercept-bot—Aahh!"

The missile slammed hard into the tri-fighter and detonated.

Viper Ten watched the explosion, then looked for the surviving bombers and tri-fighters on his scope. "Form up," he ordered. "Twelve, you fly solo escort on the first bombing run. You'll have a surprise advantage. Thirteen and I will escort the second run."

"Copy, Ten."

"Copy."

"Okay," Viper Ten said, "let's go visit the eastern wall."

Eastern Gun Bore
Fortress Omicron
0431 Local System Time

The legionnaire captain struggled to his feet. That the wall was still standing was a testament to Republic engineering.

Reports quickly came in regarding the damage to the vehicle access door. Another hit like that, and the dark legionnaires outside would have a way in. And there simply were not enough legionnaires on hand to overcome those odds.

"Captain," a comm systems officer said over L-comm. "We're detecting a second run inbound. One tri-bomber escorted by a pair of unknown model tri-fighters."

"Get every available leej firing aero-precision rockets at the incoming bomber."

"Captain," the comm systems officer said in a low voice. "By the time our A-P missiles are deployed... it will be too late."

"We still try, Leej," the captain said, his face grim. "We still try."

"Captain!" another comm systems voice called out urgently. "Picking up another craft. Naseen-model light freighter. It's broadcasting kill team credentials and flying a course that brings it within range of one of our advance anti-air launchers. Orders?"

It was a split-second decision. There was so much deceit happening today. So much subterfuge. This freighter could easily be just another Republic asset being used against the Legion on Tarrago Prime.

"Let them go," the captain ordered. *And may God help them.*

Black Fleet
Third Wing, Fourth Squadron, "Pit Vipers"
Tarrago Moon
0440 Local System Time

"Run one successful," Viper Twelve called out as he banked away from the wall, keeping the now depleted tri-bomber in his field of vision.

"Copy that," Viper Ten answered. "We're coming in on our attack vector now."

"Wait a minute," Viper Thirteen called out. "I'm picking up a new ship, Naseen-model light freighter. Oba, it's moving fast."

"Stay on target," Viper Ten instructed.

Viper Twelve positioned his craft to observe the attack run from high above. He saw the Black Fleet tri-fighters in tight formation, protecting the bomber. Farther back he saw a Naseen freighter skimming just above the trees, its speed almost unreal. "That thing could outrun *us*," Viper Twelve murmured to himself.

Without warning, the freighter jumped up, drew level with the attacking Pit Vipers, and spewed an unholy amount of rapid blaster fire at the tri-bomber. The craft and its ordnance erupted in a brilliant flash of light, and the massive fireball engulfed Vipers 10 and 13, snuffing all three ships out at once.

And the second bombing run failed just like that.

But it wasn't over. The Naseen freighter rolled effortlessly and changed trajectories. Viper Twelve saw a missile streaking toward the bomber he was escorting.

"I'm getting missile lock!" the bomber pilot screamed, but his sensors had picked up the warhead far, far too late. His voice died in a ball of flame as the Naseen freighter leveled itself, did a waggle as if to salute the lone remaining tri-fighter, and then rocketed away, buzzing the eastern wall.

"Oh no you don't," Viper Twelve said, rolling down in pursuit and throttling all power to catch up. There was no way he was going to let this freighter get away with that.

He began to make up ground. This thing wasn't so fast after all.

Almost there.

Almost there.

The devastating flurry of blaster fire from the freighter's hidden tail cannons didn't even register in Viper Twelve's mind. They tore him apart inside his cockpit before he even knew what was happening, his thumb hovering impotently above his own fire control.

Black Fleet Assault Force Scythe
Tarrago Moon
0446 Local System Time

Sergeant Gutierrez observed the unexpected turn of events. Such was war. There wouldn't be another bombing run. This battle would be decided by the troops on the ground.

To me.

Gutierrez hit the side of his bucket. Had he heard that correctly? Was someone goofing over the S-comm?

To me.

Gutierrez looked to the eastern wall. Goth Sullus stood atop it, throwing legionnaires over the side as if they were rag dolls. The entry doors began to tremble, then exploded outward as if propelled by a rush of water.

"Shock troopers!" Gutierrez called over the S-comm. "Take the fortress!"

A sea of black-armored troopers poured into the opening.

Eastern Gun Bore
Fortress Omicron
0450 Local System Time

The legionnaire captain fought back the rising terror in his throat. A monster in armor—something out of the history texts—was leading a cadre of dark legionnaires into his lines. It was like seeing a leej in MK1 Savage War armor, but made new again. Who was this?

And the creature had emerged from *inside* Fortress Omicron. Meaning he had already overcome another wall and worked his way to this point. Were any of them still alive? Commander Yoon? Anyone? Were the captain and his men the last of this company?

A sensation of dark despair rose with goose flesh across the captain's skin, his leej armor unable to counteract this unnatural cold. The creature was lifting legionnaires off the ground—with nothing more than his will, it seemed—and using them as a barrier against the concentrated fire being sent in his direction. Even as the dark creature's own legionnaires fell, he walked methodically along the top of the eastern wall. Toward the captain.

There was a groaning, and a breach alarm flashed in the captain's helmet. The vehicle access doors had been compromised, and his HUD showed scores of dark legionnaires pouring inside. But they paid a price for their every step. Enemy unit positions turned black as the captain's men let loose consistent firepower. It wasn't enough to stop the flow of men, however, and they were now making their way to the top of the wall.

The dark walker, the monster in black, walked slowly toward the captain—as though the captain was the creature's lone target. The captain fired at his enemy, but soon realized that any shots fired at the dark walker only found their way into the back of the captain's own men somehow—so he quickly abandoned that tactic. He would not abide such a thing in his final moments. Instead he focused on the dark legionnaires flanking the monster.

He took a step backward, tripped over the body of a fallen legionnaire, and landed hard on his tailbone. The beast walked nearer, and the captain scrambled his legs to move away. The monstrous thing in the MK1 armor was practically on top of him... and seemed to be taking a perverse pleasure in the captain's fear.

And then, all at once, the legionnaires around the man in black fell to the ground as one.

The man in black appeared startled. He looked around as if utterly perplexed by this.

The captain seized the opportunity. His hand felt a surge shotgun lying next to the deceased legionnaire who once wielded it. He wrapped his fingers around the pistol-style grip and lurched forward, pushing the barrel into the armored ribs of the man in black.

"Die, you kelhorn—"

The shotgun's booming report drowned out the rest of the captain's words. The man in black went spinning to the ground, landing hard on his back, black smoke rising from his armor.

Then the captain felt a heel strike the small of his back, and his face was pushed into the ground. The surge rifle was kicked away, and his arms were secured behind his back. He was rolled over, and looked up to see a dark legionnaire pointing a blaster at his head.

"Don't be stupid," the dark legionnaire said. "We're all Legion here. Wire me your L-comm passkey so we can put a stop to this. No sense in so many leejes getting dusted now that it's over."

The captain hesitated. Tactically he might be out of the fight, but his men could still make these dark leejes pay. But... for what? And for how long? They would continue to fight until there was no fight left. Until they were dead. And there was something about the way the dark legionnaire spoke that compelled him. *We're all Legion here.*

The captain made his decision. Omicron was lost.

"Introduce me," the dark legionnaire asked. "I'm Command Sergeant Gutierrez."

"This is Captain Arwen," the captain said over L-comm. "I've surrendered the eastern wall to Command Sergeant Major Gutierrez."

The dark legionnaire took over from there. "This is Command Sergeant Gutierrez of Shock Trooper Assault Force Scythe," he said over the comm. "I know how it goes. KTF. Fight to the last man. I'm Legion, too. But if you're honest with yourself, you know that the Legion has been under assault from the House of Reason, the Senate, and all those points out there that slept through school and got leejes killed. No more leejes need to die today. The salvation of the Legion begins now. Lay down your arms, and you will be treated fairly. Ooah."

Arwen spoke again. "I know some of you are thinking of holding out. If you need an order to surrender, this is it. If you want personal advice... the fight is lost. And I'm tired of seeing legionnaires get dusted."

The captain looked about, and saw his legionnaires begin to lay down their arms. And the sergeant major was true to his word. The leejes were treated with respect. The kill stopped. At least on the east wall, where it was hopeless. The captain knew that the rest of the company still had a chance, and they'd fight until that chance was completely denied.

Sergeant Gutierrez grabbed the captain underneath the shoulder and helped the bound legionnaire to his feet. "I knew you weren't a point after that trick with the main gun. You'd better get out of here. My men will take you to safety before the commander fully wakes." He glanced back at the beast, who was stirring, his wound not fatal. "KTF, leej."

"KTF," agreed the captain. He started off with his escort of dark legionnaires, then turned back. "Sergeant Major. When you were Legion... what was your call sign?"

"Exo," answered the shock trooper.

08

231st Gun Battery Assigned Orbital Defense Command
Fortress Omicron
0250 Local System Time

Much of the base was still intact two hours before the shock troopers would storm it en masse. Despite the bomb damage across the surface structures, and the damage from air-to-ground attack by the enemy fighters, the lower levels were sealed. The blast doors across the facility had done their work.

Captain Thales made his way back through the sub-lunar halls cut into the stone, passing corpsmen carrying wounded. As soon as he'd made his way through a force field, he was able to shuck his helmet and get in contact with fire control.

"Still no word on the admiral?"

"No, sir," replied the junior officer. "Command base house was wiped out by one of the bombs. Right now you're in command, but the lieutenant colonel in charge of the legionnaire battalion is ready to take over until a more senior navy officer can come up from Tarrago Prime."

Thales let that hang for a moment as he mopped sweat from his brow. He knew Navy-Legion interaction often got sticky and tricky... but right now they were in a fight. And the Legion was the absolute best at fighting. As an artillery officer, it was his job to support the Legion.

He nodded to himself as one of the nearby corpsmen covered a dead gunner with the man's jacket. The body bags hadn't arrived yet.

"Tell him he's in charge," Thales said. "And also tell him we've most likely got two spies running around the base. You've got the gun batteries. I'm going to try and track these jokers down before they do any more damage. Until then, I want you to seal fire control up. Protocol eight. No one gets in or out. If they have a target, Lieutenant... it'll be you guys. I'm heading to Internal Security."

"Roger that, sir."

House of Reason, Security Council Chambers Utopion

"Has there been any success in reaching the Seventh Fleet?" Orrin Kaar asked the gathered Security Council members.

An opulent lunch of chilled luteclaw and beezel eggs occupied the center of the meeting table. Kaar watched as some of the more corpulent delegates piled their plates high with the succulent fare.

"None," answered Vice Chair A'lill'n as she spooned a socially acceptable amount—much too little—onto a gleaming white plate. "Based on what we received from the Navy, it is likely that the Seventh Fleet is somewhere in the Tarrago system."

"And therefore unreachable by comm." Kaar let out a sigh, though in truth he felt this to be good news. With the early complications, the Seventh Fleet showing up now would be less than ideal. Better to buy time to secure the moon and Tarrago Prime and then lure the fleet to its destruction. That would provide a clear path to Utopion itself, and a new beginning for the Republic. One where men who were not afraid to lead could prosper. Men like Orrin Kaar.

Kaar looked around the table. Every delegate member save himself was stuffing his or her face with food that most of the galaxy couldn't afford if they saved for a month. They were entirely content to sit back and let Kaar—and, it must be admitted, A'lill'n—make determinations for the entire council. When the New Republic rose from the ashes of the old, they would have just that—Kaar would lead them all.

And the galaxy would flourish.

"It would seem," Kaar said to the room, "that all we can do at this point is wait for news from Tarrago. The Seventh Fleet is all we can spare at the moment, with Admiral Devers's Third Fleet already in action. Unless we wish to leave the edge and mid-core unprotected?"

Those delegates who were listening shook their heads.

"Legion Commander Keller, has your kill team been recalled?"

Keller's image flickered through the comm. "The order has been given to their team commander."

Kaar frowned. "That sounds to me a very noncommittal response, Commander."

"There is a chain of command, Delegate Kaar. The order will be relayed to the kill team, but as you know, there is difficulty communicating with the Tarrago system. It may be too late."

The eyes of the other council members looked to Kaar for a response, but it was A'lill'n who gave the answer. "You have done your part, Legion Commander Keller. However, if the kill team completes this unsanctioned mission and destroys a major Republic asset... someone will have to pay the price."

Keller's expression hardened. "Understood," he said, though his tone indicated he did anything but.

231st Gun Battery Assigned Orbital Defense Command
Fortress Omicron
0300 Local System Time

Internal Security was three levels down and on the opposite side of the gun bore around which the fortress was built. Thales made it there even though a large section of the bore in the area had taken extreme damage from the one bomb that had managed to hit its target.

To Thales, it was a wonder the gun would even fire out of this bore with all the damage. But according to the LT in fire control, it would. Damage control teams were already hard at work swapping out massive systems boards that interfaced with the solid-state guidance magnets built into the sides of the tunnel.

At one section, the bore lay open to the vacuum beyond a temporary force field the damage control team had set up. Thales donned his wonky artillery helmet and made sure he had a good seal before passing through the barrier. The team acknowledged him, and he set their comm channel after identifying it on their shoulder markings.

"I'm just gonna visually inspect the bore while I'm down here. Don't mind me."

They didn't and returned to their work.

He stuck first his head, and then his body, out into the gaping cavern that was the orbital gun bore in this quadrant of the dead moon.

It was like looking into a bottomless pit.

The distance to the opposite side of the bore was over two hundred yards, and all around the perimeter, massive maglev blocks waited to accelerate and guide the rounds to their targets. Thales leaned out further, fighting a brief wash of vertigo as he looked down. It was dark, even though the tunnel was lit the whole way down to the moon's core.

The bomb had likely been set to explode at a certain altitude setting, and that was the only thing that had saved this bore from going offline. Instead of hitting anything, it had merely dropped down the center of the massive tube and exploded in midair.

"They should've set for contact detonation," Thales muttered to himself. That would've taken all four gun bores out at once. They would've wiped out fire control in one stroke.

Except maybe that hadn't been their plan. Maybe they'd only wanted to disable the one gun that could hit their fleet. Take fire control by force, or stealth, and then take possession of the other three gun bores, ready to hit anything else within those arcs.

Something else bothered him, and normally he was the type to stay and tease it out until he had it. He was a problem solver that way—or, as the most likely now dead base commanding officer had thought of him... a *thinker*. Like that was somehow a bad thing as far as the higher-ups of galactic culture were concerned. But right now he needed to get to Internal Security and find out where the two assassins had gone off to, so he pulled himself away from the almost mesmerizing view of the bottomless gun bore and said goodbye to the damage control team.

At Internal Security he found no one alive.

They were all dead.

And that same HK malware had scrambled all the screens and terminals.

Thales drew his blaster and advanced into the dark security center. One officer was reclining in his chair, swiveled away from his station, blaster on his hip. His head had been blown off. One shot.

They got him first, thought Thales.

To his right a tech with headphones on, probably the comm operator for this section, had gotten it in the back. Whether he'd known it was coming or not was unclear. The third man in the station had at least drawn a blaster. It lay a few feet from his body, unfired.

When Thales had cleared the area, he knew two things.

One, he was dealing with someone, or *someones*, who were very good at killing. The headshot on the section chief was pro. And two, they'd come here after Deep Sensors to knock this node out before they went on to their next target.

The next target most likely had to be fire control.

Except fire control was locked down. Protocol eight. Virtually inaccessible by physical means.

And it was way down there, at the intersection of all four gun bores, in the middle of the massive hollow core of the dead moon. A bunker with only one route in or out. That route had a series of eight high-security blast doors that could not be opened from the outside. Anyone even trying would be subdued by gas, or war bots, or ventilated by two automated high-powered tri-barrel N-50s that sensed on thermal and motion. Any unauthorized personnel at the last barrier were targeted and terminated, no questions asked.

And that was only the last line of defense. The four lifts leading down-bore from each fortress all opened onto a security station guarded by a platoon of crack Legionnaires. Only *if* you got past them did you move on to face the gas, blast doors, war bots, more blast doors, and the murder guns.

And everyone in fire control knew you were coming the whole time. And they were authorized to—and this is where it got crazy, but since Thales was an artillery officer and this whole moon was basically one giant gun system, he knew—the fire control officers were authorized to detonate the entire moon in order to prevent the gun from falling into enemy hands.

Yes.

The entire moon.

But of course that would never happen. Because no one would ever invade the Republic, much less the sector capital at Tarrago. And there was no way to get through security into main fire control.

Except...

Five minutes later Thales was back at the spot where the damage control team was just finishing their work.

"Question, Sergeant..." interrupted Thales.

The damage control team sergeant groaned as she stood up from her work. She wiped her hands on her uniform and waited. She seemed in no mood for officers.

"When you guys got down here..."

"Guys?"

She'd report him for that. Great. Whatever.

"All right," he sighed. "Sorry. Long day. I apologize. Deeply," he added sarcastically. "Okay. When your team arrived. That maglev was still in its mounting bracket chain?"

She seemed to forget his offense, or rather didn't take it too seriously. She was just busting his chops. She could've cared less.

"No, sir. It had fallen inward. This whole area was exposed vacuum. The explosion must have forced it off the mounting chain embedded into the walls."

Thales thought about that for a second. "But that's not supposed to happen. Right?"

"No, sir. Not at all. But it has. Rarely. When they did the initial readiness inspection on the bore after the attack, they spotted this one. So we got detailed to come in and fix it." She waited. Obviously she wanted to get back to finishing the job he'd just interrupted.

He looked around the small space they'd been working in. The maglev panel had just *fallen* inward. It hadn't been *blown* inward. It hadn't bounced off the opposite wall of what amounted to a small niche built along the side of the bore.

He bent down and inspected the panel. After a few seconds he found what he was looking for.

"How do you..." He was gonna say "guys" but caught himself. "Get this off? When you do maintenance?"

She pointed to a pneumatic suction device attached to a small portable lift nearby.

"So you wouldn't make these marks." He pointed toward the top of the panel, where the panel and the floor formed a seam. There, the maglev panel, a very substantial piece of equipment, had been damaged.

At that point the sergeant got interested. She ran her gloved hand across the damage.

"From the blast?" she asked.

Thales shook his head.

"It's on the inside. Like someone used a device to pop the panel out of its mount and let it fall inward."

"Why?"

Thales stood, walked over to the opening, and looked down into the gaping maw.

"Because they wanted to drop onto fire control."

"That's a long fall," she replied incredulously.

And then he was running for the lifts.

Halfway there, running along a curving corridor, he felt the ground began to shake. Dust came down everywhere. There was a loud rumble.

"All base personnel. Report to your battle stations. We are under attack. Enemy ground assault forces are attacking the base. Repeat..."

Even with the turbo lifts it took forever. Along the way, Captain Thales had time to communicate with the company commander's adjutant and inform him that they had a problem down in fire control. He was told in return that the main gun was getting firing orders that made no sense—and it was firing.

The line suddenly went dead—the adjutant had clicked off. The man had sounded efficient but stressed, and Thales had the impression that the officer didn't appreciate the gravity of the situation and so had chosen to attend to other pressing matters. Then again, the adjutant probably didn't know about the two crustbuster weapons that could annihilate the moon in less than thirty seconds if fire control felt threatened.

And he was in the middle of an invasion. So there was that.

At the bottom of the core, the elevator opened out onto an innocuous platform with gravity decking. Access tunnels from the other bores led to this same platform—it was the only way in or out. Or so he had thought, until today. Down here there was near weightlessness, and if those two assassins had dropped down the tube with a minimum amount of gear, they'd have been able to land right on top of the fire control bunker—a straight shot, with no damage.

Thales's mind swam. Ahead of him the bunker waited, suspended in the void of a hollow core. A lone bridge made its way out there, and a fortified security station guarded the entrance to the bridge. The legionnaires knew he was coming.

"Advance!" called some acid-voiced legionnaire from across the wide distance between the lift and the security station. Powerful floodlights sprang to life, bathing everything, including Thales, in a bone-white cold light.

Thales raised his hands, suddenly and uncomfortably aware of the blaster on his thigh. He could see these keyed-up leejes taking that as the needed provocation to blow his brains all over the platform.

And they'd be right to do so, he told himself.

But he walked forward to the station without getting shot, and the legionnaire sergeant came out.

"State your business."

"We may have infiltrators down here," Thales said. "I'm with the 231st. Captain Thales. OIC for Navy. As of right now. I'm going in there to take command of fire control. You should have an authorization from Lieutenant..." Thales couldn't remember the kid's name.

The legionnaire sergeant merely stared at him. Any emotions—hatred, warmth, whatever—was hidden behind the iconic helmet they all wore. *They call it a "bucket,"* some distant part of Thales's mind remarked.

"Ain't no one's been down here. Ain't no one gettin' through, sir. Your ID signature checks out. Head down the bridge and never mind the war bots. Don't screw around by the emplaced guns or they'll go live on you. It's that serious. Fire control will open the door and you can go on in."

For a moment, Thales thought about telling the legionnaires to come with him. If there were two assassins in there, or trying to get in, they wouldn't stand a chance against a platoon of trained killers like the legionnaires.

But these men would never leave their assigned post. That would be like getting them to say that water wasn't wet.

"Last contact with Lieutenant..." He still couldn't remember the kid's name. He nodded toward the bunker.

"Five minutes ago. It's all quiet down here." And then the legion sergeant added, "Which kinda sucks."

It wasn't the two fearsome latest-gen war bots that freaked Thales out. The gigantic killing machines merely watched him pass without comment. It was the guns.

The automated tri-barrel N-50s. Not even the thin, transparent, domed bridge—which seemed to impossibly connect with the fire control bunker suspended in the middle of the core—was as scary as the two soulless heavy blaster killing systems.

Maybe because they were AI-run. Artificial intelligence had always bothered Thales. Like it couldn't be reasoned with. Like there was no soul to appeal to on the other side of an instantaneous and violent death.

From the bridge, he could see the nearest gun breech of the four attached to the bunker. It was a massive gleaming impervisteel system that impressed the hell out of the artillery geek side of him. Attached to the breech was a massive cylinder magazine the size of a corvette. Ready to rack and reload the rounds the orbital defense gun fired faster than anyone thought possible.

This was not some one-shot super-weapon like so many movies liked to show. Some giant beam that destroyed a planet in just a few seconds. This thing could blow up an entire fleet inside a minute, hitting each ship with its own individual round. It didn't fire as fast as an automatic heavy blaster, but close enough. Except that it fired rounds the size of trees. All of them sleeping inside those enormous cylinder magazines.

That impressed him.

The war bots bothered him.

The N-50s scared him to death outright.

Why?

He didn't know. Maybe it was the legionnaire sergeant's warning not to mess around with them. And of course the AI thing. Maybe it was the fact that if there was even the slightest mistake they would just activate and hit him with a short burst of thirty blasts.

They wouldn't miss with even one shot.

And there was nowhere to hide, because all he was doing was following a narrow tube that led into the heart of the bunker.

He'd never been so glad to hear a blast door slide aside with a hissed *whoosh*. And then he was through. The fire control lieutenant greeted him. The kid looked worried and nervous. And he seemed genuinely glad somebody else was in charge.

Thales didn't have to imagine why. This kid had singlehandedly knocked out a Republic destroyer. There would be hell to pay, and *someone* was going to pay it. That was the way the navy was. Everyone knew that.

"We need to get all the external lights going on the bunker and get the inspection cams and drones up," Thales said. "I think—"

That's when the lights inside the bunker failed. A moment later everything switched over to red emergency lighting.

"Someone's violated the seals from the magazine. They're inside the battery." Lieutenant Nayron had his datapad out as he and Thales waited near the main entrance to the bunker. Currently there were only six crew assigned to the main gun. The other five were scattered throughout the facility.

"Can they get into fire control from there?" Thales asked.

Nayron tapped and tapped. Thales could see that he was bringing up schematics.

"Maybe," he said slowly. But Thales didn't like the lack of confidence.

"One of them must have excellent code slicing skills," he said. "The trail I've been following has shown that."

And for the first time, Thales realized that the inconceivable could happen. An external threat could get control of the orbital defense gun.

Then what?

If a response force showed up—the Seventh Fleet, most likely—then an entire Republic fleet would be sitting ducks.

"We may have to destroy this facility."

The junior officer looked up at the captain in horror.

Thales, blaster in hand, smiled sickly. "I know. It's bad."

Then he explained to the junior officer his reasoning. The man just listened, shaking his head but not objecting. In the end he merely remarked, "We'll be killed." His voice was a soft whisper.

"If we can stop them before they take control... then we don't have to." He paused. "So where would they be going? Where could they get control of the gun?"

A few minutes later they were in main fire control. The officer brought up a screen. "Processors," he began. "If he's a code slicer, he could do it all from there. And it makes sense why they broke in through the magazines. This conduit here?" He pointed to the glowing white schematics on screen. "This comes in right under them. We use it maintain the bearings on the magazine gyros. They could cut in here and be right in processors. Only other way is through this room and back into target acquisition.

And right now we're sealed inside a vault. Unless I open this door... no one's getting in."

Thales stared at the screen.

"That's their only way in?"

The LT nodded.

"What's your armory like here?"

"Six rifles. Six pistols."

Thales doubted a bunch of gunnery techs were going to take out two highly trained killers.

"Hatch is through there?"

The junior officer nodded again.

"If you lose the processors, can we still fire?"

There wasn't even an ounce of hesitation. "Definitely. We can pull processing power from all across the base. It's a simple re-route. About five minutes' work."

"Where's the firefighting hose?"

Thales didn't even give the assassins a chance to surrender. As soon as the gunnery techs had unsealed the hatch that led down into the processors, he nodded to the tech operating the flow valve and dropped the nozzle of the powerful hose down the hatch, letting the slack he'd taken up go with it also. He threw more and more of the hose down after it.

The hose swelled quickly as water flooded through it. They'd had to disconnect it from the hydrofoam firefighting system that was generally meant for electrical fires, and reconnect it to the main water supply valve. Ice-cold water now flooded the racks of processors below.

There was a static bang. Someone swore. And then every processor went off like a firecracker, short, sharp, and all at once.

The iron-sharp smell of the water was replaced by the smell of burnt flesh.

One of the techs shut down the electrical grid in that section, and Thales and the LT went in, Thales leading the way with a blaster.

They found the two assassins. Both dead. Electrocuted.

For now, the Republic retained control of the orbital defense gun on Tarrago Moon.

One Voice Park
Utopion

Orrin Kaar walked among the cultivated plants, using the paved footpaths to avoid dampening his shoes on the newly watered lawn. One Voice Park was built to serve as a meeting place for House of Reason delegates and Senate Council members. A place where they could hear from constituents, lobbies, dignitaries, activists, and the media. All in the open, in keeping with the spirit of transparent government.

The real deals, of course, happened behind *closed* doors.

Regardless of its failure to achieve its express purpose, Kaar had always enjoyed the park. Atmospheric controllers spent untold amounts of energy making sure that the weather here was always perfect. But now, as Kaar examined his datapad, ordering Admiral Devers's voice message be converted to text, he found that his own mood was anything but perfect. A storm of disappointment thundered and boomed inside of him as he read.

Ground Attack on Fortress Omicron has stalled. Significant losses. Victory in doubt.

Kaar looked into the beautiful, artificial sky and cursed.

PART III

09

Levenir Orbit
The Galactic Core

"Absolutely incredible," Cade Thrane said to himself.

He hadn't made much progress in decrypting the message any further. Sure, he had inched toward a few more seconds of audio, but he couldn't comprehend what he was hearing, and computer analysis didn't seem to have any more luck than he did. But the young code slicer *had* come upon something that had him in a state of wonderment. It was the ingenious way the comm burst "floated" on top of the comm relay system. It mixed standard and deep-space transmission protocols and worked like... like a homing missile. Locking on to its target and then recalibrating and recalculating as it went.

Theoretically, as long as there was at least one comm relay within deep-space reach, it could receive the message. Then the message would convert itself to a local comm relay to get farther in, changing its stripes as necessary.

It was a masterful bit of work that marked a leap forward in the evolution of galactic communications. Certainly, when a sizable section of the comm relay was down, as was the case in Tarrago, it would still take a while for messages to get through. But they did get through.

This should be standard comm tech. Leave it to the Republic to withhold something like this from the rest of the galaxy.

This was a technique Thrane could use to his advantage. It would take maybe ten minutes to rework his own comm system to operate like the "ghost relay," as he'd taken to calling it. And then he could reach anyone at any time.

He only wished he could crack the encryption.

The code slicer snapped his fingers. Another set of eyes on the encryption—from someone he trusted—might speed up the process. Of course, Thrane would have to be careful not to reveal too much. Just get some leads or opinions on the best way to get going.

Garrett Glover was the slicer he had in mind. The wonder kid had fallen off the grid after getting mixed up with pirates, but if anyone could help, it would be Garrett.

After twenty minutes, Thrane had refitted his comm system and sent a burst with standard mouse-slice encryption. Easy to break for a coder worth anything, and making him instantly identifiable to someone who knew what to look for. Now he just had to hope the comm address he had for Garrett was still a good one.

Black Fleet
Bridge of the *Imperator*
Off Tarrago Moon
0457 Local System Time

"Admiral," murmured the comm officer charged with monitoring the private channel between Goth Sullus and the fleet. "Message."

Admiral Rommal immediately stepped over and keyed the contact. It was only a voice, the same voice he'd been talking to, and the man's menacing calm was unnerving.

What did you expect? Rommal asked himself. *Rage*? *Anger? Some promise of pain and suffering*?

But the calm in Goth Sullus's voice was unmistakable. "Admiral... I shall deal with the orbital defense gun myself. Move the fleet in to take Tarrago now. Engage the fleet upon their arrival. They shall be here soon."

And the link was cut.

How did he know that? Yes, the plan had always anticipated the arrival of the Republic's Seventh Fleet, but no one actually knew whether they would come storming in immediately, or first gather their forces in some nearby system for a counterattack. On the planning schedule, they had anticipated this might take days.

So how did he know?

Not even Crodus and all his spies, who seemed to be everywhere, knew.

How?

Admiral Rommal strode back to the real-time tactical display in the center of the lower bridge. He studied the map for a brief minute. It seemed alive, which seemed ironic in light of all the death it represented.

The situation, in-system, at the current moment was this. The fleet had three fully operational battleships. Three wings of fighters with tactical support complements. And three full divisions of shock troopers—one engaged on Tarrago in support of the primary objective of taking the shipyards, one meeting heavy resistance against the final defenders at Fortress Omicron, and one more ready to be committed as needed.

Right now, Rommal would throw that third division into a drop on the fortress if he felt it would do any good. Except Goth Sullus had said he would deal with it himself.

Of course, the plan had always been a trap. Lure the Republic's Seventh Fleet into a battle.

Right here, and right now. They were coming now.

According to him. The man in black.

Don't think that. Don't even think that. Goth Sullus. Don't call him what everyone else does. Because maybe he can hear you. Which was an insane thought.

But according to him—Goth Sullus—the Seventh was coming.

That was key.

Rommal's aides and adjutants hovered about him. Watching his face. Knowing that the order they'd been waiting for ever since operations had begun... was about to be given.

And still for one minute longer he studied the board. Waiting for something...

Then...

"Concentrate most of our jamming assets on blocking any comm with the fortress. We cannot let the Republic know of the situation there. Total blackout. Launch all wings. Bring the fleet about."

Suddenly everyone was scrambling. Speaking orders into comm stations. Setting plans in motion. All that could be known was already known. They'd merely needed the order to begin.

Rommal straightened, adjusted his tunic, and watched the tactical displays all the more.

Republic Seventh Fleet
Bridge of the *Freedom*
Hyperspace, En Route to Tarrago
0500 Local System Time

Admiral Landoo sat down in her command chair and checked the bridge jump clock once more. Forty-five seconds to target destination.

If every ship transited jump in formation she'd have... what sounded like one hell of a fight on her hands. The Republic had never trained for anything of this magnitude. At least not in her career.

She stared out the front bubble of the bridge and saw nothing but the raw intel data on those three super-massive ships as provided by the captain of the *Audacity*. Assessment and Intel had decided to tag them as battleships.

Oh my, she thought. Actual battleships. The Republic hadn't seen action against those since the Savage Wars. She wondered what they were capable of. She'd be far more comfortable if she had more ships on her side. Perhaps she should've let *Audacity* jump with them rather than ordering them on to Utopion. But that ship was only half working. It would have been of little help against these new enemy ships and their strange fighters.

Where had these ships come from, anyway?

Thirty seconds.

"Approaching target destination," called out the bridge captain.

All across the immaculate white bridge, ethereal holographic screens stood ready to capture tactical system data in real-time.

"Slowing from jump in twenty-nine... twenty-eight... twenty-seven..." announced the helm.

Landoo had argued with the High Command that there should've been some kind of contingency for a major fleet action. She had argued that many times. It was in the record. And they'd ignored her. The House of Reason had ignored her, really. "We have fifteen full fleets," they'd all murmured at her every time she'd tried to pin them down on spending. "There's no other political entity in the galaxy that can field a force of that size."

And then they'd countered with a standard-issue platitude about concern for her safety. And a smug satisfaction that they always knew the right thing to do. That even fleet admirals didn't know as much about military planning as they, the elite governing class, did.

Except on paper there was no elite governing class. And yet it existed. It survived. And really, it thrived when others withered. So mind your manners and be a good little admiral. We'll tell you what to do next.

And she'd gone along. Gone along to get along. Made fleet admiral by buying off on their lies. And here she was flying into a battle against an enemy fleet with at least three battleships.

She pushed all that away.

She was a tough old bird, she told herself. She'd made rank on brains and guts instead of favored-alien-species-of-the-week diversity promotions. Even if she was a woman and they'd promoted her just to feel some kind of gender diversity self-righteousness, she had still required herself to be worthy of every advantage they'd foisted upon her.

If this enemy fleet wanted a fight...

"Twenty-one... twenty..."

... then they were about to get a pretty big one.

She slid her command datapad across her chair, brought up her unit roster, and readied her long fingers to key in her orders as soon as she saw what the hell was going on in Tarrago.

Atlantica, the fleet's super-destroyer, would jump in on lead. In support of that massive beast were seven destroyers.

Destiny of Purpose.

Liberty.

Arangotoa, riding picket on the port flank.

Emergent.

Victory.

Bantusu.

With *Aressima* at the rear.

"Ten... nine... eight..."

Then came the carrier group.

Anticipate, she told herself. Be where they don't want you to be. Her fingers hovered over the datapad. She could feel the eyes of everyone on the bridge turn toward the forward bubble. The quiet murmur of comm and signal, the soft lighting, all of it was supposed to be calming. Landoo wondered how calm everything would be once they started the engagement. Once they started shooting at each other.

"Five... four... slowing from light speed now!" ordered the bridge captain.

Suddenly the streaking stars stood at a dead standstill as the mighty Seventh tumbled out of hyperspace, the inevitable collision avoidance alarms going off across all ships in the fleet.

"Launch all fighters!" ordered Admiral Landoo as sensors brought up targeting data on the three massive ships bearing down on them.

Within seconds the massive supercomputers below the combat information center had crunched the bare minimums of time, speed, and distance to each ship. Holographic overlays for engagement ranges for the various weapons systems began to come in seconds later.

"Raise Omicron—I want to talk to the base commander."

The enemy fleet was passing through Tarrago Moon's orbit inbound for Tarrago Prime, presenting their starboard sides. But they were well outside the orbital gun's engagement window.

And these ships were truly *massive*. Far bigger than even the super-destroyer just ahead off her carrier.

"Admiral," replied the comm officer. "Negative contact with Omicron. They've gone dark."

Landoo target-grouped the battleships and ordered all three wings of fighters to engage. She would deal with Omicron soon. Right now the Seventh had more pressing matters to deal with.

"Landoo to fleet captains. Follow the fighters in and engage at close range. Concentrate on the lead ship. Admiral Nagu, you have tactical command forward of the carrier group."

Admiral Nagu acknowledged from the bridge of *Atlantica*.

Republic Seventh Fleet
Bridge of the *Atlantica*
0502 Local System Time

The Republic's state-of-the-art capital warship opened up at max range with her powerful forward ion gun. The beast of a weapon was mounted atop the slender super-destroyer, forward of the bulbous engineering section and the eight massive engines at the rear of the ship. The first shot sped down the length of the hull and passed over the forward command decks.

Secondary heavy turrets were unlimbered and began to fire from just beneath the cap that covered the upper decks. Charged bursts of ionized energy spat forth into face of the approaching enemy fleet. The first volley struck *Imperator*'s deflectors, blowing three decks worth of capacitors offline. Internal lighting flickered across half the hull, and the ship heeled to port as if reeling from the blast.

Crewmembers erupted in a cheer across the twilight-blue command bridge of the super-destroyer.

Admiral Nagu ordered his support ships to follow the massive *Atlantica* forward into the enemy's approaching line. In a few moments he would hold station and order all flanking ships to envelop the enemy fleet, in order to bring maximum firepower to bear on their shields. Hopefully the *Atlantica* would stand up to whatever the massive ships returned fire with.

Everything about this battle was an unknown, and Nagu did not like unknowns. It's why he and others of his species seldom left their forest world. As humanoid avians, they were happiest in their trees making their songs and art. Service in the navy had been chosen by very few from that world.

"Ion gun charging to full," said the weapons officer on the deck above Nagu's command deck. "Thirty seconds to firing, Admiral."

If we can get another shot past their deflectors, thought Nagu, then we might just do something here.

"Point defense turrets online!" cried out one of the bridge officers, a little too emphatically. The enthusiasm seemed to be catching, and Nagu found some comfort in this. It meant they were eager for battle, instead of frightened. Many of them had never had a ship shot out from under them. And neither had Nagu.

"Deflectors charging to full!"

Other deck officers reeled off status reports as the massive *Atlantica* lumbered into weapons range of the three enormous enemy battleships on the stellar horizon.

Black Fleet
Bridge of the *Imperator*
0503 Local System Time

"We're listing!" shouted the CIC as the bridge of the flagship suddenly canted off beam.

Rommal grabbed the edge of his tactical display and looked over toward telemetry. The helmsmen were fighting to restore control of the giant ship, which still reeled from the massive amount of energy it had just displaced in deflecting the shot.

Collision alerts shrieked, and other, lesser klaxons competed for attention.

Bridge Captain Andrun stumbled across the listing bridge's highly polished floor and grabbed hold of the tactical display opposite Admiral Rommal. The look on his face felt like the inside of Rommal's stomach.

"Direct hit, sir. We've lost the starboard capacitors on decks forty-one through forty-three. Should be back online according to design in just a moment. Gravitational plates went a bit haywire... but they're stabilizing. It's all a learning curve, sir. This is our first time out."

He smiled hopefully.

"But she held, sir. She took a direct shot from an ion gun and held. We're blooded, sir! We can do this today."

It was a little premature to be celebrating that, thought Rommal. But he let the man have his moment. Right now a little enthusiasm and motivation might go a long way.

Rommal nodded to show that he agreed.

"Sir..." said the CIC from tactical, "we've got fighter cover up. Squadrons two through sixteen forming up." The ship was beginning to find her balance again. "We're tracking two hundred and seventy fighters inbound from the Seventh. And two additional squadrons coming up from Tarrago Command. That puts their number at three hundred and ten."

Rommal weighed that against the six squadrons each battleship carried. He had the numbers. *Now*, he thought, *let's see who survives first contact.*

Rommal nodded as the *Imperator* settled back onto her course and quietly thundered ahead into the oncoming Republic Fleet's formation.

"Open fire now?" asked the CIC.

Rommal nodded again and watched as both groups of fighters moved away from their respective fleets, racing out to meet the incoming enemy.

Republic Seventh Fleet
First Squadron, "Gray Wolves"
Reassigned to Oblavia Airfield,
Ad Hoc Special Operations Strike Command
Above Tarrago
0509 Local System Time

"Gray Leader, this is Gray Seven. We have an incoming analysis on the lead target, currently identified as battleship class. She's a monster."

"Go ahead, Seven," replied Commander Luq.

Luq and OU7 had barely survived the direct hit on the rebel destroyer that tried to block *Audacity*'s jump. Most of the other tri-fighters and the rest of the Wolves had gone up in the blast wave after the orbital gun had destroyed the mysterious rebel ship, but in the seconds after the blast, Luq had found himself flying through a maelstrom of burning gas and expanding debris clouds shooting off in every direction, and somehow, he'd come out the other side of it with barely a scratch—though for a moment it had felt as though the ship was going to rattle itself apart.

After a quick nap in the back of a noisy hangar at Oblavia Airfield while his ship was repaired and rearmed, he had found himself assigned to a special weapons strike team. The plan was for a fighter escort, accompanied by a special ECM Lancer, to fly two bombers right in under the enemy's deflectors and try to knock out a "critical" ship system. Luq would lead that strike team, with OU7 flying escort. No "critical system" had yet been identified on the giant enemy ship, but now that the carrier group's scout frigate was lashing the three battleships with every sensor it could bring to bear, new targeting data was being developed all the time.

"Highlighting on your HUD now," said Gray Seven. "If you can get us through what looks to be a lot of point defense fire, we can lob our baby into what targeting analysis tells us is their external reactor. Might be able to knock out a significant amount of their onboard power. It could even possibly be tied in to their deflector system. We won't know until we hit it."

OU7 whirred and beeped angrily behind Commander Luq.

"My bot still says we've got to have those deflectors down before we can even get close."

"Little guy's right about that," replied Gray Seven. His transmission distorted and popped; they were passing through Tarrago's ionosphere. "Our weapons package won't penetrate deflectors, Gray Leader. But once they're down, we're all clear for a shot."

OU7 beeped and clicked, announcing a new incoming message. Luq tapped the comm authorization and switched over to group leader strike comm.

"Gray Leader here."

"Gray Leader, this is Bandit Leader. We copy your mission from *Freedom*'s air boss. Form up on us, and we'll get you through their fighter cover and follow you in for the strike."

Republic Seventh Fleet
First Squadron, "Bandits," 29th Wing
Assigned to Carrier *Freedom*
0511 Local System Time

"There's too many of them!"

"Cut that, Bandit Six."

Bandit Leader tried to keep his eyes off the incoming wall of enemy fighters streaking toward them in the foreground—and the three massive gray battleships in the background. They were definitely outnumbered two to one. Minimum. And who knew what else the enemy was holding back.

He finished dialing in his deflector settings for his Lancer and checked in with his rear gunner.

"You ready for this, kid?"

"Roger that, sir. Just lead 'em nice and slow and I'll fill 'em full of blaster holes."

Good kid, thought Bandit Leader. And a good rear gunner in a situation like this one was probably going to make a difference in whether they made it back to the flight deck, or didn't.

"Just keep 'em off of us, kid."

Bandit Leader switched to all-squadron leader comm.

"All squadrons report in."

"Pirate Lead... we're hot."

"Paladin Lead... roger."

"Knight Leader... on your six."

"Storm here. Let's do this, Bandit Leader."

"Cyclone Leader... might as well."

"Red Leader... roger. We're in."

"Blue Leader... copy."

"Hearts Leader... guns online."

"Spades... we hear and obey, Bandit Leader."

"Angel Leader... we're in."

"Joker Lead... Let's roll, Bandit Lead."

Bandit Leader settled back into his seat and reached up to activate the forward blasters. The sense that this was really about to happen tried to overwhelm him. He shook it off and set himself to killing and not dying.

The wall of strange three-deflectored enemy fighters raced up on them all at once, and both masses suddenly formed a cyclone of machines and battle.

"Here they come, boys and girls. Make 'em pay."

Black Fleet
Third Wing, First Squadron, "Pit Vipers"
Fighter Engagement, Forward of Fleets
0512 Local System Time

Lieutenant Haladis opened up on an incoming Lancer. She wanted to feel the long slow *BRAAAAAAAP* of the slug-throwing guns she'd had on her last ship, but that had been shot to pieces, and she'd barely made it back to the *Terror.*

In medical checkout, the squadron supply chief had told her they'd dropped a new tri-fighter interceptor out of stores for her. Her last ship had been an interceptor variant set up for ground attack. This one carried the standard blasters for fighter-to-fighter engagements.

And now she was shoulder-deep in the biggest dogfight in modern galactic history. This, she felt certain, was a singular moment that might happen only once in a generation.

The years ahead were to prove her wrong by orders of magnitude.

And she could've cared less at this very instant, as battle and survival and the desire to kill or be killed transformed her.

Because death was almost certain now.

Both sides had gone in screaming at top speed straight for each other's throats. At blasters range, they'd simultaneously opened up in a sudden and hellacious erratic volley of fire. Some ships went up instantly, while others broke and chased. A few even managed to slam head on into the fighter they'd only just been trying to kill in the bare seconds before both sides met. Those ships had vaporized, throwing exploding debris and vapor trails in every direction, their ion reactors cooking off and detonating in secondary explosions.

Kat had squeezed off a few short blasts on an incoming Lancer. But her wingman, Viper Two, had gone up in sudden flames. So had the tri-fighter ahead of her. So she'd pulled back on the stick and climbed to avoid debris, and she'd lost her firing window.

Never mind that, she thought, as she tracked a Raptor streaking through a scrum of fighters. She increased throttle to pick up his tail. A moment later she was squeezing off shots into his deflectors. The Raptor's starboard wing disintegrated, and the fighter went spinning end around end and then came apart all at once. He was done.

Kat broke off and fell in with a tri-fighter her HUD identified as Delta Twelve.

"On your six, Delta Twelve."

"Thanks... Viper Lead. Going in close on this one."

"Gotcha."

Kat matched the other tri-fighter as it throttled up, blasters blazing, and scored a series of hits on a Lancer. Then the Lancer's rear gunner opened up and punched Delta Twelve's center pod, and Delta Twelve exploded in every direction.

Kat's ship took some deflector damage. She rerouted auxiliary batteries to reinforce the deflectors, then scanned for more bandits as she closed in on the Lancer. She didn't feel frightened. She felt alive. And close to Dasto.

She rolled one-eighty just to get the rear gunner thinking she was going to break, then came back in at the ship with blasters ranging in on the fat twin ion nacelles. Shots broke through the rear deflectors, which were lightly powered because the pilot thought the gunner had his back. One engine exploded, and the ship came apart.

Kat took a deep breath and narrowly avoided smashing into another tri-fighter that had come in at a cross angle for an assist.

She rolled her head and scanned for a new victim.

10

Republic Seventh Fleet
First Squadron, "Bandits"
Assigned to Carrier *Freedom*
0515 Local System Time

"Bandit Leader, we just lost Bandit Six. Suggest we—"

The comm went dead.

Bandit Leader checked the roster in his helmet HUD and thumbed through his own squadron from the *Freedom*. He danced the Lancer this way and that, got a sight picture for the forward blasters, and smoked an enemy fighter.

"Three," he whispered into the ether of the inter-ship comm.

He had three kills so far.

Maybe, he thought, this is just that. A game to play all by myself. Because of course, there's no winning this, is there?

"All squadrons—"

He jerked his ship out of the way of two incoming enemy fighters and rolled off hard for an opposite heading.

"Break off and commence your attack on the lead battleship."

"What if they forget about us and close with *Freedom*?" said Hearts Lead over the all-squadron comm.

"They've got to get past *Atlantica* and the destroyer squadron. Plus *Freedom*'s got another surprise waiting for them. Let's give 'em a choice. Their ships, or ours."

Black Fleet
Bridge of the *Imperator*
0518 Local System Time

The CIC stepped close to Admiral Rommal. Casualty reports were coming in from the squadrons.

"Sir, they're breaking away from the initial dogfight engagement. They're coming for us now. We can put up two more squadrons for cover and allow the strike to continue against the Republic Fleet. Our turret defenses should be sufficient."

Admiral Rommal studied the datapad the man had just handed him. The tactical analysis was sound, sensible, and could deliver the desired outcome of this phase of the operation within the hour.

But Admiral Rommal was a cautious man.

"Tell them to fall back and cover our approach to the fleet. If we can knock out their fighters now, that will make destroying their fleet much easier when the time comes to close."

The CIC stared at him for a long moment. Not a challenge. Not even really a stare. It was as though the man was running the math inside his own head. Checking and rechecking the whole scenario, because it was just far too important to leave to the machines.

And far too important for any one man to decide all their fates in just the space of an order.

Finally he seemed to settle on something he could live with.

"As you wish, Admiral."

Republic Seventh Fleet
Bridge of the *Freedom*
Rear of the Forward Line of Engagement
0518 Local System Time

"Put me through to the air boss."

Admiral Landoo waited the half second it took to pull the officer from his duties and get him on the comm. She herself was studying tactical in the combat information center. She'd moved back to this command node to better assess the battle at range. Deep sensors provided a more complete analysis, and it was a much better command center from which to control the battle.

"Control" the battle. That seemed a joke to her right now. As if a battle can ever be controlled. It already seemed to be turning into a barroom brawl. They'd lost a third of their forces in the dogfight. The critical question in the next few moments was which way this new fleet would play it.

Chase them back to cover their shiny new ships.

Or...

Come in for the kill and close with the awesome point defense capabilities of the destroyer squadron, with *Atlantica* and her powerful ion gun as the anchor.

"Ops, Admiral," came the air boss's reply.

"How long until we can launch?"

Pause. She could hear the murmur of static-laden updates coming in from the dogfight now moving over the enemy battleships.

Those are people, she told herself as she watched all the ghostly holograms suddenly mixing, disappearing, and breaking off. *Your* people.

And they're getting cut down to lay a trap.

It's the only way, she reminded herself. This is all new. We had to play it safe. We needed a surprise. An edge.

"Another fifteen minutes and I can get both squadrons off the deck within five minutes. Or I can get 'em up now in fractions. It's your call, Admiral."

"No. Continue with the plan. I want everything ready to go all at once."

"Aye aye, ma'am."

Admiral Landoo turned to her strike coordinator. The officer was wearing a helmet that allowed her to view the battle in rendered real-time. The admiral had to place her hand on the girl's shoulder to get her attention.

"Yes, Admiral?"

"Status on our special delivery from Tarrago?"

"He's getting a lot of air cover, ma'am. We're almost through the main screen. He'll be ready to drop in the next forty-five seconds."

The admiral watched the strike board beneath her. If they got this one through, they might just get off easily. Taking out one of their ships right now might just check their advance.

"Admiral..." It was a junior comm/sensors liaison officer. "*Audacity* has just jumped in. Her captain signals she's ready to fight."

Landoo steadied herself against the rail that surrounded the display. All around her lights glimmered, holograms swam with real-time updates, and static roared and flared from incoming comm traffic. The darkness of the combat information center was a murmuring facsimile of the battle it watched.

And still there was no way to get through to Fortress Omicron. Either they were dead, it was captured... or transmissions were being jammed.

"Tell him to form up with the sensor frigate inside the group."

She would reprimand him later. Right now she needed every ship she could get her hands on.

House of Reason
Utopion

Orrin Kaar chewed his fingernails. He never chewed his fingernails. They would need to be re-genned and manicured to keep up appearances. But for now, he couldn't help himself. He spit out a piece of his thumbnail onto his carpets as he watched the holovid broadcast from Admiral Devers.

This was a major naval battle. The single biggest since the Savage Wars, no doubt. The Seventh Fleet had arrived, and did not take the bait. They were engaging both Sullus's Black Fleet and Devers's Third Fleet. Admiral Landoo was entirely outmatched, and her only hope would be to retreat before her fleet was eradicated. But that chance should not have been left open to her.

Mercifully, Admiral Devers interrupted the recorded holovid, having reached his quarters to take Kaar's comm call. "Delegate, the battle is intense, and—"

"Why is Landoo not already destroyed?" Kaar barked so loud that his ears rang.

"I don't know, Delegate."

Devers looked... too calm for a man supposed to be engaged in ship-to-ship combat. Kaar reminded himself that the admiral was not a warrior. Not truly. He was a political tool. If other people were dying and he was keeping himself to the rear of the action, then perhaps he didn't feel the life-and-death struggle one was supposed to feel in these situations. Still, the admiral's reaction bothered the delegate on levels he couldn't quite put his finger on.

"Did she not receive your messages? Did she not respond to your hails demanding that she form up in front of your fleet?"

"She didn't respond to hails, and I don't know if she ever saw the messages," answered Devers. "Admiral Rommal believes a lone corvette escaped the blockade and informed her of what happened. I can't convince her otherwise, even if she did answer my hails. I—I've stopped trying. I don't know how else I... Tell me what to do, Delegate Kaar."

A corvette. A single corvette could not possibly be the difference between success and failure, could it? The fortunes of war...

Kaar calmed himself. "This is not disastrous. This can be overcome. Admiral Landoo, sadly, is among the traitorous elements you engaged at Tarrago. We'll figure out how to explain the Black Fleet at a later date. It is absolutely imperative that you prevent *any* of her ships from escaping. Do you understand?"

"Yes, Delegate Kaar."

"Kill them all, Silas."

Kaar ended the transmission knowing that success rested with Sullus's officers and not his own. Admiral Devers was in entirely over his head.

Republic Seventh Fleet
First Squadron, "Gray Wolves," Ad Hoc Special Operations Strike Command
Inbound on *Terror*
0521 Local System Time

"Gray Leader, this is Bandit Lead. Stay in tight, we're commencing our attack run now. We'll cover your approach to target!"

Commander Luq tried to ignore the star field all around him. Everything was pure chaos and no-holds-barred warfare. These strange tri-deflector fighters were swarming the Republic fighters that raced across the hulls of the massive battleships still bearing down on the Seventh Fleet. In waves, the tri-fighters were coming at them like frenetic shotgun bursts filling the space between with blazing red blaster shots. Deflectors got smashed and damage was taken, but the squadrons were hanging in there and giving back as good as they got.

"Gray Leader to Gray Seven."

"Gray Seven here."

Gray Seven was an electronic warfare and assessment Lancer configured to deflect targeting and jam enemy sensors. Special Operations Strike Command had put together an ad hoc force and assigned Gray Seven as a target-of-opportunity cohort to be used by the on-site leader.

Besides Gray Seven in the Lancer-EW, there were two Lancer torpedo bombers, Gray Five and Six, each loaded with deep penetration high-yield torpedoes, and two other interceptors riding shotgun. And Paladin Squadron was in formation all around the ad hoc strike force, peeling off to engage the wicked little tri-fighters that were racing in for the torpedo bombers.

"Are we still getting good targeting data out of that possible reactor, Gray Seven?"

"Everything looks good, Gray Leader. We confirm that's a shielding reactor near what we're identifying as the main bridge above the superstructure. We're also getting good sensor feedback on these ships. They're incredible. Packaging and encrypting for Command."

"Roger that," replied Luq as one of the Paladins exploded in front of him. "Gray Six, you follow me and Gray Two into the target. If we fail, Gray Three and Five you're up next. Good luck and good hunting."

Black Fleet
Bridge of the *Terror*
0525 Local System Time

"Captain, we've identified what look to be torpedo bombers inbound on our position."

Captain Gulza wiped away the holographic display he was using and called up the tagged enemy targets. Mainly the wave of fighters inbound. "Where?"

The *Terror*'s CIC highlighted the two torpedo bombers within the formations now advancing against the three battleships.

"Tell Commander Jaysu to knock out those fighters. Highest priority. Inform forward batteries. Make it extremely difficult for them to get through."

"As you command, sir."

Black Fleet
Third Wing, First Squadron, "Pit Vipers"
0526 Local System Time

Kat Haladis smoked another Lancer and tore away from the thick of the roving dogfight as two other Lancers interceptors peeled off to engage her.

"Viper Lead, priority tasking." It was the wing commander. "Need you to knock out these incoming two bombers. Highest priority. They're torpedo-equipped, so they're going to have a lot of cover. You up for it, Kat?"

"Targeting to engage now, sir."

Kat tagged both bombers and switched her blasters to high-intensity gain. Bombers would have thick deflectors and armor. She'd need to punch through to take them out.

"Vipers Four and Five... on me."

Levenir Orbit
The Galactic Core

It worked! It actually worked!

Cade Thrane smiled at the incoming comm message from Garrett Glover. It looked to have been sent in the same manner as his own, meaning Garrett had examined the transmission and had seen the same usefulness in the method that Thrane had. Thrane doubted his fellow code slicer would ever use the old comm relay system again. *He* certainly wouldn't.

The comm message was text only. Disappointing, because Thrane wanted to talk to Garrett about what he'd seen and done so far. Maybe catch up a bit. It could be lonely at times, making a living doing something that the rest of the galaxy seemed incapable of comprehending.

He opened the message:

> Cool transmission system! Did U build? I'm stealing, btw. Also, I enclosed some notes on the encryption. Hope they help! — Garrett

Thrane opened the attachments and began to peruse the encryption code, taking in Garrett's comments and notes like a starving man eating his first meal in weeks.

"Yes!" he shouted. "Of course! Gah, it's so obvious once you factor for—why didn't I think of that? Yes!"

He would crack this code soon. He was sure of it.

Republic Seventh Fleet
First Squadron, "Gray Wolves," Ad Hoc Special Operations Strike Command
0527 Local System Time

"Close up and follow me in, Gray Six."

Commander Luq increased to attack speed and dove toward the looming battleship below. Heavy concentrations of turret fire from across the upper decks were being hurled up at them in furious desperation.

OU7 whirred and beeped that it was increasing forward deflector power.

Luq cursed as one shot got through and seared the port side engine, knocking out the blaster on that side.

"Fifteen seconds to drop, Commander," called out an obviously shaken torpedo bomber pilot on his six.

"Hang in there!" called out Luq as he simultaneously tried to fly, dodge, and reroute damage control systems to knock out the electrical fire developing in the port engine.

Chikkka bluuuur! cheered OU7, alerting Luq that they had tri-fighters coming in.

"Ten seconds! Keep 'em off me!" warned the torpedo bomber pilot.

Luq backed off his throttle and pulled up hard to cut across the tri-fighters' firing arcs. He was getting collision alert warnings as two enemy fighters scrambled to avoid his sudden and wild charge straight at them. He pushed the throttle forward to max power and unloaded with the one remaining wing blaster.

OU7 whooped for joy. It loved close-quarters space combat.

Black Fleet
Third Wing, First Squadron, "Pit Vipers"
0529 Local System Time

Too close, Kat's mind shrieked as Vipers Four and Five took evasive action. But Kat's jaw was set. Her shoulders tight. Every fiber of her being bent forward into the targeting reticule. Willing herself to kill first.

This was for Dasto!

All of it was for her big brother. Her hero. A hero the Republic had thrown away in a useless grand gesture. They would pay now. They would *all* pay, and she wasn't getting out of the way of the Lancer that had just broken up her attack.

She rolled the fighter about its yaw axis and maintained a solid sight picture on the tagged torpedo bomber racing through turret fire across the hull of the *Terror* below.

A close moment happened. A moment when she saw the tiny bot on the Lancer spin its top sensor unit and emit a series of flashing lights. Reacting to her close pass and ludicrous speed.

It was that close.

At top speed.

Blasters blazing.

She must've scared the poor thing to death. She'd always had a place for bots in her heart. Once, long ago, she had wanted to be a bot doctor. They were the galaxy's slaves. In a galaxy that cared little for the small things, they needed someone to care for them.

But that had been another her. A different Kat Haladis. One who hadn't existed since the day before Dasto died. Meaninglessly.

But today...

... Today was not that day.

Today she was vengeance victorious. Today she was winged death.

She rolled out on course and came in right behind the torpedo bomber. She backed off her speed and lined up for the kill.

Republic Seventh Fleet
First Squadron, "Gray Wolves,"
Ad Hoc Special Operations Strike Command
0530 Local System Time

"Targeting data locked, firing solution good. Launching!" cried Gray Six over the comm. The young pilot reached over to arm both torpedoes and let them loose. After that he'd peel away and be out of this battle.

Except there was no "after that."

Kat Haladis unloaded slower yet much more powerful bursts from her overcharged blasters. The first shots slammed into the reinforced rear deflectors of the torpedo bomber.

Alarms and sirens went off, and the pilot tried to redirect battery power into the rear deflectors.

The next shots from the black-and-gray tri-fighter knocked out the deflectors altogether and caused a power surge in the cockpit. Static discharge and wild electricity ran loose, and Gray Six pulled his hands away from the smoking systems.

Then Kat was lobbing blaster shots into his unprotected hull. It only took three before the whole torpedo bomber disintegrated just above the battleship *Terror*.

Commander Luq raced back toward the next strike team.

"Gray Seven! Did we get a shot off?"

"Negative, negative, Gray Leader. No shot. I say no shot. We'll have to go over the target again."

The dogfight between both masses of fighters was now swarming across all three battleships. Lancers and Raptors were killing and being killed by the wicked tri-fighter interceptors as linked turret fire pinned down the strays and blasted them to dust and vapor.

"Gray Leader, this is Bandit Lead. If you're going to make your run, do it now. We won't be able to keep them busy much—"

Somewhere out in the dogfight, across the three massive hulls of the immense ships... Bandit Leader was gone.

"All right, Gray Squadron... follow me," said Gray Leader. "This is for all the marbles. We're going in at max intercept speed."

"We won't be able to pull away from the ship at that angle, Gray Leader, not if we're going that fast."

Gray Two, Five, and Seven formed up off his wings.

Luq did a visual inspection and said, "Increase to intercept speed and stay close." Before pushing the throttle full forward, he added, "We're going in no matter what."

Black Fleet
Bridge of the *Terror*
0533 Local System Time

"Concentrate all turret fire on that group now!" shouted Captain Gulza.

Aides and officers bent toward their stations as orders were transmitted.

Gulza stood up to watch out the windows of the bridge. He could see the torpedo bomber formation streaking in toward the bow of the ship far below.

"Viper Lead reports both interceptors down!"

"I don't care about the damn interceptors!" shouted Gulza. "Take out that torpedo bomber now!"

"Sir, gunnery can't track. They're moving too fast for our linked firing solutions."

"Tell them to switch to independent."

The torpedo bomber launched its weapons package.

"Loose comet!" shouted *Terror*'s CIC. *Loose comet* was code for an active torpedo.

"Countermeasures to full!" shouted Captain Gulza. "Helm stand by to—"

The burning hot torpedo streaked across the windows of the bridge. And Gulza, in that brief instant, knew they'd targeted the deflector reactor atop the command section.

The explosion resonated across the hull, sending a dull rumble through the superstructure,.

"Damage report!" shouted the CIC.

The damage information coordinator shouted above the din, "They've knocked out our shielding reactor! We're defenseless!"

And then Commander Luq smashed his speeding Lancer into the decks above the bridge. He hadn't meant to. Gray Five had been right. Their speed was too great to deliver the weapon and pull off the escape angle.

Gray Leader went into the target acquisition processors above the bridge.

Gray Two careened off the superstructure and went spinning off into the outer darkness.

And Gray Seven plowed directly into the bridge itself.

Both decks of the bridge were instantly holed to deep space, killing the command crew of the *Terror*.

Republic Seventh Fleet
Bridge of the *Freedom*
Rear of the Forward Line of Engagement
0534 Local System Time

She heard them cheer and whoop. Admiral Landoo took a deep breath and forced herself to concentrate on the tactical displays, seeking to maximize the advantage she'd just been handed.

They'd actually managed to wound one of the battleships.

"Tactical! What's she look like?"

The tactical assessment officer stepped away from his station to report. He accessed the holographic display the admiral was looking at and pointed toward the ghostly image of the ship they'd damaged. "We managed to knock out their deflector power. We estimate they won't be able to easily restore this unless they've got some kind of advanced backup system that no navy we know of has implemented. In other words... this ship is now vulnerable to direct fire. Some of our fighters smashed into the superstructure, and though we don't have a good picture of what damage that caused exactly, we do know the ship is vulnerable. Now is our chance, if we're going to take one, Admiral."

Admiral Landoo studied the glowing formations on the ethereal board. Admiral Nagu had crept forward with the Seventh's destroyer group, following the first fighter wave at a distance. Just beyond that the three massive battleships were holding course. Coming for the carrier group, no doubt, and apparently intending to cut straight through the destroyer group to do so.

"How long until Nagu is in gunnery range?"

"Five minutes, Admiral."

Silence.

Everyone on the bridge held their breath.

The admiral straightened and took in her bridge crew. They were all so young. So unready for this battle. A battle that had never been dreamed of in all her years of Repub Navy War College.

The brushfire conflict had always been the scenario.

Overwhelming odds to put down local upstart navies.

Or pirates.

Or raiders.

Even smugglers.

And yet, she thought to herself, these are the cards you've been dealt.

So play them now.

Black Fleet
Bridge of the *Imperator*
0535 Local System Time

"Damage report for *Terror*."

Admiral Rommal was still waiting. Everyone across the massive two-storied bridge of the *Imperator* was scrambling to compile reports—everyone but those who had stopped to stare, unable to pull themselves away from the visual spectacle of the damaged *Terror* beyond the bridge windows. Comm traffic was all around the admiral, like a thousand buzzing insects competing to be overheard.

Rommal walked to the port windows that looked out onto the *Terror*. Half the ship had lost power, and there was a fire in the command structure. And all around them, the battle continued.

He controlled himself.

An officer controls himself, he whispered in his mind.

In the Republic Navy, appointed officers acted like minor royalty. Not so here. Not on Rommal's watch. His staff and crew were doing their best with what they had to work with in the whirlwind of battle. People, *his* people, were dead and dying over there on the *Terror*.

Give them time, he reminded himself.

And then there was Goth Sullus.

You did not want to fail... him. Whatever he was. You didn't want that.

And yet this is a battle. And failures are planned for in a battle, because they are so often so much a part of it. In battle, people and equipment get destroyed and plans go horribly awry.

The admiral ran through his own tactical decisions. Was there anything he'd done that had caused the *Terror* to take what was shaping up to be three direct hits to the command structure?

Nothing. And yet ...

"Admiral." It was the CIC. "Looks bad, sir. *Terror*'s lost her external deflector power grid."

Rommal winced at that.

They would have to shift *Terror* to the rear and cover her with their deflectors. Protect her and use her as ranged fire platform once they'd engaged the Republic's main fleet.

Where the hell was Devers?

"How long—"

He was about to ask for a timetable until they could get their deflectors back up, but the CIC cut him off, because there was more.

"That's not the worst of it, sir," interrupted the CIC.

He leaned in and spoke in a low and confidential tone. Instinctively Admiral Rommal bowed his head to listen.

"We lost the whole command team. Looks like a Republic fighter smashed right into the bridge seconds after the deflectors went down."

"Gulza?" the admiral murmured.

"Dead. Everyone. Everyone is dead, sir."

"Who's in charge right now?"

The CIC pulled up a new menu on his datapad. "That would be Commander Vampa. She was on the hangar deck when the bridge collapsed."

Admiral Rommal nodded, pursed his lips, and tried to remember anything he could about the officer. But each ship had ten thousand crew. It was impossible to know everyone.

"Her file," offered the CIC, "indicates she's efficient but ruthless. Drummed out of the Repub Navy for moral offenses. Commanded a hammerhead corvette that got shot out from under her at Kaankar Nebula. Awarded the silver star for bravery."

"Then she sounds like just the right officer for this situation. Field promotion to captain. She has command of the *Terror*. Tell them to drop behind the fleet until we can get their deflectors back online."

The CIC tapped in a series of orders and said, "It's not all bad, sir. Our casualty loss assessment on the Republic Fleet indicates we've managed to knock out at least eighty percent of their available fighters. The carrier used all her cards in one go. We can rearm now and go in against them with full fighter cover. They'll have very little to fight us off with."

At least, thought Admiral Rommal, that was something.

Republic Seventh Fleet, Carrier Group
Bridge of the *Freedom*
0538 Local System Time

The tac assessment officer hovered above the admiral. Mentally willing her to make a crucial decision in the next few seconds.

"Second Wing?"

"On deck. Ready five."

Admiral Landoo lifted her chin and stared off into the darkness of the combat information center. Shadows moved among the screens and readouts here deep inside the massive carrier.

They'd been transporting a new wing out to Tarrago. One hundred new Raptors with pilots. They'd had to bring the fighters up from the auxiliary cargo bays, but the chiefs had moved heaven and earth to get two full carrier squadrons out of transport storage and ready for combat. And Raptors were the best the Republic had.

"How many survivors from the first attack?"

"Less than thirty are going to make it back to the deck. Who knows how many are combat-ready after a turnaround rearm. We'll have wounded too, but we have backup pilots. So..."

"Tell them to hold station above the group until we get Second Wing off the deck. Then bring 'em in for rearm."

She stared down once more at the board. The glowing red holographic battleships were coming closer.

"Launch both squadrons now. Inform Admiral Nagu to close and engage."

11

Republic Seventh Fleet
Second Squadron, "Gunfighters"
Ready Five, Carrier *Freedom*
0540 Local System Time

Admiral Landoo's order came across the general comm and resounded throughout the briefing rooms, passages, and hangar bays surrounding hangar deck six. Flight boots thundered down passages.

The pilots of Buccaneer and Gunfighter Squadrons, each with fifty Raptors apiece, had been sitting in their big briefing loungers going over all available data on the enemy fleet they were about to face. Or not. Some preferred staring off into space, a look of certain fatality writ large on their stony features.

Everyone knew the casualty reports from the first engagement. They'd seen the extensive losses.

Over eighty percent of the first strike had gone up in vapor trails. Eighty percent of an *Omega* strike—the fabled strike to end all strikes, the Republic's not-so-veiled threat... or so fleet doctrine had long assured them. In moments, everything had changed.

The pilots had been confined to the briefing rooms to keep the hangars clear as their ships were brought up from lower storage and armed, and the air was thick with fear and adrenaline. These pilots had expected to do no more than dead haul out to their new duty station aboard the carrier, come out to Tarrago, and run shipping overwatch missions and the occasional pirate interdiction.

Now they were being tossed into a pitched battle between capital ships. A full-scale Alpha strike against an enemy fleet. But would it be enough? The fabled Omega strike had gone down over the target. An entire fleet's worth of tactical fighters... gone. Would a mere Alpha strike, consisting only of a single carrier's fighters, be enough?

Never in their wildest dreams had the pilots in these rooms imagined they'd be in this dire situation, facing such odds.

Least of all Atumna Fal.

She was different than most of the other humanoid Tennar in one important way. She was a member of that one percent who had skin the color of a burnt orange.

It was rumored that Gomarii slavers would pay in mithrium for such a prize as a Tennar with that rarest of skin colors.

But Atumna Fal was an ensign in the Republic Navy, not a harem slave for some warlord along the galaxy's edge. She was a fighter pilot.

She wiped a bit of sleep from her eye with her right tentacle and yawned like some great jungle cat.

"Hey, girl," said the pilot in the seat next to her. "I can wake you up good and shiny."

Race Mandu was always trying to put the moves on her. On anyone. He liked to think of himself as one switched-on ladykiller. And it wasn't just Race. Every Raptor jockey in the squadron had been trying to put the moves on the small, tiny, and very curvy Atumna Fal.

She rolled two large and beautiful eyes at Race and batted his hand away with her other tentacle.

But she smiled inwardly. The attention was kind of nice. She hated the average Repub beta male with all his mincing social justice hesitations. Apologizing for asking a girl out. Apologizing for trying to kiss her. Apologizing for kissing her. Apologizing for last night. Apologies, apologies, apologies.

She wanted a man, not a wimp.

Even though she wasn't partial to other Tennar men—a warrior class with eight tentacles as opposed to her two—she still missed their "Me man, you woman" tribal virility deep down in the seafoam green depths of her world, near the temples of Ahm.

Thankfully, becoming a fighter pilot had surrounded her with a ready supply of testosterone-laden alpha males from many other races. They reminded her she was a woman. And a dangerous woman at that.

"The order just came down, Race. We'll be called to our ship in the next three minutes. Sorry, flyboy. Maybe never. "

"It don't take long," Race assured her.

She laughed and dismissed him.

And then the final order to report to ships came.

"Gunfighters up! Scramble, scramble, scramble. All pilots report to your ships on hangar deck six."

Pilots grabbed datapads and flight bags. Flight helmets were stuffed under arms as everyone ran for the exits.

Race pulled on Atumna's slender shoulder as she turned to leave. His lantern-jawed face was stone-cold sober now. Icy blue eyes searched her own.

"Be careful out there, little sister."

She smiled up at him quickly. She knew the effect she had with her devastating brown-and-gold-eyed otherworldly smile against skin the color of fall on all the worlds in the Republic.

"Forget safe," she giggled over her shoulder as she edged toward the aisle, away from him, and toward her ship. "Be the best, or die like the rest."

She winked, then raced for the flight line.

Black Fleet
Auxiliary Control of the *Terror*
0542 Local System Time

The newly minted Captain Vampa watched as techs booted up most of the auxiliary control stations deep within the battleship. Fleet protocol called for not keeping this station manned until crew reserves were at full. Now they were trying to bring it to life after the entire command bridge had been wiped out.

The great present weakness of this fleet, thought Vampa, arms folded below her chest, was crew availability. Obviously there would be casualties in this battle. They'd known that. But too many casualties, and they'd lose control. Or, she thought darkly after watching the horrific damage via closed-circuit feed of the main bridge, too many of the right *kind* of casualties.

And now she was in charge.

Just like that.

A cruel smile formed in her mind. Yes, even *she* knew she was utterly ruthless. The High Command that had eluded her in the Repub Navy had suddenly come to her in one horrific moment, here in this brand-new fleet attempting to wrest the galaxy from the Republic's trembling fingers. She found it all very ironic. They'd fired her, and now she was about to destroy them. To her, this whole fight wasn't about regime change, or a new order. To her, this was about revenge and power. Naked power and nothing more.

And that suited her just fine.

And if she was going to hold on to her command, then this was her moment to prove to Admiral Rommal and...

His name is Goth Sullus, she heard a voice remind her. A voice she allowed to speak to her. To tell her what her compass was. A voice that could force her to do the things that needed doing, even when that frightened refugee girl she'd once been didn't want to do those things.

Vampa had noticed that everyone in the fleet had some kind of strange and unspoken mental block about referring to him, but she'd forced herself to name the man in black.

Goth Sullus.

And if she was going to keep command of the *Terror*, she needed to prove herself, to him, now.

And to do *that*, she had to get this ship operational and back in the fight in the next few minutes. Already *Imperator* and *Revenge* were pulling forward to meet the Seventh Fleet's charge. Tactical showed more than a hundred next-gen fighters departing the Seventh's carrier, still hiding behind the destroyers.

She wondered if Rommal was freaking out right about now.

No one had planned on a second carrier strike. And that rebel Repub Third Fleet with the brash admiral was nowhere in sight.

"What's our status on squadron rearm?" she said. It came out as a demand to make things move faster as opposed to just a request for a mere status update.

Her first officer raised his head from internal comms. "We're almost ready to launch, five minutes..." There was a pause.

She watched him. Waiting. Waiting for him to say it. Willing him, with her depthless gray eyes, to bend to her superiority.

She hoped he was struggling with her obvious dark beauty and not the fact that she was now his captain. Because yes, she was beautiful. She knew that, because it had hampered her career. Instead of seeing a competent officer, Repub Navy admirals had either seen someone they wanted to sleep with, or someone they hated because she, unlike them, was a statuesque model with a dark beauty about her. She'd have been more successful had she been squat and butch—just diverse or minority enough to make rank for all the wrong reasons.

But she was what she was. A real live woman who used her beauty like a great hammer to bash in the skull of anyone who stood in her way.

And they all, in their own ways, had penalized her accordingly. She'd watched them climb up and above her, smirking smugly as they'd done so. Knowing they'd beaten her on nothing more than herd mentality and fear-mongering. Talent and beauty need not apply.

She wouldn't let that happen here. Not in this brand-new fleet. This was her chance. And she was taking it.

"Captain." The man had finally found his tongue.

She held his gaze for a moment longer, making sure he acknowledged her superiority in rank. Then she raised one corner of her mouth in a small gesture of amusement. Just so he absolutely had no idea where he stood with her.

"We need that cover up in the next two minutes," she shouted across aux con. "Helm, make for flank speed. We're not sitting this battle out."

She saw the helmsman pause and stare at the first officer, as if seeking permission. But with a simple turn of her head and a glare, both men returned to their controls and made the ordered adjustments to speed.

The enormous ship thrummed a little deeper beneath their boots. She could feel it on the deck, and in her stomach.

Vampa returned her gaze to tactical.

She felt the first officer sidle up next to her. "Captain, we..." He hesitated. Then seemed to find his strangled voice. "Our deflectors are offline. We will be defenseless." His tone was one of grave concern.

Vampa studied the Repub formation the fleet was approaching. The super-destroyer *Atlantica* was closing fast on *Imperator* and *Terror*. The other destroyers were fanning out to begin ranged turret fire.

She leaned forward and tagged *Atlantica* with a gesture.

"Once she engages *Imperator*, she'll use her main guns to get through the deflectors. Standard Repub targeting protocols call for massed battery fire on the first target to lose its deflectors. Our battleships can take a lot. We have a lot more armor and mass than they do. But what if *two* battleships don't have deflectors?"

The first officer studied the holographic ghosts of the ships on the display. In just a few moments both groups of ships would be within range of each other. And still he didn't say anything. She could tell he was cautious. Which was good. It would balance her recklessness.

She knew that about herself.

She knew she needed someone to rein in her wilder and more daring plans.

"It could confuse the AI targeting protocols," said Vampa, as though beginning a battle lesson of some sort. "In a perfect world the gunners would override on the basis of chained targeting-for-opportunity fire. Sensing the chance to knock us out, too. But what they don't realize is that they will weaken their overall ability to knock out our flagship by splitting their destructive capability. So my plan is to come in at them on this angle and give them our bow as a target. Less profile, and our forward armor and superstructure will mitigate our internal damage."

"We'll buy time for *Imperator* to get her deflectors back online."

She smiled at him seductively.

This was another one of her tricks.

Sex.

The man flushed as she allowed him all the possibilities she could provide. She had him. She watched him swallow, thickly. But it was what he did next that forever sealed him to her. Convinced her that she'd randomly found just the right ally in her quest for power.

"And we look like heroes to Rommal and..." He whispered as if to himself. "*Him*."

That block against speaking the name of Goth Sullus.

She let it go and returned to studying the converging forces on the tactical display. She was inwardly pleased with herself.

"Exactly. Tell the batteries to engage *Arangotoa* and *Victory* as we come alongside to flank their formation. If we can knock out both, we'll be able to broadside what remains of *Atlantica*. That's our game plan."

The first officer snapped to attention. "I'll inform the battery commanders, Captain."

No hesitation.

Perfect.

And then he was off, and Captain Vampa leaned closer to all the assets in play on the holographic displays, willing this battle to happen exactly the way she wanted it to.

She smiled as she waited for the coming slaughter.

Black Fleet
Bridge of the *Imperator*
0555 Local System Time

"Closing, Admiral. In range with forward guns in thirty seconds."

A hushed silence—apart from the constant electronic murmur of status reports from sections and squadron leaders across the fleet—fell over the bridge.

Admiral Rommal walked toward the main bridge window that looked out across the immense gray ship and the triangular bow in the distance. Holographic displays lay over all this. Currently the CIC had the display set to show gunnery arcs and ranges with constantly updating probability hit indicators. Everything was in constant motion. And yet the vast and immense stillness of space remained vast and immense and still, out there beyond this tiny little battle. This microcosm of life and death.

The Republic super-destroyer and seven destroyers were slowly closing in. Each side dancing to see how close they could come to the orbital defense gun's protective, or destructive, range. For all the intel currently being crunched and processed by both sides, no one knew what was going on below Tarrago Moon's surface.

No one knew who had control of the gun.

And yet this brand-new fleet, currently and simply identified as only the Black Fleet, had the tech and even the numbers to dominate in any scenario currently being played out. All the theories and the probabilities they'd wondered about... about their plans, equipment and even themselves... were being tested in the real-time crucible of battle.

The next test was just seconds away.

Fleet-to-fleet engagement. At range, and eventually, at close broadsides. The casualties would be enormous. On both sides.

Rommal could feel the crew waiting. Waiting for his orders to begin in earnest. As though the most massive dogfight in Republic history had not just taken place in the last hour. It was as if the galaxy now required some new blood spectacle to outdo the floating debris spreading away from the battle.

As if it were all beginning anew... once more.

He ran through his weapons one more time.

Two ships.

Two main ion guns apiece.

Four anti-matter torpedo launchers.

Forty heavy laser turrets—ten forward, fifteen per side—per ship.

Sixty light turret point defense batteries—thirty per side—per ship.

Most of the weapons wouldn't be viable until the massive ships were right alongside one another. And by then the most powerful weapons, the ion guns and the torps, would be all but useless. But for now... in the forward charge right into their spear point... they were absolutely perfect.

"Inform *Revenge.*"

Silence. The Republic's fleet was looming larger out there. The super-destroyer dwarfed all the other ships in its squadron.

And even now a second launch group from the carrier was streaking past that distant squadron. So, the Republic had held back a surprise... and now the fighter odds were back to even again. And technically, the Republic's new Raptors had held their own against the Black Fleet's tri-fighters.

"Target the super-destroyer. Fire when ready, Captain."

Ten seconds later, the two massive guns far below the command bridge, and poking out from the rise in the main hull, spat forth two high-intensity fused bursts of hyper-charged unstable ion matter superheated into a dense plasma core with a furnace temperature of thirty five-hundred Kelvin. The metallic high-pitched shriek of both guns shook the battleship to its core.

The battle, the real battle, had begun.

And deep in his heart, Rommal knew things were going to get far less polite than lobbing superweapons at range. In fact, he knew for a fact it was going to turn into a street brawl in the dark, with knives out, shortly.

Rommal watched as both ion shots rolled forward like two micro suns racing unheeded into the darkness between the fleets. Seconds later there was a flash as one splashed off *Atlantica*'s forward deflector array. The second one barely missed the long ship.

A second after that, *Revenge* landed two hits on the enemy super-destroyer's bow.

Republic Seventh Fleet
Bridge of the *Atlantica*
0601 Local System Time

"They've fired!" shouted someone in the seconds before the damage klaxon began to howl. "Brace for impact!"

Nagu distantly wondered if this new fleet, whoever he was facing, had developed some kind of alternative technology. If they'd pursued one of the thousands of exciting new weapons tech research trees the Repub had spent time and money to develop only to never implement. There was so much valuable, and dangerous, R&D just waiting in labs from one side of the galaxy to the other. Nagu had been a big proponent of turning that research into reality.

But they'd always managed to ignore him. The "they" being the House of Reason.

He watched both shots coming for his ship with a kind of quiet fatalism. Still thinking about R&D in the moments before the catastrophic damage began.

Well, we'll find out now, he thought to himself in the quiet half second before impact.

The forward deflectors collapsed all at once. Then a third shot struck the forward command structure, right below the bridge, and Nagu was sent flying, scrambling for a handhold, as the lights went out. Another massive impact landed somewhere in the aft sections of the lengthy super-destroyer. Engineering, maybe.

"Lights!" Nago shouted amid the sudden chaos that filled the bridge. He felt the ship listing beneath him, and he was suddenly aware that he was probably going to die. Klaxons roared and red emergency lighting flared to life in the thick darkness.

"Forward deflector down!" someone needlessly shouted. The tactical officer, he thought.

Nagu struggled to his feet and stumbled over to damage control. Power had come back. Readouts indicated serious damage. They'd lost forward torpedoes and guns. Engineering was breached, but power was still online.

"Damn," muttered Nagu. They'd lost their ability to fire forward.

He turned to the tac officer. "Order helm hard to port. Waist guns return fire. Fire at will!"

A moment later a sensor tech shouted out, "Loose comet! Loose comet! Tracking three... now four inbound on the formation!"

Republic Seventh Fleet
Waist Gun Battery Commander, *Atlantica*
0602 Local System Time

Commander Hu in fire control beneath the main spine of the super-destroyer rotated in his gunnery chair and brought down the targeting computer. He ranged the lead battleship.

"Unlimber the guns and fire on selected target, at my command."

The battery coordination crew all around him sprang to life as the main heavy laser turrets dropped down from the bottom of the hull beneath the long spine and rotated to acquire targets. Each gun was housed in a squat, flat, half-story-sized battery housing from which two stubby circular barrels nosed out. Shots began to pump from each barrel, alternating to keep up a steady stream of fire at the target.

Commander Hu's target was the oncoming *Imperator*. As the *Atlantica* hove over to broadside, the other destroyers in the formation continued forward into the maelstrom of fire now coming from each battleship.

Two torpedoes slammed into *Victory* amidships. Hull plating exploded out and away, trailing in the wake of the destroyer as vital internal systems lay open to naked space.

"Look at the size of that thing," one of the gunners called out over chat as another torpedo struck the *Atlantica*. Somewhere off in the hull, a distant explosion rumbled. And even though the *Imperator*'s deflectors were standing up to the intensive volume of battery fire coming from the squadron, shots were getting through and landing amidships.

"Maintain target acquisition and intensify fire!" shouted Hu across the comm.

Black Fleet
Bridge of the *Imperator*
0604 Local System Time

"Sir," whispered the CIC amid the seeming calm of the bridge. Beyond the windows a terrific fireworks display lit up the darkness as if for their benefit... a show to be watched, an entertainment not real. Never mind all the death and destruction going on inside those ships. "Captain Vampa is entering the battle with the *Terror*!"

There was a pause as Rommal turned to stare at the man, a question seared plainly across the iron-carved sharpness of his face.

The CIC understood. "Her deflectors are still down, sir."

In just moments the battleships would enter firing range for the heavy turrets.

"She'll be shot to pieces!"

The CIC acknowledged this gravely.

"Tell her to fall back and provide fighter cover. We've got two full squadrons inbound and our deflectors are collapsing. We need more point defense support with those two squadrons heading straight at us."

The CIC nodded and turned away to relay the order to the *Terror*'s command crew.

Republic Seventh Fleet
Second Squadron, "Gunfighters"
0605 Local System Time

The space all around Ensign Atumna Fal, the maw between the fleets, was filled with chaos. Raptors going up in sudden balls of flame and vapor. Tri-fighters crashing through the explosions. Heavy turret fire from the battleships that was beyond intense.

"Gunfighter Nineteen, you've picked up two—watch yourself."

Atumna cranked her head around to look out the back of her Raptor as she pulled in to a hard bank and climb. Red blaster fire chased her up through the star field.

She barrel-rolled back the other way and shook one of her pursuers. The other stayed all over her six, smashing away at her rear deflector with its blasters.

Again she rolled, but this time she came out on a new heading, diving away from the plane of the battle. As the tri-fighter gave chase, Atumna suddenly backed off her power, pulled up hard, and shot back into the thick of the battle—and straight at two more tri-fighters. She increased speed once more and shot past them, only narrowly avoiding a collision. The tri-fighter chasing her was not so lucky. It smashed into one of the fighters she'd slipped past, and both ships went spinning in opposite directions, coming apart in the middle of the battle.

Atumna was breathing hard. That had been closer than anyone could've imagined.

"Nice move, Nineteen," called out Gunfighter Seven, also known as Race Mandu. "Follow me in on the lead battleship—we'll make a run across her forward deflectors. Full burst all the way, little sister."

She fell in with Race, off his starboard wingtip. They climbed above the elliptic of the battle, then shot back down toward the split triangular bow of the lead battleship, blasters blazing.

"Watch that portside turret fire," said Gunfighter Lead matter-of-factly over the squadron comm.

As they came in at an angle to the bow of the sprawling ship, a river of massed fire came from the Seventh, smashing into the battleship's tremendous deflectors. The energy readings were off the charts.

And then, suddenly, the lead battleship's deflectors were down.

"Her deflectors are down!" someone whooped over chat.

"Roger," called out Gunfighter Lead. "Switching to attack runs *now*! Gunfighters, pair up and stagger. We need to take out their turrets. On me, Seven and Nineteen. We're going for their main ion guns."

Atumna pitched her fighter over and followed the squadron leader up the hull of the huge gray ship.

"Targeting portside main ion gun, Nineteen."

That was her target. She'd let him hit first, then follow up.

She saw the massive guns looming farther up the hull of the ship and steadied herself to line up for a pass with her blasters. Ahead of her, Gunfighter Lead began to open up with hot searing blaster fire that walked across the smaller structures surrounding the immense main gun housing.

Atumna fired next. Her shots seemed to do little against the armored battleship. She saw hull platting melt far beneath her, but no suddenly terrific explosions. Nothing to crow about.

And then they were pulling up hard and climbing away to avoid smashing into the enemy ship. Defensive turret fire chased them into the heights of the raging battle as more Raptors swooped in through the smashed deflector grid, streaking to make their runs on the battleship's turrets.

Black Fleet
Auxiliary Control of the *Terror*
0609 Local System Time

"Slowly now," began Captain Vampa. "Take us away to port and present our waist guns."

The first officer acknowledged the captain's order and watched as helm bent to the command. It was dark down here in auxiliary control, and it felt almost natural to whisper. Especially with the deception in plain sight they were trying to pull. Edging closer to the enemy fleet, off its flank, bringing waist guns to bear on their profiles... that would be devastating. They just had to go unnoticed until the moment they fired.

"Battery commanders, target the super-destroyer. Helm, continue course past the enemy's flank. Stand by to launch our fighters once *Victory* and *Arongotoa* turn to engage."

Republic Seventh Fleet
Waist Gun Battery Command, *Atlantica*
0608 Local System Time

"Commander... enemy battleship to port. Sensors indicate her deflectors are down!"

In the fire command cupola beneath the spine of the ship, the fire control crew was treated to an epic view of the battle now swirling all about them. Raptors chased tri-fighters in and among the destroyer squadron while other Raptors swarmed the lead battleship.

A salvo of ion gun shots from the two battleships slammed into *Destiny of Purpose*, striking the hull at multiple locations. One shot went clean through the rearmost engineering sections forward of the main engines. But the *Destiny* continued to return fire at the lead battleship.

"We got this!" shouted Hu. "Continue targeted fire as per AI protocols."

The *Terror*, which had been coming in head on and was now at profile, opened up on the super-destroyer *Atlantica*, raking her hull with her powerful waist gun batteries in a devastating broadside. The *Atlantica*'s hull ruptured, venting oxygen, as more fire tore through her armor. Secondary internal explosions across the starboard side ripped through bulkheads and blast doors, killing large sections of the crew instantly. Others fought to survive without life support.

Command switched the deflector array in a desperate attempt to absorb some of the blistering barrage coming from this new direction, but close-range volley fire tore through still more hull plating across the ship's upper decks, tearing the long spine of the ship to shreds. The main drive took a pounding, and what targeting computers would record as a missed shot smashed directly into the lightly shielded fire control cupola hanging beneath the spine, vaporizing Commander Hu and the fire control team instantly.

And this was just the beginning.

Fresh salvos of heavy turret fire from *Terror* began to chew through vital systems and internal quarters. Hangar deck two exploded, destroying four decks worth of crucial systems in each direction.

But the *Atlantica* was a big ship. She would hold for a few minutes more as she absorbed the combined brunt of all three battleships.

With the death of the fire control team in the gunnery cupola, the targeting AI switched over to command battery gunners via pre-devised protocols in order to unify their fire on the nearby *Imperator* at best selected range. It was a fatal flaw in programming, and the guns missed the opportunity to inflict lethal damage against the un-shielded *Terror*.

Black Fleet
Bridge of the *Imperator*
0613 Local System Time

For all the Repub's faults and inability to integrate modern and innovative weapon systems across their fleet, their cyberwarfare capabilities were excellent. Probably due to the House of Reason's need to control all forms of electronic communication in order to maintain its hold over the populace.

So when four torpedoes were fired in the first salvo, *Atlantica*'s electronic warfare center had hacked all four and sent them off in useless directions away from the battle.

Admiral Rommal had anticipated that.

He had thirty-six more torpedoes to fire, but he was waiting. Holding them back until they could begin to score internals on the flagship. Once that ship was wounded, their torpedoes would have a much better chance. Especially if they knocked out the ship's powerful electronic warfare center.

The *Imperator* shook violently.

"Damage report!" yelled the CIC as everyone held on. It felt like the massive ship had suddenly been shifted to port.

"We've had an explosion in engine housing six."

Rommal scanned the power management display to his left. Flashing damage indicators denoted the area in engineering that had been hit.

But whether it was from enemy action or a breakdown, who knew?

"We've got casualties in engineering!" another officer reported. Rommal listened as his staff scrambled damage control and medical teams. We're hit, he told himself, but not out.

He turned back to the holographic overlay. *Terror*, off to port and ahead of the fleet, was pounding the living daylights out of *Atlantica* in a series of furious broadsides from her waist guns.

Captain Vampa had disobeyed... and yet she was singlehandedly turning the battle into a slaughter for the fleet. He made a note, if he survived, to deal with her.

Two destroyers were now breaking off from the squadron and turning to engage her defenseless ship.

Rommal weighed his options. He could fire his torpedoes at the *Atlantica* and most likely knock it out of the battle right now. Or he could try to cripple one or both of the destroyers and wait through the extensive reloading and arming process it took to get new torps in the tubes. At least three minutes.

"Torpedo fire control," he commanded, "target the two destroyers breaking off. Two salvos. One each."

Republic Seventh Fleet
Bridge of the *Victory*
0614 Local System Time

"Battery commanders reporting ready to fire, Captain!"

The destroyer had turned to engage the massive battleship off the fleet's flank. That she was unshielded and concentrating fire on the flagship *Atlantica* was making the approach to contact much easier than facing the relentless fire coming from the other battleships.

Captain Karka selected target concentrations across the holographic schematic of the looming battleship. "Here, here, and... here," he said to his fire control officer. "This is where we seem to be doing more damage on the other ships."

Not for the first time, he wondered why this battleship wasn't firing back at either his ship or the *Arongatoa*. Both were closing in for close-range concentrated fire. They would do devastating damage to her.

"Share targeting data with Captain Noss. Fire at will."

"Sir!" A sensor operator bypassed the executive officer on the bridge to communicate directly with the captain. A clear violation of Republic protocols, but not unheard of. "We've got four fast movers inbound. Can't track or identify because *Atlantica*'s ECM warfare system has been knocked out, but I'm calling loose comets, sir."

The captain turned to face the operator. "Can we get a fix?"

"Trying... They're closing like torpedoes. Fast and erratic. I advise we switch our deflectors and reallocate turrets to point defense management."

"Negative. Mr. Goma... you may fire on the battleship when ready. Engage with all guns."

In that moment it was impossible for Captain Karka to imagine that the fleet didn't have his back completely covered. Not being the superior force on the field had never been a part of his naval experience in the Republic.

Batteries from both destroyers opened fire into the almost near-perfect attack profile the length of the battleship presented.

A moment later he heard the sensor tech shriek.

"Brace yourselves for—"

The first torpedo smashed through the deflectors easily. That was the special ability that old-school kinetic weapons had—deflectors did little to stop their strike. That first torpedo holed engineering and exploded exactly as it was supposed to. Five full decks were ripped apart, killing what remained of the engineering section, including the power management team struggling to maintain and restore reserve power.

All deflectors immediately collapsed due to some system malfunction redundancy.

The next torpedo streaked in and slammed into the starboard hangar decks, punching through to the main transportation corridor. Gun batteries nine and ten were knocked out instantly.

At almost the same time, *Arongotoa* took two torpedoes in the engines. It exploded down the length of the ship's spine, and engineering went up like a fireball, killing more than five thousand crew within seconds.

Captain Karka watched in horror as his sister ship went up like a supernova. A moment later the shock wave hit *Victory* and sent her sprawling over to port.

"Helm!" he shouted in the sudden darkness of the bridge, with only the madness of light and fire on display through the windows. Many of the crew were screaming, or crying, and some were already running for the emergency escape pods without him having even having given the "abandon ship" order.

As if they knew.

As if they knew all was lost now.

And then, as his growing horror reached a whole new level, those strange alien fighters came off the broad hangar decks of the massive enemy battleship ahead. Waves of them. At least two squadrons streaking straight for his dying ship.

I'm dead.

"Abandon ship!" he shouted as he scrambled to get off the tilting bridge, racing for the captain's escape pod as stations overloaded and exploded and sirens shrieked warnings of vacuum exposure.

12

Republic Seventh Fleet
Bridge of the *Freedom*
0620 Local System Time

The CIC was pointing at where both *Victory* and *Arongotoa* had been. He swept his hand out to show which routes the enemy's fleet and superior fighter cover now had into the carrier group's center.

Admiral Landoo's carrier group.

The prize of the Republic Navy.

"What do we have left?" she asked. The resignation and fading hope in her tone made the question sound more existential than tactical—but she meant the fighters in both squadrons and the survivors from the last strike.

And because the CIC was an excellent officer, he knew exactly what she meant. "Maybe... a full squadron. But they're all across the battlefield. We can't bring them to bear at any one point as per standard fleet engagement doctrine."

"And Admiral Nagu?"

"His remaining destroyers are taking a pounding, but they're still in the game. *Atlantica* is a big ship. She's been hit pretty severely—fires on multiple decks, one hangar remaining, engines dead—but they've got power and lots of guns."

A boom somewhere by the ship's prow sent him stumbling. He quickly regained his footing and returned to tactics. "We have one detachment of legionnaires. We could attempt to board this ship." He pointed toward the *Terror*. "But I don't know how much good any of it will do at this point, Admiral. We're not in a battle anymore. We really have no clear path to victory here."

Admiral Landoo had concluded as much. She'd just been waiting for the man to say it. And now that he had, a silence fell over them all.

For a long moment she stared at the board and all its holographic minutiae of starships and fighter groups swirling in to kill one another. Forward, at the leading edge of the battle, was a maelstrom of chaos and destruction. She could only imagine the carnage. And yet they were fighting on. Waiting for her next decision. Waiting for her to order a retreat.

"We need to begin to evacuate Tarrago."

She let the words hang in the silence of the bridge. The rest of the bridge crew was stunned that she'd even spoken them. Only the murmur of sensors and the low chatter of tactical comms could be heard.

When no one on the bridge moved, everyone waiting as if frozen in some unbelievable moment of amber, she went on. "Specifically, we need to evacuate the governor and all senior officials. And their families, of course."

"What about the citizens? Leading citizens, specifically," some junior said in the ensuing silence. It was a fair and legitimate question. And the woman probably was a point from the House of Reason. So of course... they were always taking care of their own.

"We have neither the resources, nor the capabilities, to conduct a planet-wide evacuation at this time. Of course the Repub will return within a matter of days, with several fleets, to retake this planet. So I expect they shouldn't suffer... too much."

Landoo was one of the few senior officers in the navy who knew what a colossal lie that was. What she'd just told them all was, in fact, one of the Repub's biggest, and most manufactured, of lies. And one of its most closely guarded secrets.

"Alert the government. Tell them to be ready to evac off of Central Hall. We'll use the *Audacity* to pull them off the landing platform there. Tell Nagu to hold the line as long as he can until we can collect the survivors. Then be prepared to jump at a moment's notice. And, I will remind everyone, all of this is superseded by one fact. We cannot lose this carrier. That blow the Republic will *not* accept."

Bridge of the Corvette *Audacity*
In Formation with Republic Carrier Group
0620 Local System Time

Desaix had his orders. Take the *Audacity* back in and pull the government types out.

He'd lied to the admiral; much of the ship was still offline from the refit. But there was no way he was missing this battle. For most of it he'd been back in Deep Sensors, watching as much of the forward battle as he could from there. Here, back under the shadow of the looming super-carrier, things had been relatively quiet.

He tapped the comm on a nearby panel. "Engineering... how are we coming on that portside thrust-displacer array? Workaround in place?"

Approaching the landing tower platform at Central Hall would be tricky under fire. And without portside thrusters it would be a lot *more* tricky. But what other option did the fleet have? His ship was the only one that could do it.

This wouldn't even be part of the battle. Still, everyone had to do their duty.

"We've got it as good as it's going to get, sir," replied the engineering repair team leader back near the power-management relays. "But it's not guaranteed. And if you go to full, there's a chance it could lock up and we won't be able to disable it. We've had to jettison some armor near that system, so... any damage will be right up against the inner hull. And if it locks up, we literally have to blow the whole system to regain control. Honestly, sir..." There was a long pause. "This is absolutely suicidal. You should understand that, completely, sir. I'm serious about this."

Desaix didn't bother to respond. He walked forward along the narrow passage that led back to the flight deck, passing techs bent over their various stations. Some looked up at him with worry. No one looked up at him like they were excited about what needed to be done next.

He arrived at the flight deck.

Both pilots were busy with the nav, plotting their approach and exit from Tarrago Prime.

"All stations reporting ready for departure?"

The co-pilot turned and gave him a thumbs-up. He still had his headphones on, and he seemed to be listening to some fleet-wide traffic. "We've got fighters inbound," he said, his eyes far away as he relayed the message. "They've broken away from the battle. Coming for the carrier."

Great, thought Desaix. *The battle's finally coming to us and we're getting sent off to rescue some bureaucrats.*

"Take us out then. Inform the carrier we're departing."

The pilots bent to their tasks, and within seconds the hammerhead corvette was shifting away from the massive carrier and down into Tarrago.

In the distance, those strange alien fighters, the ones the fleet was now referring to as tri-fighters, were racing toward the carrier, and the carrier was launching what little remaining fighter cover it could throw up against them. Point defense turrets were rotating to engage.

Black Fleet Shock Troopers, Third Group
Kesselverks Shipyards
0425 Local System Time

The firefight, after the running battle through the morning-dark shipyards in and among the sleeping giants of starships under construction, was over. Bombassa's section and the rest of the platoon had stormed the Repub marine barracks guarding the gates that gave access to the shipyards. Fraggers first, and then they'd rushed, team by team, under heavy fire from a crew-served N-50. In minutes, both guard towers were taken and the dead were being dragged out to be lined up in rows.

That was when General Nero arrived on scene.

Bombassa was leading his section in getting one of the crew-served N-50s back up and oriented out to repel an inevitable attempt to retake the shipyards. Drone intel said the marines were staging a few streets away, and the assault could come at any moment. A few Repub Lancers had tried some close air-support runs on the mechs, taking out a few, but they'd been knocked down by the anti-air torpedoes Third Group had brought with them. There weren't many ground-to-air weapons left, but supposedly some team was now hacking local defenses and the automated turrets would be online shortly.

One of the few remaining mechs, a Hunter-Killer Scout Walker lumbered across the wide yard before the gate. The HK-SW would make a difference, thought Bombassa, when the marines came at them again. Dawn was just an hour away, and they were ahead of schedule.

General Nero and his command staff surveyed the damage.

Bombassa had much respect for the man. Even in the Legion he'd been a feared and legendary combat commander. But he too had run afoul of the system in some way that remained nebulous. And now, here he was. He'd jumped in with the troops. Less like a general, and more like a real leader.

"You got to admire that man," Bombassa said in his low, deep voice. The troopers in his section didn't reply. They'd learned that Bombassa was the quiet type. They'd been through six months' training on Tusca at the fort out in the wastes in order to be turned into a high-speed, low-drag fighting unit. But unlike the legionnaires, the shock troopers had small talk drilled right out of them by the almost malevolent cadre of TACs and scarred drill sergeants who ran the sadistic training regimen. Rumors were that many of them were Tyrallian war criminals. NCOs who'd fought at places like the Sayed Massacre and the Maraan Slaughterhouse.

When the crew-served N-50 was secured and manned, Bombassa caught sight of his LT huddled around some commandeered supply sleds with the rest of the command staff.

"What do you think is next?" asked TAF44.

Bombassa knelt down and laid his subcompact assault blaster on the ground. He switched off night vision on his bucket because there was enough light from the security illumination this close to the guard station. Instinctively he began to disassemble his brand-new but recently well-used weapon for a quick field cleaning.

TAF44 took a knee and watched the horizon, taking in the gate, the other troopers, and the most likely avenue from which enemy contact would come next.

This too had been drilled into them, not unlike the Legion. No moment was ever wasted in the shock troops. Even when making seemingly idle chatter.

Bombassa disconnected the short barrel from the lower receiver of the blaster and laid that aside. "Counterattack is what the plan calls for," he said in a low voice. "But there were provisions for targets of opportunity... so maybe that's what they're discussing for us next."

Taking the lower receiver, he delicately teased out the firing crystal and assessed it. The HUD in his bucket recommended replacing; it had seen a lot of action in just the short time he'd been using it across the shipyard. Bombassa had double-tapped maybe twenty workers—third shifters who'd had no idea what was happening—and had then gotten, all alone, into a serious firefight with three Repub marines who'd inked up. They were all dead now somewhere in the dark of the shipyard.

A couple more firefights followed that, and finally the big shootout at the gate. So yeah, this crystal was done.

He swapped it out.

"You still good with all this, Sergeant?"

The question was informal. The man had used only his rank. That bit of unofficial protocol had developed all on its own, and the TACs and drills hadn't seemed to mind it much. Or at least, there'd never been any kind of official memo or punishment-based reinforcement training saying they'd couldn't.

"Good with what?" asked Bombassa delicately. But he knew. He knew what the other trooper was asking. He was just unsure why.

But here was the problem—at least to Bombassa. This new thing, whatever it was, was different than everything they'd known back in the Republic, and the Legion. Sure, everyone had complained about the Republic. And maybe that had even affected any supposed chances one might have had of climbing up the nebulous ladder of the Republic's arcane social structure.

But this new organization... the shock troopers and the fleet. They'd all signed on because they weren't *just* going to take back the Republic from the House of Reason and all the cronies and phonies who ran it for themselves. They'd been promised something *new.* Something like nothing the galaxy had ever seen before.

And whatever this *new* was... it didn't like criticism.

It liked unity. It liked purpose. It liked accomplishment. But in the few examples, and stark ones they had been, that had occurred since they'd all begun to train out there in the salt and burning iron wastes of Tusca, that one silent message had come through loud and clear to everyone.

This new thing *doesn't like to be criticized.*

The first example had taken place early on. Before they'd been given identifiers. When they'd all been known merely as recruits. "Re-cruits." Said like it was a dirty word.

One of their own had left a nasty message about the harsh conditions and pointed out the brutal nature of one TAC in particular. Ellersdurf. A brutal malevolent bullpig of a man who always carried a flat rubber strip to slap people with.

Within two hours of first formation the next morning, the offender had been dragged from their ranks and whipped without mercy. Whipped. Who'd ever heard of such a thing? In the modern age of a galactic republic... who'd ever heard of a man being whipped? Flogged within an inch of his life, really? Who'd ever even *heard* of such a thing?

And yet they'd all seen it.

And then they'd dragged the lifeless wreck of blood and torn flesh away, and he'd never been among their ranks again.

There had been other incidents. Nothing had escaped the constant surveillance of their leaders, and implementers, of this grand new military force. They must've had eyes and ears everywhere. Because nothing got by them. Nothing went un-noted, and especially, nothing went unpunished.

So when TAF44 asked if Bombassa was "good with all this"... well, how does one answer? thought Bombassa to himself. One knows how one *once* might've answered a soldier's simple ironic complaint, or question, about the powers that be and their approach to the mission. The proper response must've been as old as time immemorial: complaining, and yet still getting the job done. That had always ever been the soldier's lot. To complain.

But not here.

Motivation here wasn't just defined as high or low. Here, in the shock troopers at least... it was akin to a cult. Sacred. Holy. Revered.

Without question.

"It's all good with me, 44," replied Bombassa wisely.

That was the smart answer.

Anything else was taking your life in your hands. Because who could know for sure that 44 wasn't some kind of informer? A member of some kind of secret police no one knew about, inserted within the ranks of the shock troopers. A thought police to police the thoughts, and loyalties, of them all—in order to keep the motivation high. And the mission on point.

Then again, maybe it was just a soldier's question about the big picture, and the meaning of it all. Maybe it was just conversation in the dark after a night of killing.

Maybe the guy was just dealing with all that had been done.

Who knew?

The LT came toward them now. He was circling his fist while tapping something into his field datapad. Bombassa had finished cleaning his weapons, so he fitted the barrel back onto the lower receiver and gave it a twist so that it locked into place. He ran a quick systems check and rallied with the LT a moment later.

"Listen up, Big Man." *Big Man* was what the LT who'd been a Legion officer called Bombassa. Bombassa liked the LT. He was sure he'd been in the scouts back in the Legion, so that made him good at craft. "I need you to follow the other NCOs over to the shipyard motor pool and grab us three vehicles. We've been tasked. We're gonna try and grab a high-value target of opportunity before the Repub can pull him off Tarrago."

"Can do, sir," replied Bombassa. The sadistic TACs had liked that. Liked when orders were responded to with that phrase. It was rapidly, if not already, becoming unofficial SOP. Standard Operating Procedure.

"KTF, Big Man."

There was a pause.

"We don't do that anymore, sir," replied Bombassa jokingly. He hoped... jokingly.

The LT laughed. Bombassa could tell his officer was pumped for this mission. The guy was a killer. And a good leader. So of course he wasn't part of the Thought Police that didn't exist. Probably. Hopefully.

So there was that, and the implications of all things being more than what they seemed. And yet, to Bombassa, doing something new... was worth it. At least for now. As long as he never had to go back to Kimshana. Cursed may it be.

Eastern Gun Bore
Fortress Omicron
0529 Local System Time

Goth Sullus was on his feet. There was a hole in his armor where the surge shotgun had blasted him at point-blank range. A small flow of blood seeped through the armor's opening and trickled down his side, leaving round splatters on the deck of the eastern wall.

"Lord Sullus," said one of his elite shock troopers, his personal guard. "We must get you back to your shuttle for medical attention."

"No." Sullus straightened himself. The expression on his face suggested the effort required to stand erect was enormous. "I will not leave until control of the orbital defense gun is ours."

The elite shock trooper took a step back. "Yes, sir."

"Shock trooper," Sullus said. "You will accompany me and my guard into the fortress. We must reach and secure the fire control center at the moon's core."

Exo swallowed. "Yes, sir."

Black Fleet Shock Troopers, Third GroupCasino District En Route to Central Hall
Tarrago Prime
0530 Local System Time

The convoy Bombassa was following in the rearmost supply sled was under heavy fire from all directions. At first things had been slow going. Getting three sleds that could haul most of the platoon—they'd lost three troopers in the drop on the shipyards—had taken a few minutes, and getting everyone organized and loaded up took a few more. Then they'd gone out the main gate and weaved through a vast sprawl of supply warehouses that surrounded the shipyards.

The morning dark had at least given them some cover. But Bombassa had no doubt that the inhabitants of the city knew by now that some kind of attack was underway. There had been city-wide alerts and sirens blaring out over the morning darkness. Intel indicated that troops were being massed to retake the shipyards.

And as a red dawn began to awaken in the cloudless skies over Tarrago Prime, some trooper muttered over S-comm, "Red skies at morning, sailor take warning."

Bombassa had read books about sailing. Sailing was his someday retirement plan. He knew what the phrase meant. Storm coming. Later today. But coming nonetheless.

The LT had given the orders as they'd loaded up. Downloaded a file into each of their HUDs with mission objectives, command and signal, and real-time drone intel updates as everything progressed. In short, they were tasked with capturing the Republic governor at Central Hall. The governor, who would presumably be attempting to get a handle on what had happened in the pre-dawn dark.

Now, as morning light washed across the fantastic streets of the lower city, the heavily armed convoy of legionnaires entered the narrow streets of the casino district. Which was where they saw their first citizens.

Bleary-eyed gamblers, stumbling out of cavernous casinos still holding drinks, stopped to watch the troops pass by in their commandeered sleds. And though these troops seemed similar to the famous legionnaires, there were subtle differences that no doubt left the watchers uneasy and tense.

Farther down the street they passed the still burning wreckage of a Lancer that had been shot down. It had come in low, the pilot struggling to keep it from crashing, and had burned a scorched path through the lush foliage of the central landscaped median before finally smashing into the front steps of a Tyranian marble–clad gambling palace. Some emergency personnel still remained around the downed fighter, and a white sheet lay draped over someone nearby. Whether it was a pilot, or some passerby, Bombassa didn't know.

Halfway up that street, moving fast and racing for the governor's residence at Central Hall, they were ambushed by Republican marines. The LT, TAF01, was in the lead vehicle.

The vehicle that just took an anti-armor round.

The vapor trail of the round came from the darkness of a nearby casino. A moment later blaster fire was everywhere, all over the street, from all quarters, chewing their commandeered supply sleds to shreds.

The shock troopers were covered by improvised armor they'd managed to requisition from the shipyard.

Small hull-plating sections that had done the job nicely with a minimum of welds from the torches they'd brought for breaching. But now the lead vehicle was overturned and smoking. Dead shock troopers were spilled out across the creamy white streets of the city, and blaster fire careened and ricocheted off into lush tropical topiary and shrubbery that was suddenly on fire. As was a legionnaire who'd crawled from the wreckage.

"Go, go, go!" Bombassa shouted at the driver. "Move forward! Get through this now!"

That was standard procedure for ambushes: get out of them.

Shock troopers were opening up from the back of the supply sleds as marines could now be seen firing from the wide-open maws of the casinos.

As the sleds pulled alongside the overturned lead vehicle, Bombassa ordered the drivers to halt. He dismounted and scrambled beneath the repulsors to reach the burning wreckage. A few surviving shock troopers climbed, or were helped, onto the two sleds, while men shouted out targets over S-comm.

Sergeant Bombassa spotted the LT. He'd been torn in half, and his fancy new armor hadn't done a damn thing to save him.

The sergeant grabbed the LT's datapad and subcompact blaster, draping the sling over his shoulder as he scrambled back to the driver's compartment of the sled, dodging blaster fire all the way.

"Move!" he shouted angrily at the driver. "Get us out of here now!"

Command Center
Fortress Omicron
0538 Local System Time

Exo wondered how far his broadcast over L-comm would be effective. Legionnaire resistance was scattered. Surrender had made more sense for the legionnaires mustered at the eastern wall, where the flood of shock troopers had given extra weight to his words. For those *inside* Fortress Omicron, it probably wouldn't be received as much beyond propaganda. And that meant more legionnaires would have to die today.

Exo ground his teeth. *Let this be the last of it, then. Let this be the jolt needed to wake the Legion from its subservient slumber.*

He didn't know who he was speaking to. God. The universe. Anyone who could make it so. It was simply an expression of his innermost feelings. One that rapidly evaporated when they reached the platform at the bottom of the bore for the orbital defense gun.

The firefight wasn't a surprise. This was a fortified position they knew they'd have to go through in order to reach the fire control center in the middle of the moon. The heart of Fortress Omicron. So when they stepped off the lift at the bottom of the bore, and were greeted by immediate fire from the leej platoon assigned to guard the bridge to fire control, they were expecting it.

A crew-served N-50 opened up devilish fire on the first elite shock troopers—Sullus's personal guard—who charged onto the platform. There was little room for tactics. Ground would be taken through attrition. Even as the lead shock troopers fell, riddled with charred holes from the N-50, their frag-launchers had already announced the departure of their massive grenades.

Fwomp! Fwomp!

The two fraggers were aimed directly at the N-50 crew. One struck the leej gunner in his bucket, cracking his visor a split-second before exploding. The force of the blast tore the leej apart. The second fragger bounced off the far wall before detonating, sending searing pieces of shrapnel at the hunkered-down leejes around the barricades.

More shock troopers flooded the platform, using the sacrifice of the two elite guards to gain a strong offensive foothold.Still, this was going to be a bloodbath. Both sides exchanged blaster fire, with legionnaires and shock troopers alike succumbing to scorching wounds.

Exo remembered his L-comm.

"This is Command Sergeant Major Gutierrez," Exo said. "I urge you fellow legionnaires to surrender before anyone else has to die. The eastern wall has surrendered and are being treated humanely. The same will be true for you."

"Go to hell, traitor!" came the reply.

An errant blaster bolt streaked toward Exo. He ducked behind a cargo crate.

"You are speaking to them," Goth Sullus said to Exo through S-comm.

"Yes, sir." Exo wondered how Sullus knew that. He hadn't shared the L-comm frequency with anyone else.

"And they have decided *not* to surrender, I take it."

"No, sir."

"Very well."

Goth Sullus strode to the forefront of the battle. Blaster fire seemed to fling itself away from him. As he neared the first trooper he made a gesture, and the man was flung into a wall, eight feet up. He slid to the ground, his body limp. A second later the hatch leading into the bunker imploded inward, and Sullus alone walked into the bunker.

There was more blaster fire. But not for long.

Goth Sullus emerged.

The dripping of blood from his damaged armor continued. Exo was certain he was gravely injured. But whatever... *power* he had was enabling him to continue on in battle.

They moved across the bridge, which was guarded by a series of blast doors. Each was breached using powerful charges detonated by Sullus's elite guard. The gas that was deployed against them was just as easily overcome; their armor purified it from the air.

And then came the two cyclopean war bots.

The first of the guards went down in a hail of bright blaster fire. The other troopers took cover as the war bots set up a blistering crossfire. Even Sullus was behind cover. Gutierrez watched the man. His head was bowed, as though he were drifting off to sleep. Something Gutierrez had seen leejes do in every situation from HOLO jump to actual artillery strikes.

One war bot slowed, its gears and servos smoking, as though it were refusing to obey its own mechanisms. And then it turned its heavy blasters on its counterpart. Seconds later that war bot exploded.

Sullus stepped forward—and at the same instant, the murderous war bot regained its senses. It pivoted, and both its blasters came to bear on the man in the black Mark I armor.

Sullus flung his gauntlets wide as though he were ripping some object down its length. And the war bot's massive piston-like "arms" came away from its body.

The thing began to smoke, then it caught fire.

The shock troopers moved on.

Three more blast doors and they found the N-50s—the very thought of which had frightened Captain Thales.

With his guard moving behind him tactically, Sullus lumbered into the N-50s' arc and held out one hand. A hurricane of fire blurred from each heavy blaster system.

Sullus forced the shots to ricochet away from him and smash into the ceiling and walls. He strode forward, directly into the hail of fire, his hand still out in front of him, palm facing out.

Then he closed his fist, and the guns went instantly dead.

Sullus stood before the final blast door.

His shoulders slumping, his chest now heaving, he raised his hands, and the door slid aside. Barely.

Beyond it, the fire control crew, and Thales, waited with blasters in hand.

Sullus swept one arm across them all, scattering them like tiny toys. Some died from broken necks. Captain Thales felt like he'd been hit by a loaded mining sled. When his head slammed into the back wall, it was lights out. Several of his bones had been broken.

And that's when Goth Sullus finally collapsed to one knee, as if sensing there would be no one and nothing else with which to contend.

As if there was very little left of who it was he'd once been.

Black Fleet Shock Troopers, Third GroupStaging Area for Raid on Central Hall
Tarrago Prime
0547 Local System Time

"Nightstalker Six, this is TAF02," said Bombassa once more over S-comm. They'd had negative contact with command since arriving at the staging area. They were supposed to link up with two other elements that had taken separate routes through the city to reach Central Hall, but so far, no one but what was left of Fourth Platoon had arrived.

They'd abandoned the smoking and heavily damaged sleds that had survived the ambush and gone in on foot to the alleys surrounding Central Hall. Now they were two blocks away, with drone recon above giving them a pretty good idea of who, and what, was guarding the front entrance.

"Nightstalker, this is TAF02. Do you read me?"

Still nothing.

In his HUD, Bombassa was looking at a holographic sandbox of the front entrance. Two companies of marines stood ready to defend the place with their lives.

Over two hundred men.

What remained of Fourth Platoon was twenty-six shock troopers. And while Repub marines weren't legionnaires... they were tough monkeys nonetheless. Plus there were two light mechs on patrol in the streets nearby.

"TAF02..." The transmission was coming in broken and distorted. The high-pitched whine of blaster fire in the background was evident. "This is Nightstalker Six. Contin..." The transmission broke up. And in the sudden wash of static, Bombassa heard someone calling for a medic. Then an explosion that almost seemed to knock out comm completely. Then another explosion.

Obviously the assault to take back the shipyards had begun in earnest.

Then a new voice, imperious and hard, was on the channel with Bombassa. "TAF02, what is the status of TAF01?"

Bombassa almost blurted out that his platoon leader was dead. Killed in an ambush. But the voice, whoever it was, hadn't used any kind of protocol identifier. It just demanded answers. Intel, really.

"Cannot comply. Identify yourself now or get off this channel!" ordered Bombassa. He stared up and around, checking his shock troopers' placement and spacing along the alley. One fragger could do a lot of damage right about now, but it couldn't be helped. They were surrounded and shoulder-deep inside enemy territory. And from the sound of things, it wasn't going all that great at the nearest friendly position they had to fall back to.

Not for the first time did Bombassa wonder if he hadn't made some kind of colossal mistake. Because what if this all went sideways?

What if?

"TAF02, this Nightstalker Actual. Again—confirm status on TAF01!"

Bombassa swallowed thickly. He was in communication with General Nero now. Which meant everyone was really busy back at the shipyards.

"Sir," replied Bombassa. "Oh-one is dead. KIA in an ambush en route. We have arrived objective but don't have the numbers. We're looking at a mech-reinforced company of marines sitting on the front door. Requesting new orders."

There was a long moment of ambient open-channel noise. Men and weapons barked and screamed bloody murder. Bombassa could hear the heavy thump of the crew-served N-50.

"Sergeant!" General Nero was back once more. Bombassa could see him in his mind, moving among the troopers and rallying them, focusing them, leading them.

He was the opposite of every point that had ever tried to get him and all the other leejes killed.

"We have drone recon on your objective. Stand by, we're softening the target. Once it begins... move forward and enter the facility. Intel indicates the target is inside. I don't need to remind you... capture is mission crucial. Do you understand, TAF02?"

More blaster fire.

Someone shouting for a medic.

"Can do, sir!"

13

Black Fleet Shock Troopers, Third Group
Kesselverks Shipyards
0548 Local System Time

General Nero dragged a wounded shock trooper back from the barricade with one hand while firing his blaster with the other.

They were being overrun from almost every direction. Legionnaires had arrived to pull some kind of counter-strike.

And yet for this to work they had to hold the line here at the gate until the capital ships could make orbit. This line could not be broken. They *had* to hold until the fleet got close enough to provide further support.

Physically larger, and powerfully built, Nero had loomed above the other shock troopers the Repub marines had been trying to kill in assault after unsuccessful assault. And even though his shock troopers had beaten them back, they'd taken losses they couldn't easily replace.

Right now, he wished he had the troops he'd sent out into Tarrago Prime on opportunity missions. Chances to make more of the day than what they'd already achieved now seemed like the over-ambitious failures that had dogged his career in the Legion.

And yet there was still a moment here. A way to salvage all of this. If they could just hold off this next attack.

Someone tossed a fragger right over the barricades. Nero was closer than anyone else, and he saw it roll to a stop near two shock troopers firing back at the marines.

He dropped the dying man he was trying to save and reached down, praying the thing wouldn't go off in his face. If it did... well, then that was it, wasn't it? He felt the explosive in his hand and pushed away thoughts of it simply blowing up right now. He side-chucked it as fast as he could back at whoever had thrown it.

He heard the close explosion and dodged sudden sniper fire to get back under cover.

It was that kind of day.

"Get that fifty working!" he shouted over S-comm. Damn, he thought, at least give us some cover.

He switched to a private channel with one of his most trusted NCOs. A grunt he'd known from the Legion since he'd been a captain in some hellhole no one cared to remember. He always kept a hotkey for his best NCO when things absolutely needed to get done.

"First Sergeant Indiro!" he bellowed across the ether of S-comm.

"Here, sir," came the reply.

"There's a Repub corvette in dry dock near your position. I need you to board that corvette and access its point defense systems. Sending you a target location now. Deploy the anti-torpedo flares and tell the ship's AI to drop everything on the selected target. I need this in the next two minutes, Sergeant, or some kids are gonna get killed doing something foolish like obeying my orders."

There was a pause. A moment that seemed overridden by all the carnage and chaos of the brutal firefight. As men died and blasters whined while charge packs hit the gritty pavement all around the battle at the gate. As killers reloaded with thoughts of nothing other than making sure the other guy was good and dead.

Hang on, boys, he thought. This one's for all the marbles. That was what was in the pause.

"Moving, sir," replied First Sergeant Indiro. "KTF."

Black Fleet Shock Troopers, Third Group
Tarrago Prime
0552 Local System Time

"Standby, TAF02..." was all that came back from Nightstalker Actual.

A star scream split the air high above their heads. All the shock troopers in the alley, stacked and ready to rush the grounds of Central Hall, craned their buckets skyward and watched as the beautiful smoking stars lit the morning sky. The multi-colored smoke trails had come from off to the east. Back near the shipyards. Now, as the stars arched overhead, their sudden smoky glory blotting out the focus on air raid sirens and emergency sirens raining across the city soundscape, the dying stars began to fall down toward them. Upon them. And across the grounds and steps leading up to the grand entrance of Central Hall.

"Oh my..." someone whispered over S-comm.

"Ready to move, troopers," Bombassa alerted everyone in his deep whisper over S-comm. "Switch to thermal and stay close, watch your fire and call out your targets. Next rally point is the lobby of Central Hall. Secure the exits and..."

And now more flares fell down at them like slow thunderbolts. They hit the grounds around Central Hall and exploded into a million fireworks gone suddenly haywire.

"*Move forward!*" shouted Bombassa. And... "KTF!"

The sudden firestorm caused the Repub marines who had survived it to pull back inside the main lobby of Central Hall. The shock troopers surged through the hail-storm of smoke and burning phosphorous, crossing the main avenue into the Central Hall grounds unimpeded. They took the steps that led up to the central courtyard where strange and enigmatic sculptures, sculptures that had once represented diversity and correct thought, were now made even more bizarre by the drifting smoke and bonfires of everything that could not be planned for.

Fifty meters ahead lay the main entrance.

Bombassa passed an abandoned N-50 emplace-ment. He slung his subcompact blaster over his shoul-der and disconnected the mounting clamps for the mas-sive gun. He hefted it out of its mount with one hand and grabbed its heavy-duty battery charge pack with the oth-er. Both were weighty, but Bombassa had once benched more than any legionnaire in the 131st.

Barrel forward, he led his squad into the swirling smoke that surrounded the lobby entrance to the mas-sive state administration building.

Two Repub marines in full combat armor with the open-faced helmets, rifles at port arms, saw him first. Their mouths fell into 'O' shapes as their bodies shifted into firing positions to engage him with their blaster rifles.

Un-aimed, he ventilated both marines with the pow-erful heavy automatic blaster. Then he sprayed the tall lobby glass, frosted with conceptual pictograms and words that had lost all meaning. He had no idea if he was hitting anyone, but he was certainly keeping heads down in there so his men could get good and close to toss in their explosives. In moments they were lobbing fraggers and bangers into the darkness beyond the shattered glass.

Good boys, he thought as he continued to unload, slowly drawing a line of heavy automatic blaster fire across the smoke-draped lobby.

Then he dropped the gun, unslung his subcompact blaster, and gave the hand signal, along with a verbal over S-comm, to sweep the lobby.

Double-tap stab in effect.

Like a line of spectral wraiths appearing in the mists of a morning that would never become day, they entered the silent lobby and did the killing work that needed doing.

There were dead marines on the floor. And wounded marines too. Others were falling back to defensive positions deeper inside the endless bureaucracy and mazes of hidden power for the few.

Bombassa watched as one of his troopers targeted a marine crawling across the floor. The trooper fired then rushed forward, sticking the subcompact blaster into the marine's upper back. An industrial black diamond blade shot out from underneath the stubby barrel of the blaster, and the trooper pushed it in with a swift economy of motion that spoke of both professionalism and a kind of mercy.

A trooper on his six covered him as this happened. They moved forward to find variations on the scene repeated all about them.

The battle that came next was both violent and sudden. In moments they were pinned down behind massive pillars that ran the length of a wide ceremonial hall. Blaster fire and smoke swirled as marines and shock troopers shot each other down. But the troopers had the upper hand. One of the squad leaders flanked with three men and wiped out the remaining marines.

"TAF44," ordered Bombassa once they'd secured a tight perimeter at the end of the hall, "use that terminal and locate the governor. I need to know how many marines are left in this facility... if you can find out. Squad leaders, I need to know if we can access the elevators and what the stairwells look like. Let's move, we're running out of time."

Two narrow corridors led behind a wall that rose into the heights of the opulent hall. The flag of the republic was stamped into the marble up there. Troopers paused to swap out charge packs and adjust gear, while others ran off to scout access routes into the upper levels.

A moment later TAF44 had the info. "He's on the executive safe floor. And I got no idea, Sergeant, on how many marines we might have up there because they're using their own comm... but it seems they issued a general evacuation alert to all building personnel to make their way to the landing platform on the ninety-first floor. Hammerhead's comin' in to pull 'em off the roof."

Two of the scouts returned from the elevators. Locked out. And one stairwell had been demo'd. The other was ominously quiet.

"How long until that corvette's due?" Bombassa rumbled over comm.

"Nine minutes. They'll load the governor first. No doubt they have some private boarding passage for him secured already. We've either got to grab him inside his safe floor, or knock out the corvette, and I don't think anyone brought a Scorpion surface-to-air."

Bombassa ran though his options. They could demo as much of the building as they could with explosives on hand in order to destabilize the landing platform and deny the corvette an LZ. Or they could breach the elevators and attempt to somehow ride one upward. But the marines would be in control of that. And if the marines had surveillance, they could end their rise short of the goal.

The one remaining stairwell looked like the only available option. Bombassa checked his remaining troopers. It would be a slaughterhouse in there. But there was the mission. And who knew how valuable this governor would be in the final tally.

And that's above my pay grade, thought Bombassa as he checked his blaster once more. More by habit than need. Giving himself another minute to find any way other than the hard way.

"We move into the stairwell by twos. Cover and move. Rifles up. They drop a fragger then cover. Once we get contact, we rush. Fast. Get close. Make it violent. We can force them to give ground all the way up if we keep moving no matter what."

No one complained.

But they all knew it was suicide.

There were only twenty of them left now.

Seven minutes until the corvette docked with the landing platform.

And ninety-one floors to go.

How many minutes to load the governor and as many high officials as they could? Maybe another fifteen minutes.

Or would they take the HVT and run?

"Let's go," ordered Bombassa.

Bridge of the Corvette *Audacity*
Tarrago Atmosphere
0604 Local System Time

"Message from the governor's secretary, sir. He says enemy forces have entered the building. We need to pull him out now."

Desaix was busy trying to keep his ship together. They'd been jumped by two tri-fighters coming through the atmosphere. Turret targeting had decided to go inoperative and they were coming through heavy cumulus on final for Tarrago and the pickup.

So of course the gunners were on optical targeting. And of course the wicked little tri-fighters were dancing in and out of the clouds to make runs across the *Audacity*'s rear deflectors.

"Rear deflector malfunction, Captain," announced the co-pilot. "We got nothing back there!"

As if on cue, the ship shook from a barrage of high-pitched blaster fire. The strange tri-fighter howled off and away through the front cockpit window, disappearing into a boiling cloud mass that looked like some golden high-altitude canyon.

"We lost our ventral repulsor array. Chief says it can be fixed PDQ."

Well that's not going to help things, thought Desaix.

"Hold course. ETA to arrival?"

"Five minutes."

"Tell the marines to be strapped and ready to secure the platform. We'll take the governor and as many as we can. First sign of trouble, it's gear up and we're outta here."

Black Fleet Shock Troopers, Third Group
Central Hall Stairwell
Tarrago Prime
0605 Local System Time

Hard-charging and moving full-tilt, what remained of the strike force to capture the governor took each floor as fast as they safely could.

"Sergeant, this is Nightstalker. Corvette in sight. Need to move, time's running out!" The urgency was implicit.

Halfway up, they met the first defenders.

A small listening or observation post that seemed only half interested in doing their actual job. One of the marines literally yelled down, when the shock troopers were five flights below, "Who're you guys?"

Bombassa shouted out the name of an old unit he'd been in an attempt to buy them a few more feet to get close enough to start killing.

And one of the marines literally whooped for joy that the Legion was here.

As they closed the distance up the stairwell, they heard one of the marines calling it in to his CO. A second later he shouted down, "Halt and identify. I say Doorstop..."

Bombassa knew they were now waiting for the countersign. Some innocuous word that would let them through the perimeter. He motioned for everyone to keep moving forward. They had something on their side for just a minute more. Indecisiveness, momentum... whatever. Use it, Bombassa yelled at himself as his men surged forward.

"Victory!" shouted Bombassa, knowing that any word he chose would be the wrong countersign. But maybe it would be enough for his men to at least get a few more feet out of the indecisiveness in order to close so that the defenders couldn't pop a fragger and drop it on them.

Best-case scenario, his troopers could do them before they'd sitrepped their CO. Best case.

Blaster fire lit up the dim, emergency-lit stairwell above Bombassa. S-comm confirmed a moment later that both marines were down.

And no doubt the CO would now be flooding the stairwell with a reserve force to buy time for the governor to escape.

"*Move! Move! Move!*" shouted Bombassa over the comm. "Go for broke! It's our only chance now."

Move faster than the enemy can react.

Ten floors above, one of the reserves tossed down the first fragger. It exploded, killing two troopers. The others ran upward, pushing hard, sweating buckets to get as close as possible to their enemies. Marines were flooding into the stairwells above and below.

Just a few steps above Bombassa, a door slid to the side, and an open portal of light flooded the landing. As the first marine stepped through, following the nose of his light blast rifle, Bombassa put three center mass shots on target, dropping the marine against the gray concrete wall.

Tired, his legs already turning to jelly, Bombassa pushed up the steps, firing into the open portal. Because no doubt they were working in teams. Keep them back, he thought. And fraggers work both ways. He unclipped one from his belt, popped the contact, underhanded it out into the hallway beyond the portal, and flung himself against the wall.

It exploded.

Marines were pouring up the steps from below. Bombassa looked down to see his platoon's moving rear guard firing to keep them back. And up above it sounded like a close-quarters blaster fight gone psychotic.

A trooper fell from above, disappearing into the dimly lit levels far below. Bombassa leaned out, aimed his weapon skyward and fired. He struck a marine looking down to watch the man fall. Right in the chin.

Bombassa turned to check the hall he'd tossed the fragger down. He fully expected to see some marine coming for him with a popped bayonet at the end of his rifle. But he saw only smoke, fire, and dead and dying marines. He signaled the rear guard to move, and they cleared that floor.

Two floors up, troopers were shooting point blank into marines rushing down the stairwell. Both sides knew it was too mixed to use explosives now. Troopers were firing from one landing right into the next. And the marines were returning the favor.

And this is where the difference is made, thought Bombassa.

For most of the combatants, this was literally the most vicious firefight they'd ever been in. For the few marines that had actual combat experience, it had often been blasts on target from a distance, or pirates seeking to save their lives by shooting it out in the corridors of some junk freighter. They'd never fought legionnaires in CQB.

Or wild predators.

Both would have been the same.

The one percent of the one percent of the one percent was a terrible thing to be at arm's length with.

And these shock troopers had trained as former legionnaires, knowing that one day they'd come face to face with the Legion they'd once served.

Rage. Anger. None of that played a part in the desperate stairwell fight no one would ever mark down in history's record. These former legionnaires—who'd cast it all aside for something new, who'd let the dice fly—didn't need to be taught that only one man ever walks away from a fight. And that man was the one who caused the most pain and suffering to the other man in the shortest amount of time.

The training at Tusca had reached levels some had called sadistic. Why? Because one day the Legion and the troopers would meet. One day. It was inevitable. It was like a violent summer storm brewing on the horizon. Coming for you. And everyone could see it.

TAF34, one of the troopers under Bombassa's command, was hit already. Right in the chest. Upper right quadrant of his armor. The blaster had shot hit him like blue thunder out of a clear sky. The guy who'd shot him was not more than ten feet up the stairs.

And for some reason TAF34's right arm, the arm holding his blaster, wouldn't respond anymore. Wouldn't aim the weapon or pull the trigger needed to kill the man who'd shot him.

All that was background. TAF34 literally threw himself up the stairs and slammed his bucket headfirst into the marine who'd shot him. Like some wild bull, half mad and blind with rage. Except TAF34 was neither. His blaster wouldn't work. That was okay. He had other weapons. Bucket to the marine face was one.

Blood spray.

The marine to his left gave him a shoulder that felt like a battering ram. Now TAF34 was in and among a squad of marines who would've told you they were heartbreakers and life takers any night of the week on leave in any of a hundred bars where the flesh is on fire and the drinks are ice cold.

TAF34 pulled his combat knife with his off hand. He pushed that under one guy's armor, under the soft spot between chest and belt. And pulled it wickedly out and away like he was cutting some cord he didn't even think about. The man fell back into his squadmates, screaming bloody murder because he knew he was dead.

But TAF34 wasn't finished just yet.

One marine leaned over from the upper stairs and tried to butt-stroke the mad black-lacquered bull rampaging into their front ranks.

Which was a stupid thing. Butt strokes worked on tribal natives on distant backwaters where body armor wasn't a thing beyond bone necklaces handed down generation to generation. It was typical indigenous pacification thinking. But the butt of the marine's blaster merely glanced off TAF34's bucket and caused the marine to fall forward into the raging bull, who plunged a combat knife into him like a H8 addict surging toward an overload of chemical nirvana. The marine fell to the floor as his life ran out all over his armor and onto the stairwell.

At this moment in the battle, TAF34 had been shot two more times. Once in the leg. Once in the chest.

The leg had opened a wound to his femoral artery, and he was going to die in about three minutes. Except he wasn't even aware of this. He was using his own blaster rifle like a mace now. He was raising and smashing it down into any marine near him.

Other troopers, including Bombassa, followed close behind in turtle formation, shooting at everything all around TAF34's mad charge into the marines' ranks.

As TAF34's blaster rifle snapped atop the head of one marine, who went down like a sack of potatoes, a fragger from farther up landed on the railing, bounced past the remaining marines and rolled toward the steps leading down to Bombassa and the other troopers. TAF34 kicked it away from them with his good leg, and felt his wounded leg give way in the same instant. It was only at that moment he realized how blood-slick the inside of his armor was, and that he was being pain-tranqed as his armor tried to save his life.

The marines dove away from the kicked fragger, which had rebounded off the wall and back onto the landing, mere feet from where it had been kicked.

TAF34 rolled over onto it and hugged it to himself as it exploded.

Both the marines next to him also died.

And why, and really who, was TAF34? No one knew. But he had his reasons all the same. So his new brothers fought on to make sure his sacrifice wasn't in vain.

Bridge of the Corvette *Audacity*
Tarrago Atmosphere, Approach to Tarrago Central Hall0610 Local System Time

From the tiny bridge of the corvette, Tarrago Prime, by morning light, looked like some city under Republic bombardment. Individual freighters were climbing off and away into the roiling clouds, thrusters at full, spooling up to make the jump to light speed as soon as possible. Below, fires had broken out in several buildings, and across wide swaths of the city dark smoke roiled out of control as city services, stretched to the breaking point, tried to respond and couldn't.

Crowds were rioting, or looting. And there was a massive battle still underway at the shipyards. But even from here, and listening to the battle above, Desaix knew that Tarrago was lost.

Two destroyers were reported destroyed in close volley fire with the enemy battleships. The carrier was trying to cover the remaining ships so they could reach the jump point and get out of the system. Once the governor was aboard the carrier they'd abandon the system altogether—but until then, naval and marine personnel were buying time and escape windows with their lives.

The *Audacity* docked with the landing platform atop Central Hall, though she didn't actually land, because she was much bigger than the available space to put her down. As soon as they were secured, with the big engines howling to maintain position and the repulsors throbbing wickedly like tribal drums in order to maintain altitude, the governor was rushed out under heavy marine guard and boarded back near quarters at the aft of the ship.

Across the platform he could see people being barred by the marines from entering the landing area. People who were hoping to get on his ship and get off Tarrago Prime.

Desaix received an inter-ship comm alert. "Captain, this is Governor Toltai. I authorize you to depart immediately. The situation is too critical to remain one moment longer."

Desaix watched as the marines tried to keep the people back. He could see children. Wide-eyed and frightened as their frantic parents screamed at the marines to let them pass.

"Captain!" shouted the governor over the comm. "As an appointed official by the House of Reason, I demand—"

Desaix cut the link.

"Patch me through to the marine commander!"

A moment later he had the man. Looking out through the cockpit window he could see the armored and armed officer stepping back from the collapsing barricades swollen with refugees.

"We can take five hundred."

He saw the man turn and stare at the mass of seething desperate people.

"Might be more than that, Captain," replied the marine. "Letting them through now."

"Get your men aboard too," Desaix added before the man cut the link.

Across the vast empty platform, the marine officer shook his head, straightened, and saluted. Then he spoke to his men, who stood aside to let the mob surge forward.

The desperate mob ran toward the hovering *Audacity*. One man, who looked frightened to death, picked up a little girl and held her in front of him. Desaix knew the man would force her ahead of him if he had to. He would get his little girl on aboard, casting her fate to the galaxy.

The little girl was holding a wobanki doll. Her face was frozen, as if in disbelief.

"Chief," said Desaix once he'd gotten through to the loadmaster in lower cargo. "Open everything up. We'll take them all."

"It's not safe, sir."

"Doesn't matter. Get everyone on board. She'll hold."

Desaix cut the link and patted his ship. She'd held before. She'd hold again.

"C'mon, old girl. One last time for me."

Black Fleet Shock Troopers, Third Group
Central Hall Safe Floor
Tarrago Prime
0615 Local System Time

There were only five left.

Five troopers from the platoon that had set out to capture the governor.

Updates were still coming in from Nightstalker Six. The defense of the gate had held against the latest push to dislodge the defenders. Now it seemed the Repub was pulling out, or even surrendering already in some places, according to reports. But it wasn't over yet. Legionnaires were trying to blow up the shipyards.

There was some chatter that if the Repub still held the orbital defense gun they might turn it on the shipyards in order to deny this new enemy the chance to build more ships. And if that was the case—if anyone fired the massive gun at the planet—then it was over for everyone on Tarrago Prime. That thing would leave a smoking crater ten miles wide.

"Nightstalker Actual says your mission priority is still high, TAF02," relayed the comm operator.

Bombassa watched as his remaining men used a cutting torch to slice into one of the walls leading onto the floor that protected the governor. There was no intel as to whether the governor was in there or not. Drone recon on the corvette had gone dark. The one assigned drone had been taken out by automated point defense fire.

The cut into the security wall was almost finished.

The other troopers stood back, pocketed their gear, and readied their weapons and bangers for breach.

Bombassa held up two fingers, indicating two flash-bangs and then breach. He pointed out the order of who would go first. Or rather who would follow him through first.

He got acknowledgement clicks and nods.

The trooper cutting into the wall stood back, waited for a nod, then kicked down the weld. As the slice of wall fell inward, he stood back, handed his cutting torch to Bombassa, and readied his weapon.

Two bangers were flung through by other troopers. Their armor went offline for a second to harden itself against the negative EMP side effects of the explosives.

All they heard was the low crinkle of crumpling metal, like breaking glass, and then a yawning silence. The suits soft-booted as they threaded the smoky gap in the wall, trying to pick out targets on the other side.

But there was no one.

The floor was clear.

It was palatial and well-appointed, and there were even trays of fine food and drink still laid out, as though the troopers had only just interrupted some embassy party being thrown among the overstuffed couches and imperial leather chairs. Mirrored halls and richly decorated rooms gave way to an admin center beyond a wide kitchen.

Moving tactically in turtle formation, covering every angle, every entrance, every blind spot, they found the sealed blast door beyond the industrial-grade kitchen. A small placard indicated this was the supply and service entrance that led out onto the boarding platform.

One of the troopers bent to hacking it. He plugged in a cable from his bucket, and the display appeared to overlay his real time HUD as a virtual keyboard framed itself near his gauntlet. There was no way a cutting torch was getting through this beast of a blast door. Bombassa stowed the cutting torch on his harness and waited.

The trooper must have been a pro level code slicer, because he had the door open in thirty seconds. Beyond its massive girth, a long and shadowy service ramp crawled up onto the platform high above. They could hear the loud whine of the corvette's massive thrusters at idle. And beyond that, what sounded like a stadium of screaming fans raging at some loss. There was even blaster fire.

"How we gonna knock out a ship, Sarge?" asked a trooper.

Bombassa shook his head. He had no clue. The mission had been to snatch. Snatch meant take from a residence. Knocking out a Repub warship hadn't been part of the op order.

And yet the unofficial motto of the shock troopers had become... *Can do.*

"There'll be marines guarding the boarding ramp to the ship. Take care of those. That's the best we can do. If we can board it, then we'll take the ship. If we can't board... then we'll destroy it or call in fire from the battleships by tagging it with the target designator on your weapons. But wait until I give the order to do so. Roger?"

Acknowledged all around.

"You did good today, troopers."

They came out tactically. Moving and engaging stunned marines who hadn't figured on anyone getting through the perimeter defenses below. Defenses that had been left behind to die in place.

Three marines went down before they began to put up a decent defense. But there was nowhere for anyone to hide. The landing platform was wide and open, and the last of the evacuees were scrambling up the boarding ramp. In other words, the firefight turned into a street showdown. Like something out of the frontier past. when Terran marshals had been all there was for justice on a dozen colony worlds.

Bombassa knocked their officer down with a shot to the chest that left a burning hole in the man's armor.

The lowermost cargo door of the corvette began to rise into the closed position. The engines grew into a monstrous howl as marines and shock troopers went down.

There were three troopers left when the repulsors engaged to full and set a bombastic tribal beat hum-pulsing through everyone's skulls and armor.

Another trooper went down.

Bombassa let his weapon go and ran, its sling keeping the slapping weapon against his body. Now he was at a full-tilt dead run, arms and legs pumping.

The corvette began to slowly pull away from the high landing platform. Black plumes of smoke ran up into the sky to meet gray clouds that roiled and burst in sudden showers. The first big fat drops of rain began to fall on the platform.

Marines were firing at him as his powerful legs pumped and his hands pulled him forward for all he was worth. And then he was out over the platform and flying across the narrow void that had only just opened between the departing ship and the platform.

No net.

No ropes.

No second chances.

At a grunted vocal command, the armor magnetized his gauntlets for free climbing as he sailed across the widening gap.

One gauntlet held on as the ship climbed away above the cityscape, engines howling, wind trying to drag Bombassa off and down into the burning city far below.

His rifle slipped and then tumbled off into the city canyons. He was holding on somewhere near the massive engineering block at the rear of the ship. Or where he thought engineering must be. Through rents in the armor he could see the inner hull.

The burning city was shrinking away rapidly below him, even though the lumbering ship was only slowly climbing away from it. Republican Lancers raced past with Black Fleet tri-fighters giving chase, firing blasters as they went.

Bombassa now knew what he hated more than HOLO jumps. This. He hated this with all his soul. He was a savage. At heart he was a savage who hated the future and longed only for the land and sea, and a bit of wind with which to sail.

But he pushed all that back to some other part of his mind, as he'd always done in the years since leaving Kimshana, and pulled the cutting torch from his belt. He flicked the onbutton and watched its burning, twisting length grow from the housing canister, like the sword of some mythic and ancient warrior. Then he slashed at the outer hull, hoping he'd find some place thin enough, and unarmored enough, to make a decent cut.

He found the spot. The armor had been stripped away from a massive panel, probably to access the portside thruster array. He cut through, and the panel tumbled off into the gray storm and silver sunlight as the ship climbed through what had to be approaching ten thousand feet.

Bombassa pulled his boots up, contracting his abs, and pushed them up and through the opening. He felt his feet find some kind of shelf. He magnetized his boots and then crawled up, hand over hand, after them.

He was inside the darkness of the outer hull. He switched to low light vision and began to crawl through piping and circuitry, looking for an external maintenance hatch to violate.

14

House of Reason
Utopion

To Orrin Kaar, Admiral Devers looked frantic. And though it took effort to resist the urge to dress down the admiral for his failure to control the situation, Kaar knew that now was not the time. He needed to soothe the admiral's delicate ego and sensibility.

"I'm losing ships!" Devers called out. "This is a disaster!"

"Such is the price of war, Admiral," Kaar said gently. He hadn't thought of Devers as the type to care about the loss of men under his command.

"I'm not sure how much longer *my* super-destroyer can hold up!"

Ah. The cause of the admiral's care suddenly came into focus.

"Then fight, man!" Kaar shouted. Not unkindly. Like a coach rallying his players.

Devers sniffed. "That's not all. The Republic kill team destroyed the shipyard. Entirely."

Kaar stood up from his desk. "What?"

"I don't know... I don't know how they got past the blockade but they did. Sullus's shock troopers are supposedly hunting them down, but I don't think they'll catch them."

Kaar formed a steeple with his fingers and pressed it against the bridge of his nose. He let out a long sigh. "Without that shipyard, we will find ourselves at a standstill."

"Or worse," said Devers. "With just a few of the remaining fleets massing into an armada, Tarrago could be won back."

"You speak of that which you do not know. There are no other fleets."

Devers opened his mouth to object, but closed his mouth again on seeing Kaar's severe look.

"At least," Kaar continued, "no fleets that can help the Republic."

Devers shook his head. "So what should I do, Delegate Kaar? Attack Sullus's fleet?"

"No!" snapped Kaar as though reprimanding a bad dog. To hell with the admiral's feelings. "Continue your current course of action. I need time to prepare the necessary political and strategic countermeasures. We are not defeated. Not at all."

Black Fleet
Third Wing, First Squadron, "Pit Vipers"
0631 Local System Time

Lieutenant Kat Haladis, the new commander of the Pit Vipers, rolled out on a Lancer's six and opened fire with both blasters. Shots smashed into the engines, tearing apart armor plating and striking deep into the engine housings of both nacelles. Static electricity discharged all across one of the pylon-shaped engines, and the ship exploded.

A message from Fleet appeared as she reached up to increase the forward deflectors while passing through the expanding debris cloud of her kill.

"Viper Lead, priority tasking. New mission. Break off from the fleet and engage the carrier with your squadron. We need to knock out her jump computers so she can't get away. Highlighting structural targeting data to you now."

Kat acknowledged and scanned the battle, reorienting herself as to where the big battleships were now engaged in close-range volley fire with the remaining destroyers. And behind those, off in the stellar distance, was the grand prize. A Repub carrier virtually undefended.

"Vipers! Break off and form on me. We've been cleared to go after the carrier."

Republic Seventh Fleet
Bridge of the *Freedom*
0633 Local System Time

The message from *Emergent* had just come in. *Atlantica* was finished. Admiral Nagu had transferred his flag to *Emergent*.

Admiral Landoo acknowledged and waited. *Audacity* was due at any moment. Then they could jump away, and everyone who could get clear was on their own. There really wasn't much they could do now. This battle was lost. A total defeat.

"We should leave now, Admiral," said the CIC. He was standing in front of her. But she wasn't seeing him. She was merely watching the destruction of everything she'd ever known.

It was as though some audio loop was playing over and over in her head.

How could this be?

How could this be?

How could this be?

"General Toleda on Tarrago Prime will surrender once we've jumped away. He's just waiting for your signal."

How could this be?

"*Audacity*?" she murmured.

"Arriving in five minutes. Once it docks and we get the governor aboard, we can jump. Shall I recall all fighters?"

"What about the destroyers?"

"Admiral Nagu will buy us time. *Atlantica* is done for. Reactor core breach in progress. She's about to go up like a candle. *Emergent* is the only one that can jump. And she's taking a pounding. Honestly, those ships won't last much longer, ma'am."

The admiral stared in horror at the holographic display. Each ship had thousands of crew. And now they were either dead or stranded. They'd be taken prisoner. Maybe.

Why hadn't the orbital defense gun fired in support?

And...

Why hadn't the new Raptors been enough?

And...

Who was this enemy? Where had they come from? What did they want?

She shook her head once and stepped back as though suddenly realizing where she was. She stared around at the darkly lit CIC with its array of tactical computers and messaging lights. Each and every one of them somehow dire. Each one telling a story of death and destruction. Techs sat before stations, closer and more connected with the ongoing carnage and horror at the front of the battle than she was.

The line Nagu was holding to get the carrier away.

If they lost the carrier...

"Let's get out of here. Signal our retreat to all units. Tell the group to stand by to jump once *Audacity* docks."

And then she heard one of the techs shout, "Enemy fighters incoming."

Republic Seventh Fleet
Second Squadron, "Gunfighters"
0634 Local System Time

There were clearly more tri-fighters than Raptors now. The battle had switched from making attack runs on the lead battleship to just trying to keep the fighters off her back.

Atumna got the recall order and didn't need to be told twice to get out of there. She broke away from the battle over the *Imperator* and raced back toward the cover of the ruined super-destroyer *Atlantica*.

Three tri-fighters gave pursuit while point defense turrets from the fearsome battleships chased her and every other Raptor pilot.

Gunfighter Lead was telling everyone to return to the carrier immediately; it looked like they were about to jump out. "If you don't make it, you're on your own," he finished. As if there would be no further comm until they made it back, or didn't.

But Atumna was too busy to even acknowledge the command. The pursuing tri-fighters were swarming her six and trying to get off shots. One hit collapsed her rear deflector, and she swore a vile Tennarian oath and dove in close to hull of the burning wreck that was *Atlantica*.

Escape pods were jettisoning in every direction. Out-of-control electrical fires raged across all decks, glowing within the skeletal remains of exposed areas of the ship. Massive sections were shrouded by vapor trails jettisoning ruined armor and hull.

She twisted the Raptor over on its belly, climbed away from the underside of the battle-scarred hull, pulled a hard loop, and came back in across the engineering section. One of the reactors exploded, throwing hull plating and wreckage into the space above the ship like some super volcano. She got so close to the disintegrating ship she could see figures running down inside the main reactor housing dome. Running for the emergency escape pods. She hoped.

One of the trailing tri-fighters smashed into the hull, and a large section of the superstructure gave way and came apart. The other two tri-fighters broke off to avoid collisions.

"Nervous!" she cackled at them and stayed close to the hull. It was her only hope to keep them off her. She shot out over the engineering section and past the dead engines of the dying giant that was *Atlantica*. Max thrust, and she raced for the carrier.

And then the super-destroyer exploded—throwing a bright flash of light across the volume of dark space.

This battle was over.

Her first... and she'd lost.

And to her, teeth gritted and determined, that wasn't the way it was supposed to happen. Atumna Fal did not like to lose.

Black Fleet
Third Wing, First Squadron, "Pit Vipers"
0635 Local System Time

The fast-moving tri-fighters streaked toward the massive bulk of the bulbous Repub carrier. Defensive escorts opened up with turret fire all around the carrier's perimeter, but in moments the sleek little fighters were in and among them like wolves, pounding deflectors and weaving to avoid concentrations of battery fire.

Kat streaked past an escort along the outer ring of the defensive network and waited for her targeting computer to find the jump control node located on the carrier. Within seconds her targeting software had identified the system and highlighted it across the cockpit glass. She raced along the carrier's length, passing force-shielded hangar bays that threw an ethereal blue light out into the depths of space.

Close fire caused her to break off.

"Those screens are still up, Viper Lead," reported one of her squadron. "We'll set up for our attack and try to punch through. Stand by."

A spindly little frigate blocked Kat's egress, so she ran a bright line of blaster fire across its command deck. One shot got through and did damage. Then she was off and away, listening as her squadron began their runs against the carrier's powerful deflectors.

"We lost Viper Seven over the target. Breaking off—" and then there was nothing. The next pair lined up, and Kat dove her tri-fighter back into the fight. Defensive fighter cover was light, but the point defense fire was heavy.

Off to her left a smaller escort exploded, cracking in half at the spine. Fleet torpedo bombers had arrived. All across the field hot burning streaks of bright energy were racing toward the capital ships. Two struck the carrier and knocked down her forward deflector screens.

"All clear, Viper Lead," cried the torpedo squadron commander. "We're out of here!"

Kat yanked her tri-fighter across the hull of a supply ship and raced to set up her attack run against the carrier. Viper Four fell in on her wing.

"I got ya, Viper Leader," replied the pilot. "Watch for surface fire from the top of her hull. She's got some wicked PDC engaged."

"Roger, Viper Four, increase to attack speed. Keep it tight. We'll only get one pass at this."

Republic Seventh Fleet
Bridge of the Carrier *Freedom*
0636 Local System Time

The CIC was alive with the chatter of reports as turret commanders called out targets. The bombers had broken off, but they'd done their damage. The carrier was now vulnerable, and the battleships were closing in, passing the spreading remains of the annihilated destroyers. They were now near-defenseless.

"*Audacity* is making her approach to dock. We're starting our jump calc now, Admiral!" shouted the CIC.

Admiral Landoo checked the status boards for the fighters that were being recovered. Only fifteen were inbound.

Again, the staggering loss of numbers was almost inconceivable.

The ship rocked violently from an internal explosion somewhere in the rear hull.

Black Fleet
Third Wing, First Squadron, "Pit Vipers"
0636 Local System Time

Kat pulled up from the strike. They'd hit the jump node dead center, putting hot fire into it and getting dangerously close to the hull to make sure the job was done right. They'd seen the explosion of venting oxygen and hull plating spinning out into the void.

She added max power to the fighter and climbed high above the elliptic of the battle. The defensive turret fire had been close and hot as they made their run; at times it had seemed like the space ahead of them had been filled *only* with blaster fire. Her deflectors had taken some serious hits, but she held course and made her run, despite losing her starboard thrust stabilizer.

That was for you, Dasto.

She didn't care if they took her out now.

Knocking out the carrier, assuring that it would now be captured by the fleet, had felt like some kind of closure. Not a victory. But an honor for...

Because Dasto had been one of their best.

And they'd left him behind at Antaar. He'd held their jump window when they'd gotten into a fierce battle against the MCR. He'd bought them the time to escape. And sure, they'd given her parents a medal. His CO had even come to tell them what really happened. How her brother had flown through heavy enemy fighter cover to clear a path for the carrier to jump under fire, surrounded by three MCR battle cruisers.

"And they just left him to die?"

She'd said that. The little girl she'd once been. Screamed that in the silence that followed. And across all the years, too.

To the man in the Republic Navy uniform who'd come to tell her parents what a hero her brother, their son, had been, the girl she'd once been had screamed at the injustice of it all. And the finality.

Which was the worst part.

The navy man had just stared at the strange little girl who'd hero-worshipped her brother. Because what could he say to her? Yes. They had let him die out there. Alone and outnumbered. For the Republic.

Later, when her parents began to die and yet still walk around like they were alive... when they seemed normal even though they were dead... later, one evening watching a news show, her father said something. Only one thing. And it made her feel so helpless. And so enraged.

Noting some bit of gallant death on behalf of the House of Reason, the narrator of the show said, "Some gave all."

And Kat's father had turned off the screen and gotten up, muttering through clenched teeth, "And some gave *nothing*!"

And this—as she climbed away from all the battle and destruction and certain defeat for those who'd slain her brother—this was payback for everything that had been taken from her.

That was for you, Dasto.

And then she began to breathe.

Bridge of the Corvette *Audacity*
0638 Local System Time

The hammerhead corvette *Audacity* came in under heavy fire.

"Cleared to dock in main bay," announced the flight control comm in the same moment the sensor techs called out, "Fast movers inbound! Loose comet! We got two tracking us, Captain."

They'd arrived in the middle of the battle. Escorts were trying to keep the enemy fighters off the carrier, and there were very few Repub fighters left in the fight. To Desaix, things looked to be going from bad to absolutely catastrophic.

"Make for the main bay and get ready to offload our cargo fast. We're going back out there."

"Negative, Captain. Carrier Ops says we're jumping out and to secure for jump once we dock," corrected the co-pilot.

Desaix sighed. That was probably for the best. The three huge ships bearing down off to starboard were immense, and bristling with turrets. They were, in fact, the biggest ships he'd ever seen.

Whoever these people were... they'd come armed for tyranasquid.

The corvette passed under the shadow of the belly of the carrier and changed course to enter the massive hangar entrance beneath its hull, usually reserved for escort ships. The way was clear, if you didn't count all the enemy fighters streaking past like gnats.

"Uh..." said the comm officer. "Captain, *Freedom* just lost her jump capabilities."

The pilot turned to check with the captain. With a nod and a wave, Desaix told the pilot to continue for docking.

"How bad?" Desaix asked the comm officer.

"Data engineer says they can reroute and use the targeting computers, but it'll take twenty."

Desaix looked at the three battleships closing fast. He didn't need the nav comp to calculate an intercept. The *Freedom* didn't have twenty minutes.

He turned back to the comm station. "Chief." He waited for the loadmaster to reply. "I need everyone off in two minutes. We're going back in."

"Uhhhh..." groaned the chief.

"Do it!"

Desaix ran back to torpedo control at the extreme rear of the bridge. That had been the only place to set up the newly installed station. "Crack the seals on those babies. We're gonna use 'em to buy some time for the fleet to get out of here."

"They don't have warheads, sir."

"Yeah, and the enemy doesn't know that," replied Desaix with his gambler's grin. He dashed back to the cockpit.

Republic Seventh Fleet
Bridge of the Carrier *Freedom*
0642 Local System Time

"Admiral, *Audacity* is clearing mooring lines. She's going back out."

Landoo knew exactly what Desaix was up to. She knew he was the type. The type to try something brave and get everyone killed in the process. "Daring" was something the Republic Navy frowned on, generally.

Except... what other option was there? If the chief data engineer didn't get a new jump solution in the next few minutes... game over.

You could signal surrender now, she thought. Save everyone's lives right now by surrendering and laying down your weapons. As it were.

Because that's what this is about, isn't it? It isn't about winning now. Nine tenths of this fleet has just been destroyed. This is about saving everyone's life right before it's too late.

She turned to the CIC.

He was telling her that the main deflectors were back online but that he doubted they'd stand up to much from the battleship's ion guns.

Mentally forming the order before she spoke it, she caressed the thought of surrender. It was simple. *"Tell them we surrender."*

Instead she said, "Get me Captain Desaix."

A moment later the comm officer nodded from tactical table.

"Captain Desaix... what exactly are you planning on doing?"

She watched via screen feed as the *Audacity* backed away from the docking platform deep inside the carrier.

"We can buy you a few minutes, Admiral. We're carrying multi-warhead torpedoes. We can keep those battleships, if they care about us scratching them, busy for a few minutes. I suspect they'll freak out once they detect our launch."

"Those are experimental, and last time I checked they're not even armed, Captain. I get armaments orders too."

Desaix waited. Composed himself. *Audacity* was clear.

"We're all you've got, Admiral. We can't let the carrier get captured. You've got the governor. I suggest, respectfully ma'am, that you clear system as fast as you can. We'll jump once we launch."

The comm link went dead. He was shutting her out. Yes, he was absolutely determined to get himself, and his crew, killed. Valiantly, if possible.

She turned to the CIC. "Let's see if we can get him some fighter cover. Volunteers only. We won't be able to wait for them once we're clear to jump."

Bridge of the Corvette *Audacity*
0644 Local System Time

Except it wasn't that easy. He knew it and she knew it. So Desaix cut the link to the admiral and concentrated on getting his ship into the fight.

"Gunners, clear us a path through those fighters. We've got to get close enough to those ships to get a launch off without them jamming the torpedoes before they split."

Republic Seventh Fleet
Second Squadron, "Gunfighters"
0645 Local System Time

There were seven Raptors left in Gunfighter Squadron.

What Atumna Fal saw, as she nursed her damaged fighter back within the fleet envelope of the carrier group, were several badly damaged escorts, a corvette disembarking from the main hangar bay beneath the carrier, and multiple squadrons of tri-fighters shooting up targets of opportunity all across the carrier group.

"Gunfighters, this is Gunfighter Lead. We've been ordered to take our ships in and get out of here. Problem is, the carrier needs a few more minutes to execute her jump. That corvette is going out to buy some time. This is a one-way mission. Opt in with a click. Anyone wanna help 'em get their package delivered so the carrier can clear system?"

Atumna felt her slender tentacle caress her comm. Without the barest hesitation she clicked in reply. It wasn't a win... but it was something. And something was all she needed today.

There were five other reply clicks.

Gunfighter Lead clicked his acknowledgement too. "To me, Gunfighters... we're going in."

The seven remaining Raptors pulled hard turns and re-formed on an opposite course heading, streaking off to pick up the lone corvette going out to meet the three looming gray battleships on the stellar horizon.

Black Fleet
Bridge of the *Imperator*
0646 Local System Time

"Sir, the carrier is within range."

Rommal waited. Waited and watched the constantly evolving tactical display. Their initial plans had never included capturing the Republic's Seventh Fleet carrier.

Destroying it... yes.

But the possibility for a capture was now within reach.

And yet, Goth Sullus had wanted the total annihilation of all Republic forces. That had been clear.

But to capture it... surely he would see that for the victory it was?

Recent experiences had taught the admiral that disobeying Goth Sullus wasn't wise. He swallowed hard.

And why was that hammerhead corvette coming out against them? That was pure suicide. Rommal didn't like that one bit.

The first officer seemed to notice this too. He cleared his throat. The bridges of these battleships were innately calm in the expansiveness compared to the close-quarters tactical bridges of the Republic. Here, and nearby, everyone in the fleet efficiently went about their business as if in... a state of quiet fear. Even though it was clear that they'd won the day.

And maybe, thought the admiral, fear was a good thing.

The first officer spoke. "We've assigned the fighters to take care of the corvette. Main guns are trained on the carrier. Her deflectors are down. Shall we fire, sir?"

Admiral Rommal merely nodded. And then, to make it official, he quietly said, "You may commence firing when ready."

Republic Seventh Fleet
Second Squadron, "Gunfighters"
0648 Local System Time

"Three from above, Gunfighter Nineteen! Watch your back!"

The tri-fighters came at the remaining Raptors like a howling coven of banshees.

Atumna rolled off her target and evaded a storm of blaster fire that would have smashed her deflectors to pieces.

"Switching to tactical fire," she announced over the comm. "Staying in close to the corvette."

All across the squadron comm the remaining Raptor pilots of Gunfighter Squadron were doing their best to keep the bigger ship clear of the swarming fighters.

"Corvette captain says thirty seconds to launch window, then they'll jump clear. Stay in there, Gunfighters," called out Gunfighter Lead.

Powerful blasts smashed into Atumna's weakened deflectors. Her starboard blaster exploded from a direct hit. Alarm bells and system warning lights went off as the ship alerted her to all kinds of catastrophic damage.

Ahead, racing down the length of the corvette hull, a stray tri-fighter trailed Gunfighter Lead, lobbing blaster shots into the Raptor's hull.

Her squadron leader's ship exploded in every direction.

Atumna fell in on the tri-fighter's six regardless of the three on her tail. Some things had to be paid back... never mind the consequences.

Black Fleet
Third Wing, First Squadron, "Pit Vipers"
0649 Local System Time

"Splash one..." Kat called out over squad comm when her rear deflectors lit up like carnival. She had a Raptor all over her and dangerously close. She rolled one-eighty and dove past the hull of the corvette.

Unbelievably, the raptor followed her and struck out once again. This time her tri-fighter's port deflector array exploded. She kicked in reverse rudder, backed off the throttle, and climbed right back toward the battle.

Raptors and tri-fighters murdered each other in the maelstrom above. The maelstrom she was racing straight into.

Didn't they know it was over? Kat wondered incredulously. Didn't they know they'd lost?

The raptor was almost on top of her now, and there was no way she could shake it. Other pilots were trailing both, calling out to Kat to break off and get out of there.

More shots slammed into her ship; warning lights pulsed and then died. Something in the back of Kat's mind announced that the ship had just suffered a catastrophic electrical failure. That in the next second, the controls would no longer respond. A slow horror grew inside her. She was absolutely defenseless and vulnerable.

And then training took over. She was already reaching up for the ejection handles when the hull integrity message flashed across the entire cockpit in a massive holographic projection that swam before her eyes in white glowing letters of urgency. EJECT NOW. The ship was finished.

She yanked both handles as hard as she could, pulling them back to her. As though she were pulling herself up from a pool she'd been drowning in her whole life.

The pod exploded away from the side deflectors and engines as Kat lost consciousness. The last image she saw was the Raptor racing beneath her, pursued by three tri-fighters howling for the pilot's soul.

And then she surrendered to the twilight land between life and death.

15

Bridge of the Corvette *Audacity*
0654 Local System Time

"We've got a firing solution, Captain!" shouted the torpedo officer over the comm.

"Look at the size of those things. They're enormous," mumbled the co-pilot as they sped at the formation of battleships heading straight for them.

"Never mind them," rumbled Desaix. "Get that jump calc ready. We pop these babies, we're out of here once they get lock."

Desaix slammed his hand on the comm. A tri-fighter streaked past the front of the ship. Behind the bridge, turrets were engaging everything they could. And all around them the Raptors providing fighter cover were going down one by one.

"Fire all of them, *now*!"

The torpedo officer didn't even bother acknowledge the command as he began the launch sequences. Everyone knew how absolutely close and desperate this was. The only play was to shoot and get out of here.

"Stand by to jump," Desaix announced over the ship-wide comm.

From the rear, massive *ka-thunks* resounded as launch hatches popped open, followed by ominous *ka-chunks* indicating the newly installed torpedoes had moved into the tubes. Seconds later the torpedoes were streaking up and away from the ship, leaving curling smoky vapor trails.

Black Fleet
Bridge of the *Imperator*
0655 Local System Time

"Launch detected," said one of the tactical officers. He handed his datapad to the first officer.

The first officer quickly stepped over to Admiral Rommal. "Sir... we've detected some kind of launch from that corvette." His tone was one of slight bewilderment, or even bemusement. "Scans indicate these are probably a type of torpedo not yet fielded in the Republic's arsenal."

Rommal raised his eyebrows. "Probably?"

The officer cleared his throat. An annoying habit the man didn't seem to be able to shake. "Could be, sir. There was *some* intel indicating they were testing ship killers for use against local pirate warlords who were purchasing old capital ships off the black markets. Since the Republic isn't interested in bigger ships, there were rumors they were planning to outfit the hammerhead corvette class with a new type of weapon capable of tackling bigger ships. If this *is* that... it could present a danger."

"Can we jam them?" asked Rommal.

"Trying, sir. But as long as the launching ship remains, they're running some kind of closed-loop quantum encryption tracking we won't be able to break in on. If this *is* that system. They're not like the regular ship torpedoes—more like an ancient guided missile. Once she jumps, it shouldn't be a problem to scramble the torpedoes. Their signals will be vulnerable at that point."

Rommal was suddenly aware of the unknown variable at play. The thought of even one of these torpedoes doing serious damage to his ships was enough to make him cautious. He didn't want to have to explain that to Goth Sullus. No. Not at all. There was too much to explain already.

He, Rommal, was the unknown variable. His caution was making him choose between what was best for him and what was best for the operation. Knowing this did little to affect his next decision. It was almost as if he couldn't help himself. As though a sudden fear he'd never known overrode the most logical choice he could make.

"Switch main gun targeting to the corvette. We'll deal with it first. Then scramble the torpedoes. The carrier will be helpless at that point."

"As you command, sir."

Bridge of the Corvette *Audacity*
0658 Local System Time

"Sensors here, Captain. They're trying to hack the torps. As soon as we jump... they most likely will."

The pilot screamed, "They're firing at us!"

The massive ion guns of the lead battleship had opened up on the tiny corvette. One hit was most likely a kill.

"Evasive maneuvers!" shouted Desaix. "Stand by to jump us out of here!"

The burning disc of energy that was the first ion shot just narrowly missed the corvette.

"Can't jump *and* ensure torpedo lock integrity," the sensor operator reminded him.

"How many seconds till they go wild weasel?"

"Hard to say. They're smart torpedoes as long as they're talking to us. They're thinking for themselves based on our data. They're trying to find the best angle and range to enter the warhead phase."

Even though they have no warheads, thought Desaix grimly.

"Can we override?"

"Negative. Not now. They're using our telemetry to engage. Again... we jump, they'll be very vulnerable, Captain."

Desaix turned to stare down the length of the bridge. Everyone was waiting for him to go ahead and order jump. Behind him, the massive battleships loomed larger in the cockpit window.

Engineering Section of the Corvette *Audacity*
Local System Time 0659

Bombassa had waited. After finally managing to get through an inner-outer hull maintenance lock, he'd popped out somewhere in crew quarters. He'd quickly shucked his armor and grabbed a naval uniform that barely fit.

As a Legion NCO, he'd taken escape and evasion courses, and he figured all the training he'd received in the month-long course on Skerith was probably relevant to his current situation.

The mission was still in play, as far as he was concerned. Locate the governor and capture him. He had his sidearm—a snub-nosed blaster that packed a powerful punch—and the cutting torch.

After locating a medical pack in a small dispensary currently not in use, he stowed both weapons inside the bag and moved out into the main passages. Every corridor was filled with refugees, and he could hear the howl of the battle between the fighters and the return fire from the capital ships ringing throughout the hull. All of this mixed with the close passes of tri-fighters—and occasionally the massive hollow *BOOOOOOM* of a starship exploding.

Eyes on mission, he told himself as he moved forward, fearing death by decompression of a holed hull at any second.

On a small ship like this, most everyone had a good idea of who was who. Asking where the governor was probably wasn't going to do anything but set off alarms. So that wasn't an option.

But Bombassa had been on hammerhead corvettes before. He'd been assigned diplomatic duty, once, long ago when he was a private. He knew there were special quarters for dignitaries forward, below the main command deck.

In a crowded central passage up the spine of the ship, Bombassa stopped to listen as someone from the crew announced that the corvette would be docking with the carrier shortly and that all non-crew were to leave the ship immediately by a series of exits that were noted. The voice also added that there would be a lengthy security screening on the carrier's hangar deck to ensure everyone's safety.

And seeing as Bombassa didn't have even the most basic of Repub credentials—they'd been made to destroy everything during training on Tusca, erasing all traces of who they once were—staying on the ship was the only way to go.

He listened to the powerful docking clamps of the carrier attach above and below the hull. Most likely engineering would be a safe, and dark, place to hide.

He began to force his way through the swelling crowd as they pushed toward the various portside hatches. In time he made it aft, where he was able to move quickly until he was confronted by two marines—part of the shipboard security contingent every Repub ship carried. They were in a side passage that ran along starboard stores, deck fifteen.

But generally they were removed from the crew. They kept to themselves. Better for security that way. Which meant they wouldn't recognize that he wasn't part of the crew. So Bombassa tried to bluff his way past them.

"We've got a radiation leak down in engineering. I'm on my way to treat for burns. Gotta go, guys."

From the looks on their faces, he guessed he'd just set off warning bells. For one thing, he figured, he wasn't wearing a navy medical uniform; he was wearing deck officer browns. More importantly, a guy like Bombassa stood out among... anyone. The marines would've noticed a giant dark-skinned titan who towered over them being on the ship at some point during their six-month rotation. He just wasn't built for stealth.

"Better call this in," said one marine to the other.

The mistake the two marines made was that they didn't get their weapons up once they realized they might have a situation.

Bombassa drove his fist in a lights-out right cross straight into the first marine's chin. It was a cheap shot from a sledgehammer. But as they'd always said in the Legion... play to win. The guy's head snapped back, and Bombassa's fist felt an awful crunch.

He distantly wondered if he hadn't broken the man's neck outright.

The second marine reared back like a snake, bringing his assault blaster up swiftly to engage. Bombassa merely continued all the way around with his punch, letting his kinetic motion and massive body follow as he threw a roundhouse kick at the side of the other guy's head with the full force of his massive boot.

Both marines were now down, unmoving.

He broke both their necks and moved their bodies behind some transport cases. He left their weapons, because carrying them would set off more alarm bells. His hidden blaster pistol would be enough anyway. Then he shouldered the medical bag he'd dropped in the assault and continued down the passage toward engineering. By now the ship was back underway, and Bombassa had a bad feeling that if it managed to jump out of this battle he'd end up being executed.

Ominous *ka-thunks* and *ka-chunks* sounded above him.

Two options now faced him. One... find an escape pod, eject out into the battle, and somehow disable the jump battery before the thing took off toward the nearest Repub-friendly port. Or two... knock out this ship's ability to jump him into enemy hands.

His decision was to attack engineering.

Bombassa had no idea how to disable anything.

Other than shoot it.

He laid down the medical bag and withdrew the blaster pistol. Then he pulled out the torch, too. Shoot everything and everyone. Cut into all vital systems with the torch.

In the end, he was bound to break something.

Black Fleet
Bridge of the *Imperator*
0600 Local System Time

Admiral Rommal watched the missiles and the corvette in holographic real time. Across the expanse of the massive battleship, the ion cannons thrummed and boomed as the corvette dodged shots and ran. Meanwhile there were twelve missiles inbound.

"All turrets, target those missiles! Nothing gets through!" he shouted across the bridge. He'd never shouted. He'd never been this desperate. But this was too damned close.

And then, in horror, he watched as twelve torpedoes suddenly became... many.

Sirens whooped from sensor controls. Beyond the massive bridge windows, space was filled by torpedoes and vapor trails.

"The torpedoes must have been some kind of multi-vehicle launch system!" the first officer shouted.

The explanation seemed lame to Rommal. And a bit late.

And we're dead, he thought. "Starboard evasive. Waist guns, screening fire!"

Maneuver alarms sounded across the ship as it hove to. Beyond the massive windows of the bridge, both *Terror* and *Revenge* were moving ponderously, heeling over to bring their devastating broadside guns in to support the screening fire that would come far too late.

"Ninety-six... no, ninety-eight missiles tracking on our position, Admiral," announced some desperate sensor officer.

All across the battleship every gun that could be brought to bear was sending up a wall of blaster fire in order to knock down the myriad vapor trails tracking in on the ship.

"One hundred!"

Bridge of the Corvette *Audacity*
0601 Local System Time

"They've split! We're clear to get out of here, Captain," cried the torpedo officer.

"Jump now!" ordered Desaix as a massive ion shot streaked past the hull. It must have been exceptionally close, because the deflector on that side collapsed just by attempting to absorb the latent passing energy from the seething mass of the charged ion shot.

"We're outta here, Captain. Hold on..."

The pilot reached up and pushed the jump levers forward.

Nothing.

"Captain!" It was the comm officer. "Carrier *Freedom* says thank you for the assist. They're clear to jump."

"I'm getting system faults all across engineering. What's going on back there?" shouted the co-pilot. He threw his datapad to the floor and scrambled up to reach the master bus to reroute jump control through the auxiliary systems.

He flipped switches in vain. Nothing was happening. Then he turned to Desaix. "We're dead in space!"

The man's look of horror was made all the more poignant by the view beyond the bridge's windows. The non-warhead torpedoes were now smashing—harmlessly—into the deflectors of the looming battleships. Even now the battleships were returning to course. Bearing down to fire on the stranded corvette.

"Sir," said the comm officer over the bridge speakers. "Inter-ship communication from engineering."

Desaix released his grip on the pilot's chair. "Send it through."

A moment of silence passed.

Then an unrecognized voice came through. It was deep and rich. And though its tone was pleasant... it would be the narrator of so many of Desaix's nightmares in the POW camp he would find himself in.

"This is Sergeant Okindo Bombassa of Third Group. Your ship's power has been disabled. Stand down and signal your surrender to the fleet before they destroy us all."

Republic Third Fleet
Super-Destroyer *Rontaar*
En Route to Tarrago
0609 Local System Time

Admiral Devers smiled as the crew went to battle stations. In his mind, he'd played the game well. Faking distress. Convincing his conspirator that he was engaged all along. He was the information pipeline, and the man had fallen for it all, allowing Devers to make the best decision for his *own* future. He'd waited to see who would win. He'd filed bad reports with that idiot Karr. And now that Goth Sullus was clearly the winner—a thing no one had been wholly sure of to this point—now he'd pop in and take the carrier himself.

It was time to tighten up the alliance and grab a little glory.

In just moments his ship, and the rest of Third Fleet, would drop in right behind Landoo's carrier.

Goth Sullus would be pleased.

And Karr was no longer needed.

Republic Seventh Fleet, Carrier Group
Bridge of the *Freedom*
0608 Local System Time

Admiral Landoo watched as Devers's fleet jumped in right behind her. At first she thought they were saved. That the Third had finally arrived. But already comm was getting a message for them to surrender. From Devers himself. It was playing across the bridge comm.

The traitor, she thought bitterly. That explained a lot.

And then the CIC nodded to her, pointing toward the systems display. The jump calc re-route was done.

"Admiral, we're clear."

Without hesitation she shouted, "Jump now!"

Republic Seventh Fleet
Second Squadron, "Gunfighters"
0609 Local System Time

Maybe she was all that remained of her squadron. She had no idea. She'd stayed with the corvette as long as she could. Once the big ships had started shooting their main guns, the enemy tri-fighters had cleared out.

She watched as the missiles were fired from the corvette, then she broke off. The battleships were coming in fast now.

Moments later, the carrier group jumped away from the battle. They would live to fight another day.

But by that time she was doing everything she could to keep her fighter from coming to pieces all around her in the vast black loneliness of enemy occupied space.

So she made for Tarrago Prime.

Warning bells and system malfunction alarms competed for her attention as she dove through the atmosphere. Her ship shook violently.

In the distance she could see the main capital. It was on fire. Strange dropships and assault transports were descending through storm clouds. A private starship tried to take off and escape. Tri-fighters swooped after it and shot it down.

Things got worse inside the cockpit. Hydraulics were gone, and fly-by-wire was barely communicating with her HUD.

First the number one engine went down. Then, over the lush tropical coast, south of the main city, the number two engine flamed out.

Her ship was nothing but a glider in the barest sense of the word. A glider heading out over a vast dark ocean.

She held the stick and did the best she could. But her speed was too great, and she hit the water hard. Pieces broke off, but the reinforced canopy and cockpit held. Her helmet slammed hard into the controls, cracking in half.

She had to open the canopy. The ship was already sinking fast into the choppy sea. High troughs were replaced by sudden waves that raced across what remained of the battered and shot-to-pieces ship.

Dazed but alert, she remembered the manual process for cycling the canopy. She reached down and began to crank it open. Seawater immediately rushed in and flooded everything. She shut off the master electrical panel as the ship slipped below the water line and seafoam and ocean crashed down on her. Cranking hard, she looked up and saw the surface of the water falling away.

It looked like silver. Like quicksilver. Moving and beautiful.

And it was a kind of peace to her soul.

That vision had been one of the first in this waking dream she called a life.

After all, she was a Tennar. Aquatic amphibians from a world of water.

The battle-scarred Republic fighter surrendered to the depths, its minimal buoyancy overcome, and fell away toward the distant sandy bottoms of an alien world. Shifting greens and dark depths called to her.

And Atumna Fal kicked free of her harness, peeled off her flight suit, and swam away into the blue shadows of the sea.

EPILOGUE

Eastern Gun Bore
Fortress Omicron

Goth Sullus leaned heavily on Exo as the two men emerged from the command core of Fortress Omicron. The repurposed MK1 armor was incredibly heavy, and Exo struggled to hold up the weight as they moved past shock troopers guarding their legionnaire prisoners of war. Some of these leejes, Exo knew, would resist. They would see it as their duty to the Legion to attempt escape and disruption at every opportunity. He hoped others would see the new dawning of the Legion. Hoped that the Black Fleet would absorb the Legion and its legionnaires. With or without Goth Sullus.

Though, Exo had to admit, Sullus had proved himself to be the most capable warrior he'd ever seen. Wounded, shot in the chest, and then what he'd done in the tunnels... it was supernatural. There was no other word for it. Exo shuddered at the thought of such a powerful being in the universe. The man's existence made him fearful, and he began to understand for the first time why some men dared not even speak Sullus's name.

But Exo would not give in to fear.

"Bring me to my shuttle," Sullus whispered, and something inside Exo's mind knew exactly where to look. Like a picture had been painted for him, though he'd seen very little of the eastern wall prior to his descent into the moon itself.

There was a Republic landing platform farther in. A place where supply shuttles would touch down to deliver ordnance and food or to take leejes shipside for leave or reassignment. Now it was empty save for a burnt-out repulsor tug. The kind that moved starfighters and other heavy vehicles around when the trip was too short to bring in a pilot and go through all the pre-flights.

Exo wished he could lay Sullus on the ruined tug and *drive* him to the waiting shuttle at the end of the landing platform. His knees threatened to buckle beneath him with each plodding step.

No other shock troopers made an attempt to help. Whether from fear or awe at seeing their leader as he was, Exo couldn't guess. He thought about ordering a gawking shock trooper to come over and help, but somehow felt that such a request would be beneath him. Certainly it would be beneath Sullus.

From above, an Elixir-class shuttle began a slow ascent. This was a Republic model, likely from the Third Fleet, which Exo heard had mutinied and defected. Two squadrons of Raptors roared by on escort duty. They looked untouched from the battle, as if they were ceremonial craft. The type hauled out for air shows to entertain the populace.

"The hero arrives," Sullus said. His voice was acid and bitter.

Exo knew enough to keep his mouth shut.

The shuttle descended gracefully, touching down between Exo and Sullus's shuttle. Its forward ramp lowered, and clouds of white gases released to join Tarrago Moon's atmosphere.

Who was this? Admiral Rommal? One of the generals?

Sullus straightened himself and began to walk on his own power. Slowly. He left Exo standing alone, mouth agape. How did the man find the strength?

From inside the shuttle a man dressed in the white garb of a Republic admiral appeared. He walked boldly down the ramp, his black calf-height boots gleaming, a white cape flowing behind him.

Exo squinted. Could it be? He magnified the view on his visor.

It was Devers.

"Point sonofabitch," Exo said, and began to slowly raise his rifle, hoping that no one would see. That no one would get the impression that he was seeking to shoot Goth Sullus in the back. He would end that point before Devers could do to these shock troopers what he'd done to the leejes on Kublar. And so many leejes thereafter.

"Lord Goth Sullus," Devers said, dipping down into a gentlemanly bow. "With the orbital defense gun secured, my forces have arrived on the moon to secure the remaining three walls. I ordered the remainder of my fleet to jump in, adding to the damage suffered by Admiral Landoo's Seventh. The Third Fleet's losses were... minimal. I hope you would do me the honor of reviewing my battle plan. I believe you'll find my variations—"

Sullus simply walked past the admiral, not even acknowledging him.

Devers stood there, his proud face etched with annoyance, his tongue pushed against the inside of his lip. He did not turn. He continued facing forward, speaking to Sullus, who walked beyond him. "I'll remind you, Lord Sullus, that ours is a partnership. You must acknowledge my contributions to this battle!"

Exo's blaster was almost up. Slowly. Almost high enough. He wouldn't fire from the hip. He didn't know if he'd get more than one shot. One double-tap.

Goth Sullus stopped and looked over his shoulder. He held up a hand... then squeezed it into a fist.

Devers's head suddenly bent sideways toward his shoulder, twisting to nearly a ninety-degree angle. An excruciating snap filled the air of the Tarrogan moon, and Exo could see the admiral's severed vertebrae pushing into the side of his neck like some macabre goiter.

The admiral stood motionless but somehow remained upright—perhaps by the power of Goth Sullus. Exo did not know.

"Your contributions have been acknowledged," Sullus rasped.

Admiral Devers fell face first onto the landing pad and expired.

Black Fleet
Bridge of the *Imperator*
0928 Local System Time

The Battle of Tarrago was over.

Admiral Rommal ordered the fleet in close to Tarrago Moon. Now that the orbital defense gun was theirs, they were safe within its range. A shame it couldn't have been made operational in time to strike at the remnants of the Seventh Fleet. But it belonged now to the Black Fleet, and that was enough.

He watched as Goth Sullus's shuttle left the secured LZ within the smoking ruin of Fortress Omicron. A moment later a comm officer announced a shuttle traffic request.

"Prepare to receive Shuttle One."

Everyone knew that was the call sign for Goth Sullus's personal shuttle. He was returning to his ship.

Rommal looked over at the comm officer. "ETA?"

The man indicated five minutes.

"Deploy a battalion of our best troopers to receive him on the main hangar deck."

The officer looked up at him, the unsure look in his eyes clear. What, exactly, was the meaning of this?

"Now!" shouted Rommal.

Crodus drag-stepped from across the bridge. "What are you playing at, Rommal?"

For a long moment the fleet admiral watched the various feeds. Repub officers and marines being frog-marched out from their positions on Tarrago Moon, and on Tarrago Prime itself. Under the close eye of shock troopers. He watched as an artillery captain was loaded onto a stretcher by medical techs. That one was from the feeds on Tarrago Moon. At the base. Deep inside it.

He knew that man's fate was uncertain at best. As was the fate of all those who had been captured.

Just like the corvette they'd hauled in by tractor. A corvette that had been singlehandedly disabled by one shock trooper sergeant. He'd watched the videos of its crew being herded off the ship, hands up, by crack shock troopers from Second Division. The corvette's captain had looked none too pleased.

No doubt Goth Sullus would want to meet this hero sergeant who'd captured a capital ship all by himself.

"What are you playing at, Rommal?" Admiral Crodus asked again.

There had been heroes today. Even Vampa, in her own bold and reckless way, had seized the moment at great personal risk to protect his flank. Goth Sullus would see her for the hero she was. Just as he would see others. The shock trooper, certainly.

But how will he see me?

He turned to Crodus.

"We won," Crodus reminded him. Probably because there was that sick look on Rommal's face. The look of command responsibility. The look that said you never really win—you just don't get as many people killed this time as you did the last. The look that's seeing only the operational failures and none of the victories. Whatever side you were on, as a leader, there would always be that look.

That was as old as warfare.

"We didn't capture, or destroy, the carrier," Rommal said. "It got away. We didn't knock out the orbital defense gun on time, and your spies seemed to do little good in defeating their advanced warning system, or delivering the operation of the gun into our hands. We lost the shipyards, too. And I'll remind you that was the primary objective of this operation."

Rommal let that hang for a moment. He watched as Crodus's mask of constant watcher changed to one of dawning realization.

The realization that your position might not be as strong as you thought it was.

His fellow admiral swallowed thickly. "And," began Crodus slowly, "what do you intend to do with all those shock troopers once his shuttle arrives?"

As if there were other ways to survive.

Admiral Rommal watched the man, realizing there were other options than the one he was considering.

Then he spoke just one word and left for the hangar bay.

"Survive."

Levenir Orbit
The Galactic Core

Cade Thrane felt sick. He had been listening to sections of the now-decrypted comm bursts with growing horror.

Delegate Orrin Kaar.

Admiral Silas Devers.

These were pillars of the Republic. The greatest the galaxy had to offer. And, it would seem, they were in league with someone named Goth Sullus, involved in a plot to topple the government.

Thrane searched the holoweb for references to Sullus to see if he could find some context. There was nothing. And soon Thrane grew fearful that even with his own encryptions, someone might be watching. Looking to see who out there might be poking their noses where it didn't belong.

He gave up the search.

But that didn't stop the upset in his stomach. Breaking the encryption had brought a euphoric sense of joy. Finding out what was inside Pandora's box had brought him existential dread. It was a burden, this information. What should he do? To whom should he go?

Thrane examined the faded fabrics of the once top-of-the-line furniture. The interior of his luxury yacht had lost its luster. It no longer shined. But this information... this information could buy him an entirely new life. A gleaming luxury yacht direct from the factory assembly line. Custom-built. He could live on a core world. Vacation where he pleased. Permanently.

And all he had to do was sell the recordings to the kind of person who would do exactly the wrong thing with them. A syndicate lord or pirate. Someone who would use their contacts to blackmail the recording's participants out of a sum of money far greater than the fortune they gave Thrane to acquire it.

"I'm a smart guy," Thrane told himself. "I could blackmail Kaar directly. I could use his own comm system to let him know what I know..."

No. This was a man willing to leverage Republic assets against the Republic's own military. He would have no difficulty sending a kill team in to end Thrane's life. Wasn't that exactly what he'd paid Aldo Kimer to do in taking down the relay stations at Tarrago? Thrane bet that Kaar never imagined anyone else would have been privy to that little secret. It only went to show that, beyond whispers in the dark, there were no safe communications. Thrane had proved that much in his achievement.

There was a lot of money to be had. But what was the good of it if the Republic fell? The Repub was far from perfect, but revolutions brought uncertainty. Millions of credits might set him up, or they might be just enough to buy him a month's worth of rations. Who could say? And what was his duty? Could giving this information to the right people save lives? Save the galaxy?

Thrane cranked up the volume on his shipboard audio system. He let the raging music carry him away. So he could think.

Who did he know? Who might be able to help?

The name of Garrett Glover entered his head for the second time that day. He'd sent Garrett only a snippet of the encryption, just enough to get him familiar. And if the other coder would soon decrypt it on his own, if he hadn't already. Garrett was that good. Which meant he, too, would know who was involved.

Perhaps... perhaps his old friend could provide some guidance. Maybe he would know what to do.

Thrane sent a comm burst to Garrett and was surprised with how quickly the other man answered.

"Hey," said Garrett. "I thought you might call. Did you decrypt the message?"

"About an hour ago," replied Thrane. "You?"

"A little before that. This is a big deal, Cade."

"I know. And there's a lot more to it than what I showed you. Like... end-of-the-world level stuff, man."

"Send it to me?"

Thrane hesitated. "Why? You gonna try to sell it? I'd... I'd want a cut."

"No," Garrett answered. "I've met some guys. Legionnaires. They're good guys, man. They need to know what's going on."

Hand it over to the Legion? Just like that?

Was this the right thing?

Would Thrane regret not cashing out on this once-in-a-lifetime opportunity? Would he live long enough to enjoy it if he did?

"Okay," Thrane said, and he felt a sudden comfort in his decision. "Transmitting the full archive now. Nothing's gonna be the same, Garrett."

"I know," the coder answered.

House of Reason
Utopion

Orrin Kaar sat somberly in his office. Admiral Devers was dead. Not from battle, though that was what Kaar would report to the Security Council. Devers would be remembered as a martyr to Kaar's purpose, that was certain. But that wasn't how it happened. The word Kaar had received from Devers's second in command was that the admiral was summarily court-martialed for failure to follow orders. Executed on the spot by Sullus himself.

So much for the two being equals.

But that didn't mean that Sullus would reign. The prize of prizes, the Republic itself, would belong to Orrin Kaar. He needed now only to remind Sullus of this. Needed to express in no uncertain terms that Sullus *needed* him... if he wished to achieve anything beyond a Pyrrhic victory in Tarrago.

A black-clad comm officer appeared on the holofeed.

"Stand by for... him," the officer said. There was fear in both his voice and expression.

Good. That Sullus was taking this call meant that the leader of this uprising recognized the role Orrin Kaar played in his rise. Certainly Sullus had the resources and wherewithal to amass an army on his own—when Kaar had discovered Sullus's activities, he was already on his way—but even Sullus would have to admit that his ascendance onto the galactic stage could not have come so soon without Kaar's help.

Goth Sullus appeared before Kaar. He wore battle armor reminiscent of the earliest legionnaire design. But upgraded. Newer. Better.

Yet Sullus seemed to struggle to stay upright. He was wounded. His voice betrayed his pain. "You may speak, Delegate."

You may speak. Kaar bit his tongue at the audacity of that comment. "I understand that you have summarily executed one of my most useful political tools."

Sullus hissed menacingly. "I will not be questioned."

"I meant to do no such thing," Kaar said, his diplomatic skills recovering him naturally. "You have my apologies. Admiral Devers was *not* a capable commander, but he *was* a priceless figurehead. Years have gone into positioning him as a trusted representative of the Republic military. He could have won over scores without your having to fire a shot. I do not question that *we* will still be victorious," Karr made a point to emphasize that this was a "we" operation, "however now it will be at a much higher cost in lives. Your war against the Republic will require more direct fighting than stealth now, I'm afraid. The Republic must be conquered outright."

"So be it."

This man's overconfidence will be his undoing, Kaar told himself. "A difficult task, do you not think, when the shipyards we've been relying on lie destroyed by a Republic kill team..."

Sullus betrayed no emotion, but neither did he speak.

Ah, Kaar thought to himself. *So he did not know.*

"Lord Sullus," Kaar said, taking a stab at a proper title, "I came not to praise Admiral Devers, nor second-guess the strategies in today's conflict, but to bury our... difficulties. Now, I can control the Legion from my position in the Security Council. I can send the Seventh Fleet into a trap. I can pave the way... if only you had the resources. Which you no longer have hope of, given the shipyard's destruction. But... there *is* still yet a way to have at our disposal a fleet capable of battering down what remains of the Republic force."

"Speak," Sullus demanded.

"Tell me, Lord Sullus: Have you ever heard of the *Deluvia*?"

Black Fleet
Main Hangar of the *Imperator*
0933 Local System Time

Shuttle One settled down to the gleaming deck of the massive main hangar bay. On the outer edges of the vast open space, other shuttles were offloading wounded and recovered pilots from the battle. But in its center, a battalion of crack shock troopers stood at attention, assembled by company to greet the arrival.

As Admiral Rommal watched the shuttle settle onto the deck, listening to the repulsors throb and shut down, he considered that even if he were about to meet some nasty fate at the hands of their enigmatic leader... Crodus was right. They had accomplished something. They had won something. Tarrago was theirs. It was no longer part of a decrepit Republic that cared little about its warriors, or their spouses who died in their arms, lying in some third-rate hospital among a thousand other people dying by the moment.

He remembered her.

Remembered how proud she'd been of him as he climbed through the ranks of the Republic Navy. And he also remembered how helpless he'd felt when she died. How powerless to prevent the death of even one person. Denied the medical treatment that could have saved her life. Denied because his connections in the House of Reason were all but non-existent.

Denied the life they might have had.

But in this moment, as the shuttle's boarding ramp lowered to meet the gleaming deck of the hangar, he remembered that she had always been proud of him. That he had always given a good account of himself. That she had taken pride in his uniform and appearance. As if it were hers. A thing she possessed.

She had taken pride in him. Pride in her man.

He'd seen what Crodus's face had implied back on the bridge. There were many ways to survive. Reports coming in had indicated that Goth Sullus might have been terribly wounded in taking Fortress Omicron. And here was a battalion of troopers who would obey their admiral if for no other reason than that they'd been turned into killing machines.

If there was ever a chance at survival... then maybe this was it.

But they had done something here.

They had won something new.

What? he wondered. What had they really accomplished?

The beginnings of something bigger. Something bigger than the pettiness of the Republic. A Galactic Republic that was nothing more than a club for elites, so they could live off the backs of the ninety-nine percent of the galaxy. *Theirs* never died of diseases that could be treated. *They* never got passed over. *They* never went without.

Or felt small and powerless.

And she had always been so proud of him.

Goth Sullus appeared, coming down the ramp. Leaning on the arm of a shock trooper.

This was survival.

And the beginning of something better, perhaps. Something bigger than a Republic. Something grander. Something imperial by orders of magnitude. Something better than a House of Reason that was little more than an anonymous mafia run by endlessly do-gooding scolds. Something run by a great man. A benevolent dictator with the power to set things right. To make the hard choices that needed making.

And in the end... an empire for them all. Maybe it was just that.

Admiral Rommal sucked in a lungful of air to give the command that would change everything. The command that would either mean their survival... or his death.

Every admiral must be a gambler. A gambler that he will win the day. A gambler who pays with others' lives. And occasionally... even with his own.

They had created something bigger than themselves here today. Tarrago was the beginning of what was to come. And hopefully... it would be better than the Republic had ever dreamed it might be.

Let the dice fly, he thought.

Rommal spoke. "All hail... the emperor."

And then he fell to one knee and lowered his head in obeisance to the future leader of the galaxy.

SAVAGE WARS

RISE OF THE REPUBLIC

Explore over 30+ Galaxy's Edge books and counting from the minds of Jason Anspach, Nick Cole, Doc Spears, Jonathan Yanez, Karen Traviss, and more.

LAST BATTLE OF THE REPUBLIC

OC **STRYKER'S WAR**

OC **IRON WOLVES**

01 LEGIONNAIRE

02 GALACTIC OUTLAWS

03 KILL TEAM

OC **THROUGH THE NETHER**

04 ATTACK OF SHADOWS

OC **THE RESERVIST**

05 SWORD OF THE LEGION

06 PRISONERS OF DARKNESS

07 TURNING POINT

08 MESSAGE FOR THE DEAD

09 RETRIBUTION

10 TAKEOVER

REBIRTH OF THE LEGION

01 LEGACIES

02 DARK VICTORY

03 CONVERGENCE

04 REMAINS

05 LAST CONTACT

06 KTF PART I

07 KTF PART II

HONOR ROLL

We would like to give our most sincere thanks and recognition to those who helped make *Galaxy's Edge: Attack of Shadows* possible by subscribing to GalaxysEdge.us.

Robert Anspach
Sean Averill
Steve Beaulieu
Steve Bergh
Wilfred Blood
Christopher Boore
Rhett Bruno
Marion Buehring
Peter Davies
Nathan Davis
Peter Francis
Chris Fried
Hank Garner
Gordon Green
Michael Greenhill
Josh Hayes
Jason Henderson
Angela Hughes
Wendy Jacobson
Chris Kagawa
Mathijs Kooij
William Kravetz

Clay Lambert
Grant Lambert
Richard Long
Danyelle Leafty
Preston Leigh
Pawel Martin
Tao Mason
Simon Mayeski
Jim Mern
Alex Morstadt
Nate Osburn
Chris Pourteau
Maggie Reed
Karen Reese
Glenn Shotton
Maggie Stewart-Grant
Kevin G. Summers
Beverly Tierney
Scott Tucker
John Tuttle
Christopher Valin
Scot Washam
Justin Werth
Justyna Zawiejska
N. Zoss

ABOUT THE AUTHORS

Jason Anspach and Nick Cole are a pair of west coast authors teaming up to write their science fiction dream series, Galaxy's Edge.

Jason Anspach is a best-selling author living in Puyallup, Washington with his wife and their own legionnaire squad of seven (not a typo) children. Raised in a military family (Go Army!), he spent his formative years around Joint Base Lewis-McChord and is active in several pro-veteran charities. Jason enjoys hiking and camping throughout the beautiful Pacific Northwest. He remains undefeated at arm wrestling against his entire family.

Nick Cole is a Dragon Award winning author best known for *The Old Man and the Wasteland, CTRL ALT Revolt!,*and the Wyrd Saga. After serving in the United States Army, Nick moved to Hollywood to pursue a career in acting and writing. He resides with his wife, a professional opera singer, south of Los Angeles, California.

Printed at Repro India Ltd.